THE COMYN'S CURSE

M MacKinnon

This book is dedicated to my husband, who walked the path right beside me every step of the way, and to the most amazing country in the world, home of my ancestors... Scotland the Brave.

CONTENTS

ACKNOWLEDGMENTS

Kathleen Kiel, my personal assistant and close friend, who gave me honest feedback no matter how awful it might be.

Victor Cameron, who volunteered to guide a total stranger on her visit to Rait Castle, the real star of this story, simply out of love for the castle and his country.

Kenny Tomasso, always there when I needed to kill somebody or blow something up, to make sure I did it right.

Margaret Hastie, my wonderful landlady in Inverness and the inspiration for Nessie.

GLOSSARY
OF SCOTTISH TERMS
(OR ANGUS, TRANSLATED)

Auld – old
Aye – yes
Bairn – child
Bide – to live, to stay
Bonnie – pretty
Braw – fine, handsome
Cannie – careful, cautious
Dain – done
Dinna, didna – don't, didn't
Fur – for
Gae – go
Gang – go, went
Gie – give
Greetin' – crying
Guid – good
Hoors – hours

Kelpie – a Scottish water spirit that can assume the form of a horse or a human and lures unsuspecting humans into the depths of the lochs
Ken – to know, to understand
Kent – knew, understood
Nae – no
Noo – now
Puggled – tired or fatigued
Sassanach – outsider, English
Verra – very
Whingin' – whining
Willna – will not, won't
Ye – you

*Loss is the uninvited door that
extends us an unexpected invitation
to unimaginable possibilities.*

Craig D. Lounsbrough

SCOTLAND, 1442

She ran blind.

Although she knew every corner, every doorway, every corridor of the keep as well as she knew her own name, tonight all was different. Her very home had turned against her. The fetid air pressed down on all sides, seeking to crush her. Shadows reached out to pull her in, to wrap her in their darkness and steal her breath. She ran on, heedless of their malice. Shadows could not harm her. What could was much worse.

The screams from below were dying now, as the voices that made them were stilled. Those who sought to destroy were themselves slain, their lifeblood running into the ancient stones of her family's castle floor, staining the rushes and turning them black as the hearts of the schemers.

And she was the cause, she whose whispered warning had turned the tables and allowed victim to become victor, prey to become predator. Nausea threatened to rise up and choke her. Never could she have foreseen the terrible consequence of her desperate words. She had murdered her own family. For this there could be no forgiveness.

She stumbled, nearly fell, forced herself up and continued her desperate flight. Up the curving stone staircase to the next floor, down corridors until the tower door loomed before her out of the darkness. She was struggling for breath now, hampered by her heavy gown, faltering. But she could not stop. To stop meant death.

At long last she reached the top, gained the empty circular chamber. The room's one arched window was indistinguishable from the gray stone walls on this moonless night, but it called to her, promising freedom. She allowed herself a tiny exhalation of relief. Here she could wait.

He would come for her—her stalwart warrior, her heart's joy. She had given herself to him freely, and he had accepted her gift and given his own—a promise to take her away, to keep her safe, to love her as she adored him. She had saved his life and the lives of his men at the cost of her family's lives. She would have done it again.

Her heart caught as she heard stumbling footsteps on the tower staircase and she melted back into the shadows of the wall. The door opened. The glad cry caught in her throat and became a whimper as a familiar figure staggered toward her. In the light from the torch held in the rough hand, she could see the dark stain on his tunic, the pain etched on his face. The pain...and the hatred.

Her father raised his sword. "Traitorous bitch!" he spat. She felt the window ledge behind her, knew *that its promise of freedom had been a lie. She was staring at her death. Still, she would not meet it in this stale tower room. Forcing herself through the arched window, she clung in desperation to its outer edge, reason giving way to the blind impulse to survive.*

The next moment the sword came down, severing her hands at the wrists and plunging her downward to the rocks below. She made not a sound as she fell, the shock and pain having robbed her of even this last shred of humanity.

Her last thought was of him.

CHAPTER 1

HARRINGTON, NJ

Im sorry im in love with someone else

Numb, Aubrey stared at her phone. It was a mistake, of course. The text couldn't be from him. Marc could be an ass sometimes, but he would never do this. To shatter her life in an ungrammatical text, to give her such news as if it were a note to pick up milk or remember a dinner engagement. She had heard of text breakups happening to other people, had always assumed that it couldn't have been much of a relationship or teenagers who didn't understand what love was.

But she and Marc were twenty-three years old, for God's sake! They were getting married in six months. They were in love! Plans had been made, set in stone. They couldn't be changed now. She looked at her engagement ring to reassure herself, trying to ward off the inexorable dread building inside her. She read the message again, the phone shaking in trembling fingers.

I havent bn happy for awhile im sure you noticed

No, she hadn't noticed. How could she have noticed? It wasn't real, right? *Was it so hard to use proper punctuation on something as important as this?* Her mind groped for a hold on something, anything but the message in front of her.

Ive bn seeing Angie and we relized we still love each other

The fist that had grabbed her heart was squeezing tighter, making it an agony to breathe. Angie. Marc's high-school sweetheart. The one he could not stop talking about when they'd first met in college, the one Aubrey had helped him to get over. The one who still lived here in Harrington, a town that was too small not to run into everyone you had ever known. When had he run into Angie?

Aubrey Cumming had met Marco Russo as a sophomore at Wyatt College, a small liberal arts school west of Scranton, Pennsylvania, and had fallen for him hard. Their first date had been spent talking—well, now that she thought about it, Marc had done most of the talking—about his storied basketball career at the Church of the Immaculate Conception High School in Harrington, New Jersey, about his plans to go into his father's farm equipment sales business after school...and about his heartbreak.

Had he even asked her about herself on that first date? She couldn't remember. She had been too busy staring into his liquid brown eyes with the foot-long lashes, feeling lucky to have snagged a date with such a paragon. This lovely, broken man who had turned to her, trusted her with his sadness. She was captivated, lost. Was there anything as pitiful or alluring as a beautiful man whose heart had been crushed by a harsh woman?

Her adoration and sympathy had struck a chord with him and more dates followed, in which she did manage to share something of her life in Bradley, a small suburb of Pittsburgh. She told him of her love of literature and her desire to move to Philadelphia after college and work in a publishing house. He nodded in understanding and stuck his hand down her blouse.

They had been exclusive for the remainder of their time in college, and on graduation day Marc had asked her to marry him. She remembered it now as the best day of her life. They would move to his hometown in New Jersey, where his parents still lived and he had a ready-made job waiting for him. Not just New Jersey, but *South* Jersey. It sounded perfect.

To a shy girl from the far west of Pennsylvania, New Jersey was almost as good as Philadelphia. The *shore* was in New Jersey! Marc had painted visions of sailboats, blue skies, summers on the sand. He had talked of the boardwalk, cotton candy and pork roll— whatever the hell that was, it sounded lovely—crabbing and clamming. Mecca! Philadelphia was only forty-five minutes away. And New York City was just up the road. The Big Apple. Home of musical theatre, shopping, the arts. It was a dream.

Aubrey had been so mesmerized by the beautiful picture he had painted for her that she'd never stopped to consider the complete absence of compromise in this decision. Her opinion on their future was unimportant, because he had everything all figured out. Their future was lit up and glorious. She had made him the happiest man in the world with her eagerness to share it with him, he had told her.

The reality was that she had moved ten hours away from her home, to a town where everyone knew everyone else and most were related in some way to each other. Anyone coming in was an outsider. In fact, if you were not *born* in Harrington you were an outsider. Forever. Your children could be Harringtonians, if they were born in Nesbitt General Hospital.

Harrington children went away to a nearby teacher's college and returned to live out their lives in the town of their birth, often in houses built on a parcel of their parents' farmland. The town had no publishing houses, no museums, only a tiny, understaffed library and one bookstore on the verge of extinction.

Marc was giving up nothing. He would be back in his hometown, the returning high school hero who would step into his father's shoes someday when he inherited Russo Farm Sales and Service. They were the biggest John Deere dealer in the tristate area, he enthused. They would be set for life. His friends were all here, and his mother could help plan the wedding. Aubrey would love Harrington, he promised, and his mother would love her.

Marc's mother did not love Aubrey, not even a little bit. She thought Aubrey was stuck up and used too many big words. Also, she was not Italian. Francine Russo made sure that her Marco's new girlfriend knew all about his first love, Angela Ferrari, whose family were related to the Russos in the distant past because their great-great grandfathers had come from the same village in Palermo. Angie was a great cook, would have made her son a wonderful wife. It was a shame he had gone away to college. *And met me.*

Marc laughed at Aubrey's anxiety, reminding her that he was the only son and his mom was just a typical Italian mother. "She'll get used to you, honey."

That hadn't happened.

Marc's mother doted on him, fed him Italian food with names she couldn't pronounce, and pretended Aubrey didn't exist. When she had asked for Francine's recipe for spaghetti sauce, she had been told in no uncertain terms that it was *gravy*, not sauce, and that it wouldn't come out right if you weren't Italian. Marc, of course, lapped up the attention like a puppy, never noticing that his fiancée was excluded from the love fest.

Now, as the shock began to recede, she began to see the little things that she had missed while mired in her fog of love. The way he was always too tired to take her to Philadelphia. How they had lived here for nine months and she hadn't been to New York yet. Even the shore was forty-five minutes away, and there was too much traffic. The fact that Harrington was one of three towns in the most backward county in New Jersey, with the highest unemployment and the lowest literacy rates.

All of those things were surmountable if they were together. But were they? Lately he had been too tired to do anything after work, too tired to listen to her stories about her job at the bookstore and the eccentric people who came in. Too tired even for sex. She had tried all the suggestions in *Cosmopolitan*—"How to Keep the Home Fires Burning," "Fifty Ways to Make Him Mad for You," "Bolder in the Bedroom"— with uneven, temporary results.

She realized that her fear and uncertainty had been growing for some time. When had she begun to feel *less*? Less beautiful, less desirable, less...his. Somehow Marc always seemed to compare her to some unattainable ideal, some impossible embodiment of the perfect woman, and to find her wanting. She remembered the way he had made suggestions on how she could better herself.

"Why don't you wear your hair up more often? Maybe a perm?" "If you used eyeliner, your eyes would look bigger." "Isn't that shirt a little...mannish?" "Maybe if you were shorter, that outfit would work better." Now, as she turned her glazed eyes back to the texts, she realized that what he had been saying all along was: "Why can't you be more like Angie?"

She remembered that the stages of grief were supposed to be denial, anger, bargaining...what was next...oh yeah, depression, and acceptance. Well, she had whizzed through denial in the space of fifteen minutes and was well into anger. Aubrey was pretty sure, as she read the text over and over again, that anger would last a hell of a lot longer than denial. And wait...why wasn't one of the stages revenge? It should be, because right now what she wanted most was to catch Marc and his high school sweetie doing the nasty together and rip both their throats out.

Her own throat tightened and she choked on a sob, and there she was, right back into denial. He didn't really mean it. He'd be back. What about all the things he'd promised? What about their children? He'd wanted five, had already named them. Marco Jr., Anthony, Giovanni, Sofia, Maria. What would their children do if he abandoned their mother before they were even born? How could she go on without him? He had brought her to this godforsaken place and abandoned her. The loneliness rose up like a black cloud and threatened to crush her.

Aubrey stared at the wall of her apartment, the wall on which she hadn't bothered to hang anything personal because it was only temporary; she and Marc would be starting their own home soon and there had been no point in making this place hers. His idea, of course. "This is just until the wedding. My mother wouldn't like it if we lived together before that. We'll go house hunting together, honey, and we'll make it our own home!" And now she realized, with dawning horror, she had no home anymore.

Her body shook with the realization. Abandoned... again. It was her worst nightmare, one she had been having since her father had left them when she was ten. He had been feeling an odd lethargy for weeks, and one day he'd looked up from his cereal and said simply, "I don't think I feel well, Mary." His spoon had clattered to the table as he toppled from his chair to the spotless linoleum, dead of a massive heart attack. And that was when Aubrey's mother left her, too.

She hadn't run away, not physically. But she had withdrawn into herself, given in to grief and despair, and embraced despondency as if it were religion. At times she seemed to forget she had a daughter. Aubrey had not recognized this new person in her home; struggling with the reality that Dad wasn't ever coming back was enough for a ten-year-old to deal with. If she noticed the growing pile of bottles in the recycling bin, the vacant look on her mother's face, she couldn't be expected to understand it. She and her mother had never been close. Together they floated through the house like ghosts, going through the motions. Polite, wooden—strangers.

Aubrey had been daddy's girl. From him she had inherited a gentle sense of humor, a love of story, and an imagination out of all proportion to reality. Her mother had provided the physical character- istics: the tall slender frame, large hazel eyes, and thick blonde hair. She had also given her an innate shyness and a tendency to worry.

With her father, she had been outgoing, efferves- cent, witty. She felt safe with Dad. He was her hero, the man upon which to base her judgement of all men. She had spent hours listening to him tell her of her Scottish heritage—of the wild, barbarian clans that clashed over and over through the centuries like waves breaking on the shore of the North Sea.

"You're a Cumming," he told her. "The blood of warriors runs through your veins—never forget that, Bree. Someday we'll go to Scotland and I'll show you."

"Someday we'll go to Scotland." It had been repeated many times in her childhood until it was embedded in her heart. "Someday we'll go to Scotland."

Now Scotland seemed a distant dream, something conjured from the imagination of a lonely child. Western Pennsylvania held nothing for her anymore. Her mother had waited just until Aubrey was safely in college to sell the house and move to Florida, where she had found a new beginning with the man who had put in her alarm system. Howard—or was it Homer? Aubrey didn't care. She was happy for her mother, but they had nothing in common; they had been strangers for a long time. Her childhood was gone, and now her future was in tatters.

She could never call Harrington home, not without Marc. She was homeless. Stuck in New Jersey...no... *South* Jersey, without the man with whom she had envisioned spending the rest of her life, sporting a degree that she couldn't use. Who needed a BA in English in a town that didn't read? A part of her realized that she was being unfair, that her predicament wasn't New Jersey's fault, but right now the last thing she wanted was to cut Harrington a break. The questions surged through her mind like a storm surf at the Jersey shore. How the hell had she allowed this to happen? When had she lost control of her life? Why couldn't he love her like she loved him?

What was she going to *do*?

CHAPTER 2

ROCKY ROAD

Two hours later found Aubrey still staring at her phone. The screen had gone dark long ago, but the words of the text were engraved on the insides of her eyelids. *Im n love with someone else.* She had never met Angie, had assumed that such a meeting would be unnecessary and too awkward. She had been grateful that the old flame remained in Marc's past, just a fading memory now that he had moved on. He never mentioned her. Aubrey had worked *so hard* to exorcise the sainted Angie from Marc's mind. It just wasn't fair!

Angie had been the one to break off their high school romance, Marc had told Aubrey. He was going away to college, she was staying in Harrington; they were just kids, and long-distance relationships never worked. It had been great and she wished him the best, but this was better for both of them. Over too many beers at a frat party Marc had confided to Aubrey that he was pretty sure she had been cheating on him with Tommy Morgan. She was a bitch, he'd slurred—a lying, cheating slut, and he was glad she was gone. He had loved her, would have done anything to make her stay, he blubbered. The tears in his eyes had called to her.

What a good listener she had been! She had held his hand and whispered consoling words to him, telling him he was too good for that girl, that she'd be sorry someday that she had given up such a prize. How pathetic she sounded in her memory, how needy! Were all women this susceptible to a man's pain, or was there something fundamentally wrong with her?

It had been good, though. Very good. They had laughed a lot, seldom fought. By the beginning of their junior year they were spending every night together, and senior year they had taken an apartment together off-campus. They had played house, skipped class to lie in bed late into the morning. The sex was better than good. Oh God! The thought of never enjoying that body again, of never lying next to him, naked and spent and steeped in happiness...the phone slipped from her stiff fingers and slid to the cheap area rug, and she put her hands over her face and let the tears flow. Her head ached and she felt nausea working its way up her shaking body.

Her phone lit up as a text came in. Marc! She fumbled it into her hand, ready to forgive him anything in her relief. She giggled as she thought of the earful he was going to get for frightening her with this stupid joke.

It wasn't Marc. The room darkened again, the walls pressing in.

Just stopped at Angus' and you aren't there. He's worried. You OK?

She was tempted to ignore the text, but that would never work with Kathleen Bianchi. Kate was a police detective and had a sixth sense about trouble and a seventh where her friends were concerned. There was no way out of this. She would hunt Aubrey down like a bloodhound, bring her to bay and force the truth out of her. Aubrey squared her shoulders, typing blindly.

Marc dumped me. For Angie.

Nothing for a long moment. Then...

That bastard! Hold tight, I'm coming over.

Fifteen minutes later the tall, lanky figure of her best friend Kate let herself in with her key. She was accompanied by the other bloodhound, Colleen Fitzgerald, known to her friends as Fitz. Kate lived with her husband Eddie in one of the new condos across town, down the street from Fitz, and she'd broken every traffic law in Harrington to get here. It helped when you were on the force.

"Brought ice cream," announced Fitz. Tiny, blonde and fiercely loyal, she was a natural nurturer. And she knew about heartbreak. Fitz was the worst judge of the male sex that had ever been born. She was consistent in her ability to pick the most rotten specimens available for boyfriends, but she bounced back from each breakup undaunted, ready to jump into the whirlpool again. The ice cream cure had been applied more times than any of them could remember, and it always worked. At least, it had always worked when *she* was the one who required consolation.

Aubrey had not moved. She sensed that someone was talking, but the words were scrambled, like the sentences she'd tried to translate in her college French class. They just didn't come together to make sense. Her mind clutched at the distraction. God, she hated French! She had worried that she wouldn't pass French IV, would never graduate, and had tried to tell Marc about her anxiety. He hadn't understood. "Just cheat," he had said, and shrugged his shoulders. Simple. Not one of his better suggestions. In fact...

Voices intruded on her flickering memories and Aubrey strained to pull her wandering attention back to the present. She looked up with bleary eyes and saw Kate sitting across from her, reaching for her hand. Where had she come from? And Fitz?

"Now," ordered Kate, "tell us."

She blinked and told them. It took a long time, because she kept bursting into tears and her words were difficult to understand through the hiccupping, but they said nothing as they heard her out. Finally she ran down like a clockwork toy and sat staring at them, shoulders hunched against the stark reality of her words, a sodden mess of grief.

Fitz was looking at the texts. "I'm going to castrate him," she said with finality. "Bastard." She got up and stomped to the kitchen, got out the ice cream and three chipped pasta bowls—the big ones.

"Before we decide on how we're going to murder Marc Russo, we need sustenance," she announced. "Rocky Road, the ice cream for the broken hearted. I'm a nurse; you know you can't go wrong with my prescription!" Fitz's voice continued to spew nonsense as she slammed the bowls onto the counter and ladled out huge scoops of her antidote. She shoved a bowl into Aubrey's unresisting hands and plunked herself down on the floor, muttering invectives under her breath.

Aubrey lifted the spoon to her mouth and took a bite, the motion automatic and uncaring. The ice cream slid down her scratched throat, working its magic in spite of her indifference. She looked at her two friends, blinking, wondering how she'd been lucky enough to find them in this alien land. There was more to Harrington, New Jersey than Marc Russo, she thought...and suddenly, without warning, she was angry. Rage bubbled up from somewhere deep in her heart, hot and oily. She welcomed the feeling, stoked it. Angry was alive. Angry was good.

"I'm not going to let him get away with this!" she announced. "I can't *believe* he thought he could just type out a few words and never face the music. What a monstrous, fucking coward!" She gestured with the spoon. "I'm going to go to his job and force him to tell me we're through to my fucking face!" Kate and Fitz watched her with approval. Aubrey never cursed. This was not the meek, drooping blob of humanity they had walked in on a short while ago. She was a spitfire, a hell-cat. Aubrey glared at them and shoved a huge spoonful of ice cream into her mouth. The result was immediate. She dropped the spoon and clutched her head as pain ratcheted through it.

"Brain freeze," said Fitz. "Put your tongue on the roof of your mouth. Tha-at's it." She beamed a benevolent smile at Aubrey. "I know it feels awful, but just think how much worse Marc is going to feel when you force him to face you like a man in front of his father and work buddies. Ooh, I want to be a fly on that wall!"

"You do know that he was never good enough for you," said Kate, her voice calm. "Marc Russo was always more in love with himself than with anyone else, even in high school. I never wanted to tell you because your head was so far up in the clouds you couldn't see it, but it's true. And he's not the brightest bulb in the chandelier. He never would have gotten into college if it hadn't been for that basketball scholarship. I know this to be true because we're related, unfortunately, way back somewhere in Neanderthal times. His branch just never evolved. You are sooo much smarter than he is."

"I don't feel very smart," mumbled Aubrey, her anger evaporating like water bubbles on a hot stove. "I feel like the stupidest human being in the universe right now." The tears welled again.

"Well, of course you do, sweetie—that's how man poison works!" Fitz snorted. "He got into your heart through your eyes. He's a looker, I'll give him that. But you aren't the first to go down that rabbit hole, and you won't be the last. It's happened to me any number of times, and here I am, ready for the next adventure with a spoon in my hand, ready to coach you through it!"

Kate rolled her eyes. "This is new for Bree, Fitz! She doesn't have the practice with awful men that you have. *You* are an experienced fuck-up with the male species," she added kindly. "Give her a minute before you drown her in tales of your horrible relationships, will you?"

"Well, you're one to talk, Kate Bianchi! What do you know about sucky relationships? You've been blissfully married for three years to your boyfriend from the fifth grade, for God's sake, and you and Eddie still go at it like rabbits every chance you get!" She stopped and gave the serving spoon a nervous lick. "Oh...um...well...I didn't mean to imply that you were *doing* it in fifth grade...or that I've *seen* you, you know, but..." Fitz jammed the spoon into her mouth and stopped talking, aided by a glare from Kate.

Aubrey let out a weak giggle, sat up, and swiped at her eyes. "How can anyone wallow effectively with you two around?" she asked in wonder. She regarded her best friends with affection. Kate and Fitz had been here not more than a half hour and already she felt better. She straightened her spine and took a deep breath. She needed to remember that there were some very good things about Harrington, and two of them were sitting in front of her right now, radiating love and concern. She could worry about the next stage of the grieving process tomorrow. Right now she was with the two people she loved best in the world, and there was ice cream to be eaten.

"So," asked Kate. "Next step—what are we binge-watching this time? *Downton Abbey* or *Outlander*?"

"*Outlander!*" answered Fitz and Aubrey in unison.

The mountains of the Scottish Highlands rolled across the television screen and the Skye Boat Song filled the room. "Sing me a song of a lad that is gone..."

It hit her with a dull thud. Yes, her lad was gone. He wasn't going to wake up tomorrow and realize his terrible error. He wasn't going to come running back to beg her forgiveness and swear his undying love. He no longer belonged to her, and she suspected he had been drifting away for a long time. There was nothing she could do about it, and the ache in her heart was not going to go away anytime soon. But here in this moment, with Kate and Fitz, she could forget for just a few moments that once again she had been abandoned. She could lose herself in make-believe, in the beauty of this mystical tale of a true love so strong it would last through the centuries. In that most magical land of all...Scotland.

Suddenly she sat bolt upright, her face going pale. "Oh, my God!"

"What is it, Bree?" Kate asked in alarm, spoon arrested halfway to her mouth.

"Angus! I'm supposed to be at work—he's going to kill me for worrying him!"

CHAPTER 3

OIL ON THE WATER

The harsh Scottish wind howled over the water, whipping the whitecaps into a frenzy and moaning around the legs of the Hound Point Oil Terminal in the Firth of Forth. At night the terminal was lost in the mist. Not until one was almost upon it did it appear like a monstrous alien creature out of the waters of the firth, evoking the ancient beast for which it had been named.

Legend had it that during the twelfth century the lord of nearby Barnbougle Castle had owned a huge hunting dog, from which he had never been separated since its presentation to him as a whelp. Locals often commented, upon seeing the two wandering over the moors day and night, that there was something unearthly about the attachment between man and dog. They shivered and crossed themselves and wondered what would happen should one of them die.

As it happened, the lord was called upon by virtue of his station to fight in the Crusades, that mad bloodbath from which so many never returned to their homeland. And it was so with the Lord of Barnbougle. In a godless land he was cut down in the heat of battle to lie face up in the desert, bleeding his life into the sand. At the same moment on a chilly promontory over a firth in Scotland, a hound began to howl, never ceasing until it collapsed in its grief and died. Since that day, say the residents of the area, the ghost of a howling hound has appeared on the point each time the lord of the castle neared his time.

Many centuries had passed since the legend was born, but the locals never forgot, and through the years some would swear they had heard the howling of the great dog when another lord took his last breath. Thus the promontory became known as Hound Point, and when modern men decided to build an oil terminal in the waters of the firth it made sense to pass along the name to the ungainly structure standing in defiance of nature above the waves.

During the day tourists crossing the nearby Forth Bridge could see the huge tanker ships docking at Hound Point to be loaded with oil bound for ports all over the world. It was a key component in the economic success of the United Kingdom, and a political pawn in the struggle between Highlanders and their compatriots south of Hadrian's Wall. Oil meant work, prosperity, and political supremacy.

Unlike the Grangemouth Refinery several miles down the firth, there was little chance of an accident at Hound Point. Oil was not refined here, merely loaded. No chance of an explosion or that dreaded environmental disaster, a spill.

But that was about to change. As the night mist closed in over the firth and the wind roared and shrieked above the waves like a demented ghost, six figures slipped into the frigid water and swam toward the terminal. The divers wore deep water wetsuits to protect from the biting cold of the icy current and they carried the tools of their trade in the packs strapped to their backs.

A crew member on the deck of the tanker *British Honour* stretched and yawned. A lot of the work on an oil tanker was monotonous, but guard duty was the worst, in his opinion. The cold Scottish winter seeped into his bones and the boredom was enervating and constant, exacerbated by the knowledge that it was unnecessary. The idea of someone attempting to steal oil was ludicrous. It wasn't in barrels, so how would a thief load it? A vessel large enough to contain enough oil would be somewhat noticeable, after all. He yawned again. Boring was better than fearful when all was said and done, he supposed.

But the men gathering below were not interested in stealing oil. Their mission was to be immediate and catastrophic, and like the legend of the ancient hound would never be forgotten. Behind them, at the end of a cable, a round metal sphere stalked the divers, supported with utmost care by two members of the team. The black ball had spikes protruding from all sides, giving it the look of a malignant porcupine.

The sphere was a contact mine left from World War II, every bit as deadly as the day it had been manufactured in a Nazi munitions factory. Prohibited by the surrender of the Axis powers from realizing its terrible potential, it had been kept hidden and guarded for just such a time as this. Tonight, its chance had come. Some weapons stood the test of time, and this was such a one.

The men honored their lethal companion with the respect it deserved. It was the most important member of their team, and the most horrifying. It had one function. The men towing it were its attendants, present only to assure its position and facilitate its purpose. Once the mine was tethered in place, they would be gone, their job done.

They had no doubt that their employer had hired them for political reasons, but those were of no concern. Like mercenaries in foreign wars through-out history, these men worked for only one objective. They were Scots, born and bred in the Highlands, but they had little interest in their history, no compunc-tion about how their actions might affect their land or their people. They had no loyalties, except to the one who was paying them. And they were the best at what they did.

Only the group leader had ever been in contact with their employer, and even he had never seen the face of the one who had ordered this mission. The men preferred it that way. Their payment would be deposited in an off-shore account as soon as the flames began to climb to the sky and spread across the firth.

The behemoth tanker was berthed at HP 2, one of Hound Point's two loading platforms. The depth at this point was twenty-two meters and the ship rocked in the water, her tanks half full. The loading process had begun the previous morning and usually took at least twenty hours to complete. As the sun rose, the tanker would be sated and ready to debark with her belly full of enough oil to fill a million barrels.

The men gathered unseen beneath its hull with their prickly companion were there to see that the tanker would never leave her berth. The ship was hours away from extinction, as were the men who rocked in their berths above, waiting for the new day and another load of black gold. Regret for human loss of life was pointless; caring was a waste of time and energy. Such were the laws of war, and the divers knew that this was a war.

The leader of the team maneuvered the mine to a space beneath the center oil tank. Another swam to a point about five feet under the hull and waited. The contact mine was anchored to the floor of the firth and floated upward until the man waiting signaled. The cable was fastened and the mine allowed to drift, a round spiky death with all the patience in the world.

The plan was beautiful in its simplicity. As it was piped into the tanks in the hold, the weight of the oil would force the great colossus ever lower in the water. When the ship's hull touched the spiny monster waiting just five meters below, the mine would be triggered and history would record the demise of *British Honour* and the Hound Point terminal.

The team shouldered its equipment and swam off the way they had come, silent and invisible. Job done, all that remained was the waiting.

At three o'clock in the morning the world is at its darkest and most silent. The night is determined to retain its grip, and even the most stubborn insomniac has given up and surrendered to the numbing peace. On the Firth of Forth the wind had died and the waves lapped against the oil tanker berthed at HP2. The only sound was the constant thrum of the pumps as they loaded the oil into the tanks.

And then Hell came to Hound Point. As the hull tapped against the mine, eighty kilograms of amatol reacted. A massive force lifted the tanker ten feet into the air almost in slow motion, and then folded it at its base and slammed the vessel back into the water like a child's toy, its hull torn and bleeding oil from a mortal wound. Fire caught the oil and followed its path across the water and onto the platform, destroying everything in its path. The darkness was split by a tower of fire that shot eighty feet into the air.

Within minutes everything that had stood above the water was in flames. The ship's metal hull heated like an oven, cooking everything on board. The guard on deck opened his mouth in horror, only to breathe in the ball of fire that surrounded him and burned his body to a charred husk where he stood. Those in their beds were the lucky ones, asphyxiated before they had time to wake up and realize they were dead. *British Honour* settled to the floor of the firth, her blackened, twisted masts reaching up from the waves like the arms of drowning men.

Fifteen miles away, the explosion sent tourists in Edinburgh stumbling to their hotel windows to watch the black smoke rising into the sky and wonder if terrorists had found them here, in the most peaceful place in the world.

They were right to wonder. War had been declared in Scotland, but the enemy was closer to home than anyone had imagined, and this display of aggression was just the beginning.

CHAPTER 4

TOUCH NOT THE CAT

The bell piped *Scotland the Brave* as Aubrey opened the door to *Angus' Auld Books*. She smiled as she always did at the sound of the bagpipes, in spite of the nausea roiling in her stomach. A combination of heartache and too much ice cream was not an excuse to miss work, and besides, sitting at home would be far worse. Here was where she felt at home, more than she ever did in her lonely, under-furnished apartment. Her Marc-less apartment.

Taking a deep breath, she passed the tartan draped counter and went through the stacks to the rear of the shop. She waded through piles of unshelved books until she reached the battered door at the back. A plaque affixed there showed a mountain lion with its paws raised in defiance, and the words "Touch not the Cat Bot A Glove" circling the edge. "Touch not this cat without a glove," the clan Mackintosh motto.

Angus Mackintosh was sitting at a scarred oak table, poring over what looked like an account book and scowling. He looked up and his face transformed at the sight of Aubrey in the doorway, breaking into an impossibly beautiful smile. The two missing front teeth somehow added to the charm. Ordinarily Angus resembled nothing so much as a cantankerous garden gnome, but for the few he deemed worthy the smile was a gift, like the sun emerging from a cloud bank, and well worth the experience. Aubrey felt her spirits lift.

"Ach, lassie, I was worrit when ye didna come in yesterday. It's not like ye not t'lit me ken if ye be poorly." The smile disappeared, replaced by a familiar glower. Now that she was proven not to be poorly, the gnome was back.

"I'm sorry, Angus. It was a really bad day." She took a deep breath, let it out slowly. "Marc broke up with me." She took another breath and held it, bracing herself for the explosion.

"Aye?" Angus shrugged. "That's guid, then."

She laughed at the simplicity of his response. She couldn't help it. Angus had never liked Marc, and he made no effort to hide his feelings. Not that he knew him well—Marc had been in the bookshop exactly twice during the eight months she had worked there, and both times he had looked warily at all the old books as if they might sneak up on him when he wasn't looking and make him learn something. He was equally suspicious of Angus, with his broad Scots brogue and the kilt swishing about his knobby knees.

"What does he wear that skirt for?" Marc had demanded the first time he picked her up from work. "This is America, for God's sake!"

Angus had withheld comment on Marc, but his bushy eyebrows told the story for anyone perceptive enough to read them. It was obvious that Aubrey's man did not read books, therefore he was superfluous at best. Guid fur nuthin.

Aubrey went back through into the bookshop and booted up the computer. She was the only one who used it. Angus avoided technology with a tenacity that was as admirable as it was annoying. She fixed herself a cup of coffee from the Keurig in the small cafe area—another of her ideas that made no sense to Angus—"Whit do we need 'at fur?" he had asked her. "We want them t' buy a book an' gang away, no?"

It wasn't worth explaining to him. She suspected that he challenged her just for the sake of arguing anyway. And in some respects he was right. The cafe corner did attract readers, but more often they came in to enjoy the ambience of an old-world bookshop with coffee and a muffin. They would look lovingly at the books huddled on their shelves, sigh in delight, and then break out their Kindles. Not exactly a great advertisement for a *bookstore*, but she was afraid that if she removed the Keurig and pastries, the sort-of customers would remove themselves and their Kindles to the coffee shop down the street. The Busy Bean had recently installed a leather couch and two arm chairs, damn them.

She sighed. It didn't really matter what they did; the bookshop was doomed. Even if all the Kindle readers saw the light, chucked their devices and bought books, it wasn't enough. A town like Harrington just wasn't the venue for a shop like this one. Angus and his kilt and his auld books stuck out like a string quartet at a rock concert, and provoked hilarious derision by the folks who passed by on their way to the video arcade or the dollar store.

Angus didn't seem to notice, or maybe he thought they were the ridiculous ones. He was a man out of his element, in every conceivable way. A Scotsman in full regalia in a town full of second and third generation Italians, sprinkled with a few mutts like Aubrey. And he didn't seem to care. In fact, he seemed to revel in his nonconformity. Everyone in town knew about Angus, but hardly anyone ever saw him out of the shop. He was Harrington's own Loch Ness Monster, famous for being elusive and mysterious.

What was Angus doing in a place like Harrington, New Jersey anyway? Aubrey wondered, and not for the first time. He'd been here when she arrived, and *Angus' Auld Books* had been old then. Was he possessed of a time machine? Or even better, had he fallen through some standing stones one day whilst hiking through the heather, *Outlander* style? It was one of the many mysteries that cloaked her old Scotsman like the shadows under Menley's Bridge, where the kids went to drink beer and make out. No matter how many times she asked him, the response was always the same: "It's nae on's business but mah ain." And that was that.

She received a slightly different version of the same answer when she attempted to engage him in any discussion about the ultimate fate of the shop. "Somethin'll come along. Ah ain't worrit." But sometimes Aubrey caught him looking at her from under his bushy gray eyebrows, and he did look "worrit" to her. It caught at her heart. She truly loved this old man and spent quite a few sleepless nights wondering what she would do without him. He'd probably go back to Scotland, she realized, and it hit her with the force of a battering ram. He was the closest thing to a father she had now, and the thought of losing him rocked her. The idea was almost unbearable, following on the heels of Marc's defection.

After straightening the books on the shelves again—how did they always get so mixed up when people never seemed to look at them?—Aubrey checked the inventory against the few sales they'd made yesterday, which took a distressingly short amount of time. Then she brought up the website she'd created with her own loving hands, featuring pictures of the Cairngorms, Loch Ness, the Isle of Skye, and a picture of Angus taken at his work table, grizzled head bent over a book. He'd never looked at the site, so he wasn't likely to see the picture, even though she was quite proud of her achievement.

The layout was beautiful, if she did say so herself, and it had received hundreds of hits, which should have been uplifting. The problem was, the hits could have been from anywhere in the world. That was the nature of the internet. Most likely a miniscule number came from Harrington. And the hits didn't bring in customers. So after all was said and done, the site was useless. But you had to try, didn't you? Besides, it was by way of being a tribute to her father, and that made it worth the effort.

Three of the Kindle ladies came in, chattering like magpies about the latest "book" they were reading for their book club, and made a beeline for the cafe corner. They were regulars, in their small way, and thus deserving of Aubrey's respect. At least they bought muffins. Angus would not have deemed them worthy of any kind of attention, as they did not read real books—except for the fact that they heaped adulation on his kilt, his sporran and the lethal looking dagger tucked into his stocking. Angus was, after all, a man.

Sure enough, here he came, swinging his plaid like a Celtic rooster.

"Weel, kimers, an' fit loch thes braw morn?" He thickened his brogue to the point of incomprehensibility, but since he said the same thing every time they came in, his admirers had learned that he was saying, "Well, ladies, and how are you this fine morning?"

They simpered at him. "Oh, fine, Mr. Mackintosh. And will you finally tell us today what a Scotsman wears under his kilt?" They all giggled. They took turns asking and never got tired of it. Aubrey rolled her eyes.

Angus chuckled as if it was the first time he'd heard that one. "Weel, 'at's nae mystery, lassies, unner his kilt a Scotsman wears 'is boots!" The answer was different each time. Leaving them in stitches, he sashayed back to his workroom. They went back to their devices and their muffins and an hour later they left, without buying anything made of paper.

Left alone again, Aubrey's treacherous mind shifted to the night before. Without Kate and Fitz, she could feel her world closing in like a vise, feel the panic rising to strangle her. Was this what an anxiety attack felt like? Staring at the Callanish Stones screensaver in numb misery, she let the emotions rise up and engulf her in a mist of anguish. Marc was gone. Her future was gone. Her livelihood would soon be gone. She felt like Gulliver, a misfit in a land not her own. She thought she had cried enough yesterday to fill a bathtub, but grief was an evil magician who could always conjure more. Aubrey put her head on her arms and let the self-pity carry her away in a new torrent of tears.

And then Angus was there, gently guiding her into the back room, his gnarled hand clutching her wrist and his plaid swinging behind him as if it had a life of its own.

"Ach, lassie, there's no point blubberin' abit things 'at ur dain an' gain, noo."

Aubrey snapped at him, unable to shoulder the burden of worry and pain any longer.

"But they're not done and gone! That is the point! The bookshop isn't making enough money to pay the rent, and I can't stay here where Marc is!"

Angus emitted a Gaelic snort somewhere between his nose and his throat. It might at any time signal disgust, anger, or approval, but Aubrey knew that it was to be ignored at her peril.

"I'm sorry, Angus. I know you're just trying to help. But you can't."

"Shut yer gob, noo." He gave her an ominous look.

She shut up and let him guide her to the corner of his workroom and push her into an ancient chair, a piece of furniture only recognizable as such by the four chipped legs that fought the laws of physics to hold it up.

She must really be in dire straits, Aubrey thought. The chair was Angus' own, his "wonderin'" seat he called it, where he spent an inordinate amount of time with his head back, eyes closed, pipe hanging at an impossible angle from his lips. She'd always suspected that "wonderin'" meant sleeping, as the rumbling noises that emanated from the corner sounded an awful lot like snores.

"Noo, rest yer heart, lassie," he said, his voice gentle and soothing. "Gie yerself some peace."

They sat in silence, letting the quiet and the shadows of the workroom envelope them.

"I can't stay here, Angus," Aubrey said again after a while, her voice calmer but still trembling. "And I have nowhere else to go."

Her Scot gave her a long, measuring look. Then without warning he stood up, pulled her out of the chair, and dragged her out of the workroom and back into the shop. "Come wi' me, lass, there's somethin' ye need tae see." Aubrey, bewildered by the abrupt change in pace, followed him. She had no choice; when Angus was intent on a course of action, nothing on earth was going to stand in his way. The Scots would never have lost the Battle of Culloden, she was convinced, if they were all as hard-headed and determined as Angus Mackintosh.

He pulled her deep into the darkest corner at the back of the shop. This was the part of the store that Aubrey privately called "the Arcanum," because the books here were old—some of them maybe ancient. Who knew when they had been written, or what secrets they might contain? Angus, probably. No one else ever ventured this far back in the stacks, and it was too dark here to read the titles anyway.

She inhaled and her nostrils were assailed by the wonderful scent that old books could give. The musty tomes had a smell that only bibliophiles would understand, a lovely aroma somewhere between chocolate and earth after a rain. She took in the combination of grassy notes, acids, and almond embracing her olfactory system like an old friend, or a lover.

A lover! Aubrey snickered, trying to imagine Marc smelling like an old book. No, he would never smell so honest. His scent would be more like a cheap perfume, perhaps "Au du Betrayal." She giggled at her wit, surprised and gratified at finding her sense of humor battered but intact. She found that in the company of her true friends, she could breathe a little better now when she thought about Marc. Friends like Angus, Kate, Fitz...and books. They would get her through.

She let her fingers dance over the spines of the old books like a blind man reading Braille, her touch feather-soft and reverent. She didn't dare pick one up, afraid that committing such sacrilege might cause it to disintegrate, collapse into a pile of dust. She wanted to so much that she clasped her hands behind her back to keep them still. The books were piled willy-nilly on the shelf, as though they had been up during the night socializing with each other, sharing their secrets while no people were there to intrude on their knowledge, and scurrying but not quite managing to get back into place before daylight arrived.

Angus shouldered Aubrey aside and reached up for a large book that rested just above eye level. He brought it down and carried it to the worktable, and then turned to face her, his expression unreadable.

"What is this one?" Aubrey's voice was low, almost a whisper, as though the book might be disturbed by any kind of human noise.

"Ah want ye tae see fur yerself. Gang aheid, ye don't need tae be afraid o' it. It means ye no harm."

It meant her no harm? A book? What an odd thing to say, Aubrey thought, even for Angus.

"But be cannie," he added. "Don't be scarit if it talks tae ye, noo."

Curiouser and curiouser! She gave Angus a long look to see if he was pulling her leg. He did that, sometimes. His lined, leathery face was set, serious. He was not joking.

She was seized by an unaccountable nervousness, a fear that her next step might change her in ways for which she was not prepared. She was almost afraid to reach out toward the odd book. A preternatural feeling of apprehension had crazy butterflies flitting around in her stomach.

What the hell was wrong with her? It was just a *book*, for God's sake, not a wild animal. Taking a deep breath, she touched the thick leather cover...and screamed.

Aubrey found herself cowering against the nearest bookshelf, some three feet away, unaware of how she had gotten there. Her eyes wide with shock, she looked to Angus. He hadn't moved, but the expression on his face had changed. He looked *satisfied.*

"What was that?" she said with a quiver. "What the *hell* just happened?"

He ignored her panicked question. "Ah was right," he said softly to himself. "It knows 'er."

CHAPTER 5

ALL IN THE NAME

Aubrey repeated, almost pleading, "What *was* that, Angus? Did you know this would happen?"

The expression on his face gave her the answer before he spoke.

"Aye," he said, the look of gratification at odds with the tension in his wiry frame. "Ah ken. At leest Ah hoped. Gang aheid," he said eagerly, "it willna hurt ye."

Aubrey felt rooted to the spot. Every one of her senses had been involved in the first attempt to touch that book. She had felt a jolt like she imagined it might feel when one stuck a finger into an electric outlet, heard a buzzing like a thousand angry bees inside her head. She could still taste the rancid remnants of burnt meat. The smell was almost overpowering—dense, foul air that swarmed with maggots and decay. And she had seen the book *move*, almost as if it were reaching out to grasp her hand. She had never been so frightened in her life.

But she trusted Angus, didn't she? He had always been there for her, had treated her like a daughter. Would he allow her to place herself in danger if he could stop it? But what if he couldn't stop it? What if...?

"Gang aheid!" he barked, affronted. "Ah woodn't let harm come tae ye, ye shood ken 'at."

She did ken that. Aubrey hesitated, then moved to stand in front of the book again. Just a book, after all. Nothing supernatural. She shook herself and reached out a trembling finger. The buzzing rose like a swarm of hornets and drowned out all other sound. The meat taste and smell of decay were back, gagging her. The book stared at her with a look of impatient malevolence, and before her horrified gaze the pages began to turn of their own accord. She tried to jerk her hand away and realized that she could not. Terror rooted her to the spot.

The rifling pages slowed, as if the book was searching itself, and as they did Aubrey felt a strange calm descend and fill her mind. Her fear drained away as if it had never been, to be replaced by wonder and a sort of eager anticipation.

The pages stopped turning. The buzzing dwindled to a low hum. Angus moved up to stand beside her, nodding approval. "Reid it," he said quietly. "It be fur ye."

"Me?" She turned wide eyes on him. "Why me? What does it want with me?"

"Reid it," he said again, the impatience returning. "Dinna be askin' questions noo, lass!"

She took a deep breath and turned back to the book. The words were written in an old tongue, by hand, and the ink was faded almost to invisibility. But she could make them out clearly, and she could understand the words as if she had Googled them this morning. A soft chill moved up her spine at the realization. She *shouldn't* have been able to read them, but she could.

※

In the year 1442, she read out loud, *the Comyn clan did lay claim to the castle that is called Raite, and so also did the clan Mackintosh. Long had the two argued over the castle, and about much other, but the Comyns having possession the Mackintosh at length conceded their ryght. Upon hearing this, the Comyn did invyte the clan Mackintosh to a grayte feast, the purpose to celebrate the burying of animositye. But there was treacherye in the heart of the Mackintosh, and the men of the clan had contrived in a plot most foul, that at a signal each would rise up and slaye his defenceless host. The daughter of the Comyn had taken the son of the Mackintosh to her bed, though she loved him not, but hated her clan the more. It was she who did give the signal for the massacre to begin. Thus it did happen, and the Comyn were slaughtered to a man where they stood, hands still raised in toast to their murderous guests. The blood ran thick on the floor and soaked into the rushes, whilst she who had no heart watched without shame. But the Comyn himself saw his daughter's stony face and knew the depths of her deceit. He did follow her to the top of the castle tower, and did there cut off her hands and send her to Hell. With his last breath he did curse the clan Mackintosh, that they would never again find peace. From that night to this the walls of Raite Castle have stood emptye and the clan Mackintosh have wandered the hills of Scotland, never to find a home. The clan was cursed thus for the foolishness of the son of the Mackintosh: none shall be loved truly, but always in vain. The curse will never be lifted until a Comyn comes to love a Mackintosh without guile, and the sin be thus absolved. The ghost of the faithless lass wanders the hall still, searching for the one who will lift the curse and free her.*

Almost as if the book knew that she had come to the end of the passage, it closed with a snap. Aubrey jumped back, rubbing her fingers. The humming ceased, and the smell of burning wood and dead flesh dissipated as if it had never been. Pulling herself together with difficulty, she turned to the old Scot.

"That's...sad, Angus. But what does it have to do with me?"

His eyes were evasive. "Ah dinna ken, lass. Th' wee book was talkin' tae ye, wasna't?"

"Angus!" Her frustration was mounting. Something was working at the edges of her consciousness, trying to get through the shock to her brain.

"Angus," she said slowly, "that's just it! Why *would* the thing talk to me? It's a book! And anyway, it's just some historian's opinion, isn't it? The book only knows what somebody wrote in it, probably centuries ago. It could be wrong!" Just saying it sounded ridiculous, as if she was discussing a real person instead of a musty old pile of parchment. She looked at the offending volume with loathing.

"Weel, noo, it isnae fur me tae question th' magic, is it?" Angus was not smiling. "An' aye, th' *story* depends on who's tellin' it. But th' *curse* is real."

"Come on! How do you know that?"

He said nothing for several moments, picking at his plaid and looking at the floor. Then he spoke, but his words made no sense to Aubrey.

"Ah've ne'er found love, lass." He looked at her then, and his blue eyes reflected centuries of loss and heartache.

Never found love? Where had that come from? And what did it have to do with that damned bo—

Aubrey gasped. "You're a Mackintosh! You think you've been cursed! Oh, Angus, that can't be...it's not possible!" Her heart broke for the old man. He'd been old when she met him. It had never occurred to her that he might once have loved someone, that he had suffered a loss. Here she had been going on about Marc, whingin' and greetin', as Angus would say, about her pitiful love life and her hatred of Harrington, as if she were the only human being who had ever suffered that kind of pain! How selfish can I be? she thought in disgust.

She wanted to hug him, but she knew that a hug was the absolute last thing he would want. So she wrapped her arms around herself instead and stepped back. Angus stared at her, unblinking.

"All right...I'll accept that you *think* you're cursed. But if no Mackintoshes can ever find love, then how are you even *here*? The line should have died out, shouldn't it?" She fixed him with a triumphant eye.

"Ye dinna need love tae have bairns, lass," he explained, his voice patient and sad. "Dinna ye ken 'at?"

She was embarrassed. "Oh. Yes, of course I know that! But do you mean to tell me that you think *no* Mackintosh in almost six hundred years has been in love? That's ridiculous! How would you even know, anyway?"

Angus sighed. "Ah juist ken." The words were final.

"Well, I don't believe it," said Aubrey. "It's ridiculous! Everything in that—*thing*— is like a fairy tale! It's just make believe! I can't believe that a whole clan thinks it's cursed because of something an ancestor did hundreds of years ago! Ridiculous!" she said again. "And what about the other part of the curse? The part where they have to wander around Scotland looking for a home? There are a lot of Mackintoshes in the Scottish Highlands, aren't there? Surely they live in houses!" She fisted her hands on her hips, feeling a bit like a lawyer who has just won his case.

Angus shook his head in annoyance. "Och aye, they bide in hooses. But they lost their castle, an' th' lands gi'en tae 'em by th' Bruce. They lost their *honur!*"

Aubrey didn't get it, but she could see that it meant a great deal to Angus. And then it struck her, the thing that had been niggling at her brain, and she looked back at the book, sitting innocent and still on the worktable. *I'm just another old book, never mind me*, it seemed to say. Only now she knew better. She shuddered in recollection. If it was all a fairy tale, why had she felt that power? Why the smell, the taste, the buzzing? She wished she had never laid eyes on that damn book. She sighed, and her voice was barely above a whisper.

"But why me, Angus? Why did it react like that to *me*?" She wondered again if Angus, for some reason known only to himself, might be having her on, might have orchestrated this whole charade.

"Hmmph," he remarked, as if he knew what she was thinking. He turned his back on her. Then he turned around and fixed her with a piercing glare. "Yer name is Cumming, reit?"

"You know it is. What does that have to do with anything?"

"Weel," he answered, drawing the word out like a fishing line with a victim that looked a lot like Aubrey flopping on the end. "Sometime in th' sixteenth century, th' Comyns gang 'n changed their name."

He rocked back on his heels and grinned at her, milking the moment.

"They changed it tae Cumming."

She sank onto a stool.

Angus poured out a generous dram of Talisker whisky into two stubby glasses and handed one to Aubrey. "A wee dram'll fix ye reit up," he pronounced. She sipped it and made a face. She'd never had scotch before. It tasted like motor oil with cigarette ash stirred in, but it was Angus' favorite and shock did wonders for the taste buds.

Closing her eyes, she gulped the whisky down and held out the glass for another wee dram. And then another. This stuff wasn't half bad, she decided after the third one had burned its way down her throat.

When she held the glass out again, Angus gave her a dour look. "Ah'll be needin' th' keys t' yer motur," he said.

Aubrey was feeling all warm and snuggly inside—until she stood up. The room began to swim before her glazing eyes, and too late she remembered she hadn't had any breakfast. To his credit, Angus guided her to the bathroom and held her hair back while she vomited up all the whisky, and then he left her alone to lie on the tiled floor, moaning and wishing for death.

When she stumbled back out into the workroom an hour later, Angus was sitting in his wonderin' chair, the book in his lap. He looked up and gave her that beautiful, toothless smile.

"Says here 'at when th' Comyn lass finds 'er Mackintosh, all th' pipers in Scootlund will begin tae play."

"That's nice," Aubrey said. She sat down on the floor and put her head in her hands. She felt fuzzy, as if someone had thrown a wet blanket over her head. She was never drinking whisky again, never ever. How on earth had they managed to keep drinking the stuff all through the wedding episode of *Outlander*? She'd developed a new respect for the Scots while she was in the bathroom puking her guts out.

"Did ye hear what Ah said abit th' pipers?" he asked, the impatience crackling in his voice.

"Yes, I heard. So what?"

He snorted. "All th' pipers in Scootlund..."

"Okay, all the pipers in Scotland." What wasn't she getting?

"Weel noo, yer wee Marco trooble is solved." He stood and hopped around in a credible rendition of the Highland Fling. "If yer t' hear th' pipers, ye have t' gang tae Scootlund!"

Ye have t' gang tae Scootlund. *Someday we'll go to Scotland.* Aubrey stared at Angus, hearing her father's words in her head. Well, why not? Maybe she owed it to Dad to go for both of them. She could research her family, have some fun, and solve her "wee Marco trooble" at the same time.

"Maybe I will go," she said slowly. "There's nothing left for me here. But it won't be because I believe in that book!" She gave him a stubborn look.

Angus beamed at her. "'At's th' spirit, lass!"

Sanity resurfaced.

"No, Angus, that's stupid. I don't know anyone in Scotland! Where would I live?"

"Ach, dinna ye fash yerself aboot 'at. Ye'll bide wi' mah friend Nessie, in Inverness."

And just like that, the decision was made. Hours later, as Aubrey drove herself home in the waning summer light, she gripped the steering wheel and contemplated the avalanche of the last two days. She'd been dumped. A book had attacked her. She'd discovered single malt whisky. And she was moving to Scotland. When had she lost control of her life? And why did it feel so right?

*If you hear the past speaking to you, feel
it tugging up your back and running
its fingers up your spine, the best
thing to do-the only thing-is run.*

Lauren Oliver

SCOTLAND, 1442

For countless centuries before Ailith Comyn's birth, her family had been at war. At war with Edward I of England. At war with Robert the Bruce. At war with the Grants, the Shaws, the MacPhersons. In previous centuries, the Comyns had been the law in the north of Scotland, controlling many castles and collecting tariffs from lesser clans. Their power had stretched from Inverlochy to Slains, and they had ruled the political scene like Highland gods. But always there had been war.

It was the war for Scottish independence that proved their undoing. Victory in battle depends upon backing the right leader, and as the thirteenth century slipped into the mists of time, Clan Comyn made a fatal choice. In a monstrous miscalculation of the tides of war, they chose to attach their fortunes to the armies of King Edward I of England, creating a lethal enemy in the man who would someday become king of all Scotland. Thereafter, the enmity between Ailith

Comyn's ancestors and Robert the Bruce was intense and malignant.

Clan Comyn's hopes of a return to power and glory were forever dashed at the Battle of Bannockburn in 1314, when the laird was killed and their lands given to Clan Mackintosh, staunch supporters of the Bruce. Like the wolves that roamed the Highlands in those days, other clans sensed blood and gathered at the walls of the Comyn strongholds, hoping for a chance to take their enemy down. There were more enemies than allies, more losses than gains.

Legends began to arise with each Comyn defeat. In 1330, men under the Earl of Moray massed beneath the towers of Dunphail Castle, one of the last Comyn fortresses, and prepared to starve them out. Five Comyn defenders fought their way out in a desperate effort to re-supply their comrades with grain, but upon their return they were captured by the superior force of the Moray. Their heads were thrown over the wall to their comrades, accompanied by the taunt "here's your beef for your bannocks." Horrified, the Comyn defenders attempted to flee but were cut down, their blood soaking into the rough Scottish earth.

Clan Comyn would never rise again. The legend of the five headless ghosts who haunted Dunphail pursued them down the years, to be added to the increasing list of defeats suffered by the luckless clan. The enemies came and went, the Comyns losing more of their power and more of their land. In the end, they were left with one castle, named Raite, which they had wrestled from the Mackintosh by trickery.

Ailith knew nothing of her clan's history, neither the glory nor the defeat. By the time she was born, in the fall of 1424, Robert the Bruce was nothing more than a tale to frighten children...the Comyn bogeyman. The enemy now was Clan Mackintosh and its allies.

Ailith's three brothers were warriors, like their ancestors before them. They spent their days in the lists of Raite Castle and their nights in their cups, waiting for the next foe to present himself. They knew nothing else.

They had no time to waste on a sister. Ailith was nothing more than a bargaining chip. A woman was raised to serve her men and to be bartered to the highest bidder, for whatever lands and alliances she could bring. Ailith Comyn knew no other way, and so accepted her responsibility as the dutiful daughter of her laird.

Until she met Coinneach Mackintosh.

CHAPTER 6

WOOL GATHERING

Sheep drifted across the road, creamy mounds of tufted wool with no purpose in mind, no concern beyond the next meal which lay just out of sight over the hill. No hurry. They came closer, curious, crowding all around her now, their vapid sheep faces sniffing, pushing. As they surrounded her the faces changed, morphing into something feral and intelligent. Close up, they exuded menace. Their black eyes glinted with hatred, their mouths opening to display sharp knives where teeth should be. They had come for her—

With a cry of terror Aubrey startled awake, unsure for a moment where she was, still lost in the awful sensation of impending peril. She found herself sitting in the window seat of the huge British Airways 767, breathing in short gasps with her eyes closed tightly in panic, mouth dry.

"Fear of flying, dear?" her seatmate asked in sympathy. A fellow American, by her accent. "I used to suffer from anxiety, too, until my doctor prescribed the good stuff, and now I'm right as rain. You should go see yours, that's what they're there for!" The tiny gray-haired woman dug into her bag and produced a massive pillbox, flipping it open to reveal a veritable trove of variegated pills. "I know you're not supposed to take other people's medication, but you look like you need it. I won't tell if you don't!" She winked at Aubrey.

"N-no, thank you. It was just a dream. I'm not afraid."

"All right, but the magic is here if you need it."

Magic. The word pulled Aubrey back to Angus's bookshop and the malicious book that had held her in thrall such a short time ago. *Was* it magic? Suspended here above the world, in a vessel that weighed tons but seemed weightless, anything seemed possible. Magic was in the eye of the beholder. She looked out the window at the puffy clouds through which the giant airliner streamed, strong and capable. Not sheep, just clouds. Innocent, like the sweet little drug dealer sitting next to her. But the remnants of the dream clung to her consciousness, ghosts born of the all-consuming terror she had felt.

Aubrey had lied. She *was* afraid. She wasn't afraid of flying, or travelling alone to a strange country where she knew no one and had no idea how she was going to support herself. Not the normal things. *Let's see*, she thought, *I'm afraid of murderous sheep. And weird smelly books that try to talk to me. I'm scared that the curse might be real, and that I'll fail*

Angus. And I'm terrified that I might be more like the Mackintoshes than the Comyns, and I'll never find love. I'm afraid I'll never trust again. And that was it, she knew. The fear of abandonment, started when her father had left her in the blink of an eye, and cemented by Marc's betrayal.

Well, as long as she knew what her problem was, she could handle it. She would simply not let another man get close enough to worm his way into her heart. Easy fix. Aubrey had always been easier around imaginary men than the real thing anyway, preferring Prince Charming, whose motives were always pure and scripted, to an unknown entity who might say or do anything. Because she was pretty, with ash blonde hair and wide hazel eyes, boys asked her out. But there was something about her that kept them at arms-length, and after a while they gave up and didn't ask again.

By the time she enrolled at Wyatt College as an English major, Aubrey had been ripe for plucking by someone like Marco Russo. A blank canvas upon which he could paint the glories of himself, the reflection of his own perceived perfection. It was a relationship that worked for a while, simply because they were such opposites, but it had been doomed from the start. She could see that now. Maybe she just wasn't cut out for romance and love, unless it was in a book or on her beloved period dramas, and that was fine with her. She had expended all her love on a family that had left her, and on a knight in plastic armor.

The only good things that had come from the miserable detour to South Jersey were her friendships with Kate and Fitz and her alliance with Angus. Because of those three, the side trip to Harrington had been worth all the pain and betrayal. And it *was* a side trip—no matter what happened in Scotland, Aubrey knew that her time in Harrington, New Jersey was over. She'd cancelled the wedding, packed everything into storage, and said her goodbyes to the only three people who mattered. She would come back, but only to visit. The one good thing about being homeless was that you didn't have to go home.

She wasn't worried about leaving Angus. He was the reason she was on this crazy quest in the first place and she had to believe he wouldn't leave her alone to stumble around on her own, unarmed and unprotected. Angus would find her wherever she was. Maybe it had been destiny that she had come upon him in Harrington in the first place.

Or had he found her? Shortly after she'd arrived in town, she had been scouring the employment section in the *Harringtonian*, finding job opportunities for "Sales associate, *Morgan's Dept. Store*," "Short order cook, *Vinelli's Trattoria*" (sure, maybe they'd share their recipe for gravy), and "Home health aides wanted for group home," when a small, cryptic ad jumped out at her. "WANTED: A body wha' needs books. *Angus' Auld Books*, Elm St."

At first she had thought it was a sales ad mistakenly placed it in the employment section of the paper. Someone trying to unload a lot of old books. But for some reason her eyes kept returning to the odd posting, and the words "needs books." Who doesn't need books? What could it hurt to check it out? At the worst, she might come home with another book or two, and she'd be no worse off than she was now. So she had gone, and there was Angus. He'd greeted her at the door and told her, "Hoors are on th' door. Ye'll pit yer things in th' wurkroom. Ye start in th' mornin', dinna be late." And that was that. Now he was her family.

Aubrey struggled to reach her tote bag, wedged under the seat in front of her. She squirmed and shimmied and finally fished it out with her foot, landing it in her lap. It was like a workout just to survive in coach, she thought in irritation. Maybe she'd meet a Duke or a laird in Scotland, and then she could travel first class, where they had such things as hot towels, and real food...and leg room.

Turning her attention to the tote, she scrounged around until she found the plastic bag which held her luggage claim tag, car rental receipt, and the information on her lodging in Inverness. Angus had arranged everything with his friend, one Nessie Mackeggie, who ran a boarding house in the city within walking distance to the train and bus stations.

"She's no' th' wee monster in th' loch, noo," he'd told her. "Er name be Agnes, bit they call 'er Nessie cuz 'er hoose is on th' hill above th' river Ness." He paused, looked sidelong at Aubrey. "A coorse, if ye cross 'er, she can give th' monster whit fur!" Then he had burst out laughing, his face crinkling in merriment. No one appreciated Angus' wit more than he did.

The mysterious Nessie had refused payment for the room, so Aubrey was more than grateful and not planning to "cross 'er'" in any way. Since the woman didn't know her and had no earthly reason to give her free room and board, she suspected that Angus had paid for her lodging, which was both surprising and moving. When she faced him down with it he had told her with bad grace that it was his gift and she should just take it and be done.

Undone, more like. She'd been reduced to a blubbering mess until Angus, embarrassed, had thrown up his hands and muttered, "Gang on wi' ye, lassie. It's only a wee bit a minny!" About that Aubrey harbored serious doubts, since Angus, embracing the stereotype, pinched every penny until it howled. There was no amount of money that was wee enough if he had to let go of it. This was the most generous gift she had ever received, and all the more wonderful for his sacrifice. She suspected he knew she had spent most of her meager savings just on the airline ticket.

Her lodging was covered for the foreseeable future, but she needed some source of income. So that meant she'd be looking for a job. Angus had told her that Nessie would help with that. If only Nessie could help her with the loneliness that was creeping into her soul, filling her mind and making her stomach roil with anxiety. Aubrey leaned her head against the window. Watching the clouds scudding past and listening to her seatmate's soft snores, she tried to empty her mind of the choking apprehension. It didn't work.

What the hell was she doing, travelling thousands of miles to a country about which she knew next to nothing, planning to stay until...until what? Until all the pipers in Scotland played the damn bagpipes at the same time? The *Scotland the Brave* door ringer was about all she could take of bagpipes, thank you very much, and the idea of millions of them all playing simultaneously was the most horrendous thing she could imagine. The sheep would rise up in revolt at the prospect of their stomachs being used in such a cavalier fashion, and everyone would go deaf from the noise.

Aubrey was not much good at wallowing. Her spirits began to lift as her imagination supplied her with the vision of a horde of sheep marching to Edinburgh in protest at being used to make musical instruments. The Million Sheep March—their signs would read "Bagpipes make baaaad music!" and "Wait until you need a sweater!" And all because a silly American had come to Scotland to lift a curse and save a clan.

Anyway, she didn't have to worry about causing the entire population of Scotland to become hearing impaired, because the pipes weren't supposed to play until homeless and lovesick Mr. MacRight came swaggering up in a kilt made of Mackintosh tartan and made her fall in love with him. Uh huh. The whole idea was ludicrous. She was flying to a foreign country to fix some kind of wrong that had been done five hundred years ago by one of her ancestors. Even saying it made her question her sanity. What was she supposed to do—stand in the airport with a placard saying "Is your name Mackintosh? Apply here!" What had she gotten herself into? But behind the anxiety and doubt there was an excitement building, a sense of adventure and possibility. Her imagination was reveling in the chance to get out there and discover what mayhem it could bring about in this magical land.

She thought of Kate and Fitz and the unwavering support they had given her in this crazy endeavor. She had told them about the book and the curse, and they had nodded as if it made perfect sense. Of course they didn't believe a word of it, but Aubrey knew what the girls' motivation was. They hoped the move would cure her of her heartache over Marc's defection. Simply getting her out of town was good enough for those two, and she loved them for their loyalty. Angus—well, Angus was just special. She would do anything for that old man, and if anything included an extended stay in a beautiful country with free room and board and a chance to do some research into her family history, then so be it. As long as the sheep kept their distance and she only had to deal with one set of bagpipes at a time. With that comforting thought, her mind let go and she slept, waking as the plane was beginning its descent into Heathrow.

"Have a safe trip, dear," her seatmate said kindly, wrestling her carry-on into the aisle. "And no more bad dreams, you hear?"

"Thank you. I promise," Aubrey answered with a rush of affection. And then the tiny medicine woman was gone, the last link to her home country. She hadn't even gotten her name.

In due time Aubrey boarded her connection, and it seemed mere minutes until they were taxiing in to Edinburgh. She was in Scotland. Her stomach tied in knots of apprehension and expectation, she descended to the tarmac and let herself be carried along with the crowd to her destiny.

Edinburgh Airport was disappointing. Not much tartan, no pictures of castles or lochs, just an airport like any other. As she passed the newsstand on her way to baggage claim, a headline caught her eye. "Firefighter Killed in Third Rig Sabotaged in six months—Parliament Blames Scottish Nationalists." It seemed to be the news of the day, Aubrey noted; every newspaper's front page screamed some version of the story. Well, so far Scotland was not much different from America. Politics and violence ruled the news everywhere in the world.

What did I think, that the top news would be about a couple of clans laying siege to a castle? Then again, sabotaging oil rigs was just the modern version of cattle raiding, she supposed. Aubrey bought a paper, thinking that she should brush up a bit on the current issues of the country in which she would be living, so she might look at least a trifle intelligent at the local Inverness pub. Her imagination had already painted a picture of the pub. Waiters in kilts, plaid everywhere, locals drinking whisky and wolfing down haggis—whatever that was. Didn't matter, it was *Scottish*, dammit!

Baggage reclaimed, Aubrey found herself approaching the miniscule rental car that would be her chariot on her quest. She hit the button on the remote key and threw her bags into the tiny trunk—or was it a boot? She was feeling the full effects of the long flight and lack of quality sleep, and she still had a four-hour drive ahead of her before she could call it a day in Inverness. She opened the driver's door, flopped onto the seat—and gaped in shock. The car had no steering wheel, no pedals! Staring in dull bewilderment at the empty dashboard in front of her, her mind went blank for a minute, and then she laughed in relief. The wheel was on the other side. How could she have forgotten that basic fact? She looked around to make sure no one had witnessed her idiocy and hurried around to the other side.

Settling herself on the right-hand side of the car, Aubrey was presented with her next challenge. It was a manual transmission, and the gear shift was now on her left. Oh, God. How was she going to negotiate the narrow Scottish roads, remembering to stay in the left lane while trying to shift with her left hand? Why didn't they have places in the States that trained tourists to drive in the UK so they wouldn't kill somebody? She sighed, released the clutch, and drove at a snail's pace around the parking lot for a few minutes, practicing and trying to get up the nerve to hit the road.

After a few hours on the motorway, her courage restored by the fact that she hadn't killed a single sheep, she felt better. Her muscles unknotted and her spine relaxed into the backrest. As the breathtaking scenery flashed past, she realized that for the first time in weeks, she felt free. She could do this. She was a Scot, after all, a Cumming, and her ancestors had once ruled the land she drove through. Aubrey began to hum *Scotland the Brave*. She was home.

CHAPTER 7

NESSIE

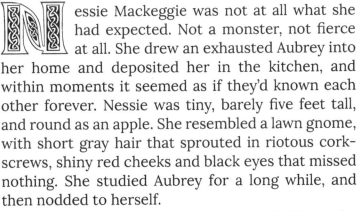essie Mackeggie was not at all what she had expected. Not a monster, not fierce at all. She drew an exhausted Aubrey into her home and deposited her in the kitchen, and within moments it seemed as if they'd known each other forever. Nessie was tiny, barely five feet tall, and round as an apple. She resembled a lawn gnome, with short gray hair that sprouted in riotous corkscrews, shiny red cheeks and black eyes that missed nothing. She studied Aubrey for a long while, and then nodded to herself.

"That Angus is a canny one," she said. "I kent he would get the job done."

In a fog of fatigue, Aubrey still couldn't help noticing that, right here in the middle of the Highlands, Nessie's brogue was much easier to understand than

Angus'. Odd. Her befuddled brain clicked onto what she had just heard.

"The job? What job?"

Nessie beamed at her from her apple face and asked, "And how was your trip? Are ye up for a bit o' tea?"

Ahh, so in that aspect she and Angus were alike, Aubrey thought. Evading the question was an art form for Angus; maybe it was a Scottish trait. Well, she was too tired to pursue it right now anyway, so if Nessie was going to play that game, the joke was on her. She hadn't the energy to care.

But it was only seven o'clock in the evening on this side of the world. Although she'd been up for what seemed like days, she knew she had to stay awake as long as she could to battle the time change.

"I'd love some, thank you." Looking around the kitchen, she gasped in delight. "Is that an AGA?"

The huge red ceramic stove beamed at her across the room, as if to say *Of course I am. Am I not magnificent?* Aubrey had only read about the iconic appliance in books, and somehow it was this quintessential symbol of Britishness, more than the right-side steering wheel, or driving on the wrong side of the road, or the sheep, that brought it home.

"Oh my God," she murmured, "this is real."

The tea was amazing, and any other time Aubrey would have done it justice, but after the first sip her body shut down. She awoke briefly to find Nessie pulling her to her feet with gentle hands.

"Time for bed, lass, there's the morning t' talk."

When she opened her eyes again, daylight filtered into her room on the hill above the River Ness, in the old house that was to be her home for the foreseeable future. She looked at the ancient peeling wallpaper, the antique wardrobe, and the giant four-poster in which she found herself. She gazed out the dormer window into a Scottish summer morning, and then she looked at her phone. Three-thirty in the morning! And it was freezing—in July! *What the hell?*

Burying her head under the comforter, Aubrey tried to make sense of it all. Was Scotland that close to the North Pole? Wrapping herself in the comforter, she dragged herself to the window. Fog covered the river and the mountains she had seen in the distance yesterday, and drops of water clung to the pane. The sun seemed to have forgotten the Highlands in its plans for the day.

Into her head came the echo of Angus' voice, "Naebody goes tae Scotland fur the weather, lass. Best bundle a lot 'o jumpers, mind ye!" Why hadn't she paid more attention? She hoped Inverness had a mall. Aubrey crawled back into bed and stared at the ceiling, trying in vain to go back to sleep. Giving it up, she pulled out her book and read until finally she dozed off again.

When she arrived downstairs in jeans and both of the sweatshirts she had brought, Nessie was bustling around the kitchen, putting enough food on the AGA to feed an entire clan. She waved Aubrey into the sitting room to meet her fellow boarders and told her that she was just in time for breakfast.

"Ye'll be havin' a full Scottish breakfast, so I hope you're hungry."

Hungry? She was starving! All she'd had was a sandwich at the airport while waiting for her car, and she'd been so nervous about the drive that she hadn't wanted to stop once she got on the road. Then she had been too tired to lift a fork. A full Scottish breakfast...maybe two...sounded like heaven.

When she entered the sitting room, four pairs of eyes turned her way, conjuring the image of a group of owls rotating their heads all at the same time. The first pair belonged to an elderly gentleman sitting in the window seat, reading today's issue of the newspaper she'd bought yesterday in the airport.

Sharp blue eyes measured her, and then went back to their reading. A soft Gaelic snort came from behind the newspaper.

"That's Old Harry Campbell," said a rather round woman seated on the couch. "Don't mind him, he takes a while to get to know people but I can tell he already likes you." She had a mellifluous British accent and exuded Yardley's English Lavender, and judging by the generously powdered wrinkles that had settled comfortably into a kind face, was at least as old as "Old Harry."

"I'm Gladys Chesher," she went on, bobbing a head of soft white curls, "up from the lake country for my summer visit. And this," she pointed to the man seated next to her on the couch, a dapper gentleman of late middle age wearing a three piece tweed suit straight out of Dickens, "this is my son, Ronald. He's a godsend, my Ronnie." She beamed fondly at the man, who gave her an indulgent smile in return and said nothing.

"And that's Maxine Bisset," Gladys finished, indicating a tall willowy woman of indeterminate age sitting bolt upright in a chair across the room. "She used to be a dancer. She's *French*," she added in a stage whisper which couldn't have been missed by anyone in the room. The woman inclined her head and favored Aubrey with a regal smile. Her silver-streaked black hair was pulled back into a severe bun at the nape of her neck, and her delicate frame was encased in diaphanous black chiffon from head to foot. She was gorgeous.

Aubrey began to feel a bit like the awkward new kid in school. She was still standing in the doorway, and the Owls were all staring at her again, which was a bit disconcerting. None of her fellow boarders seemed to be under the age of fifty, but what had she expected—a sorority house?

"And now that you know us all, who are you?" Gladys asked, her tone direct but not unkind. The others stared unblinking at her and said nothing. It seemed Gladys was the spokesperson for the group.

"I'm Aubrey Cumming. Pleased to meet you all." Aubrey smiled her most pleasant smile, the one she saved for customers who actually bought books, and looked in vain for a place to sit. No one else seemed to notice the problem, and for a moment she felt like Alice at the mad tea party. She was saved from further embarrassment by the arrival of Nessie, who announced, "Breakfast!"

Aubrey stared in horror at the conglomeration on her plate. There was an egg, fried until its yolk had long since given up the ghost. That flat thing looked as if it might be a potato, pounded into submission. Okay, that was definitely some sort of ham, and a link of sausage. Baked beans? Who had baked beans for breakfast? And what were those suspicious little round patties of something...one black, one brown?

Nessie came over and pointed to each item. "Tattie scone, egg, back bacon, toast, Lorne sausage, beans o' course, black pudding, haggis. Full Scottish breakfast. Eat!"

She ate. It was delicious, even the haggis. I'm eating haggis, thought Aubrey happily. I'm eating haggis in Scotland! She looked up to see that all the housemates were watching her again, with varying expressions. Gladys looked complacent, as if she had personally found Aubrey in an alley and brought her home to be fed and petted. Ronald looked bored. Maxine, who had nothing but tea and toast in front of her, wore an appalled look on her exquisite face, as if she were being forced to watch a baby bird eating its first worm. And Harry Campbell was staring at her with unabashed pride.

"'At's it, lass!" he chortled. "Noo yoo've hud breakfast!"

Aubrey grinned at them, her full stomach loving them all. "So, what exactly is *in* haggis?"

"Ach, nuthin' but th' innards of a sheep mixit wi'suet an' parritch," Harry explained. "An' black puddin'..."

"Never mind!" Aubrey gulped. "I get the picture." She pushed her empty plate as far away as possible. "Delicious."

"So, dear, what brings you all the way to Inverness?" Gladys' curiosity was avid, her little bird eyes glinting with the need to know. "The rest of us have been coming for years, and Harry lives here, but what is a lovely young American doing in the Highlands of Scotland, of all places...and all alone?" Her eyes narrowed. "Are you running away from something? Or *someone*?"

No one else seemed perturbed by the intrusive questioning; apparently, they were accustomed to it. The Owls stared without shame, waiting for her answer.

"Someone, I guess," Aubrey answered when the silence had stretched out and begun to be awkward. She took a breath, her mouth opened, and without warning the words began to pour out. "My fiancé dumped me for his old girlfriend. In a text. He couldn't even tell me face to face—" She stopped, appalled. Why was she telling them her private affairs? Her problems were none of their business! And yet somehow it felt good to get it off her chest, to unload her baggage onto total strangers. Was there something besides sheep guts inside that haggis? Maybe a truth serum?

"Tell us about it," said Ronald, startling Aubrey with the first words he had uttered that morning.

So she did. She told them the whole story of Marco and Angie, and how he had broken up with her through a text message. She told them about

Harrington, New Jersey, and its distressing lack of readers. And she told them about her Scottish heritage, lifting her head in sudden pride at the feeling of belonging somewhere. She said nothing about the book, or Angus, or the curse. That was something she would keep to herself; she had no desire to be hauled off to the local asylum just yet.

Aubrey finally sputtered to a stop, shocked to find that she was crying. Sobbing her heart out in front of people she'd just met! What must they think?

"Oh, my dear, what a terrible human being that Marco is!" Gladys fumed. "He deserves a good thrashing, in my opinion!" Her face radiated distress.

"What is this *text*?" asked Maxine. Aubrey explained, and watched the Frenchwoman's eyes darken in her expressive face. She shook her head and muttered something dark and Gallic.

"He was no good for you, this man," she declared, those marvelous eyes huge and sorrowful. "You are beautiful and sweet, any man would be fortunate to find you!"

'Weel, yoo've come t' th' right place, lass," said Harry Campbell with calm assurance. "Ye were smart tae come tae Scootland."

"And now you have us!" Gladys proclaimed. "So everything will be just fine."

Nessie came back into the dining room. "Dinna worry," she said calmly. "It's been taken care of. Angus is in charge, she'll be all right."

"Ach, weel then, that's guid," grunted Old Harry, and he picked up his newspaper and retired to the sitting room.

Aubrey was overcome by the warmth and kindness of her new fan club. It was unexpected and extraordinary, all the more heartwarming because she could tell they meant it. When they had all left to go about their business, patting her arm on the way out, she wandered into the kitchen to see if she could help Nessie but was told to "get along with ya, lass. There's some tour adverts in the sittin' room. Why don't ye look into some o' them? Tomorrow ye can walk down t' the High Street and have a wee talk with the people at th' Visitors' Center. They'll set ye right up."

"Thanks, Nessie. For everything," Aubrey told her, the words catching in her suddenly thickened throat. There was no way she could explain to this strange but wonderful little woman the feelings that were bubbling up inside her, warming her from the inside out. She didn't quite understand them herself.

"Ach, go on with ye!" Nessie said, and turned away, her cheeks pink.

CHAPTER 8

GREY SKIES

Darius Sanderson steepled his hands and leaned back in his leather chair, staring out of his office windows at the rain. Damn Scottish weather, he thought. Couldn't they string three days of sunshine together in this shithole of a country? Why was it always so goddam grey? If it weren't for these terrorist attacks on oil rigs, he would be in the Mediterranean, sitting on the deck of his sailboat *Levande*, drinking a perfect gin and Dubonnet, instead of mired here in Edinburgh in a world of grey and wet.

Thoughts of his yacht, a fifty-two foot beauty named in honor of his Swedish mother, added to his depression. "Levande" meant "Living," and what he was doing right now was anything but.

Much as he hated to admit it, Sanderson was a Scot. His mother Stella, for some reason he could never fathom, had met and fallen in love with Malcolm Forrester in Glasgow on a trip to Scotland during her gap year. Malcolm had stayed around long enough to father Darius, and then had abandoned mother and child to follow his real loves, whisky and punting. Darius had never met the bastard and hoped he never did. He had taken his mother's name and thought of himself as a Swede. He didn't even know if his father was alive—he hoped not. Stella's family had abandoned her, so there they were, just two more victims of bad judgement and the world's cruelty, eking out an existence in the Scottish Lowlands.

But Darius was a survivor; more, he was ambitious and clever. He had worked in a bakery, in a distillery, and finally on an oil rig, working his way up until he became indispensable. He saved every penny he made, and by the time he was twenty-five he was in charge of the Captain, the third largest oil field in Scotland. Five years later it was the largest, producing more than 180,000 barrels of oil per year. Darius Sanderson was a player.

But he was not content to run one oil field, no matter how large. The real money was in oil trading, and he began to put his fertile mind to work learning the ins and outs of the industry. In June of 2014, crude oil entered a bear market, with a price just under eighty pounds per barrel. Sanderson watched and waited. By February 2016, the price had dropped to under twenty-two pounds per barrel, and he made his move. Sinking everything he owned into oil, Darius waited. When the price went up he sold, when it went down he bought. It didn't escape him that he had become a gambler like the father he hated—the difference was that he was a *very good* gambler, and the stakes were enormous. He was savvy and ruthless, and he had determined never to be poor again.

His oil trading company, PETRO, now occupied the entire twelfth floor of the Exchange Tower in Edinburgh, but as he stared out at his perfect view of Edinburgh Castle his mind was not on oil. He was boiling with fury at the current political climate. The referendum for independence had been in 2014, and it should have been over. The "Yes Scotland" crowd had been soundly defeated and Scotland was safely back in the United Kingdom where it belonged. So why wouldn't the bastards just admit they'd been beaten and have done with it? Darius had poured a small fortune into the "Better Together" campaign, and he'd do it again if necessary, but he had better uses for his money and besides, there had been an outcry when his donation had been leaked.

It was all the fault of that damn Brexit, which Scotland almost as a whole had decried. Britain's decision to leave the European Union had given new life to the nearly dead movement for Scottish Independence, and now another referendum was looming. The "Yes" faction, now calling itself "Caledonia First," was galvanizing its political machine through the Scottish Nationalist Party, shamelessly using Robert the Bruce, William Wallace, and the Battle of Culloden to fire up Scottish patriotism and rekindle their disdain for the English.

Darius wished that Culloden had been the end for every damn Highlander in Scotland. The fairy tale romance of kilts and bagpipes and hearty men drinking whisky in the heather was just that—fantasy, like the Bogles or the Brownies. It had no chance of survival in this era, and it was time the hotheads in the Scottish Parliament realized this and gave way. Sanderson could care less about history or independence, except where it affected his bottom line, and to that end it was critical that Scotland, and her oil rigs, remain in the union.

The sabotaging of three large rigs and resultant losses, both of lives and of massive amounts of oil, was being blamed on the Caledonia First lunatics, and for good reason. If they could prove that the United Kingdom was unable to protect her northern subjects' natural resources, then Scotland would have to take care of herself. The oil belonged to the Scots, the theory ran, and if Scotland couldn't own it then no one would. Well, Darius Sanderson *was* oil. Despite his losses, or perhaps because of them, the current situation was playing into his hands. People were beginning to notice Caledonia First, and to listen. He could not allow that to happen. If everyone thought they had been stupid enough to sabotage the oil rigs, they would be crucified in the court of public opinion. Their bid for another referendum would die and they would skulk back to their villages with their tails between their legs.

Sanderson was taking steps, and it was time for the next one. Looking out the window, he saw that the rain had stopped for the moment. He pressed the bell on his desk.

"Bridget, find Oliver and get him up here."

"Yes, sir," his secretary said in her brisk, flat voice.

A moment later Oliver Thomson entered the room, his handsome face eager. Too eager, Darius thought at times. "Yes, boss?" he asked.

Oliver had been with Sanderson since the beginning, helping him behind the scenes, putting his plans into action, acting as his muscle when needed. His loyalty was unquestionable; there was almost nothing that Darius could ask of him that he would find reprehensible or beyond the pale. They had met when they both worked the oil rigs together, had sensed a need for something in each other and thereafter had become inseparable. When Darius' star began to rise, he took Oliver Thomson with him, training him to be his personal assistant and bodyguard. Ollie was like the family he had never had, closer than a brother. He was the only person Darius Sanderson had ever truly loved.

"Ollie," he said, his voice low and urgent, "I have come into possession of a damning document—one that will put the Caledonia First people out of business forever and end this ridiculous charade. It contains proof that they're behind the sabotage of the oil rigs and will almost certainly put their leaders in prison for murder." He clasped his assistant's arms and looked deep into his eyes. "I need you to deliver the document, Ollie. It's the most important task I've ever given you, and I need to know that you're willing to carry it through. For it to be connected to me would be damning. If it fell into the wrong hands it would be the end of PETRO, and of me. Can I trust you to do this?"

Oliver looked stricken. "Why would you ask that, boss? Have I ever given you reason not to trust me? I would give my life for you, you know that!" His eyes were wide, beseeching.

"I do know that, I'm sorry. It's just that I need to know you will take the utmost care to deliver this information into the right hands." Darius' voice was contrite, but impatient. He handed Ollie a plain white envelope and a separate paper with an address. "Memorize this address."

Ollie did, and then carefully tucked the envelope into his breast pocket. Without another word he turned and left, walking tall, heading for the stairs to the parking lot. Behind him, Darius Sanderson took a deep breath and settled back into his leather chair to stare into the gloom at Edinburgh Castle, outlined against the grey horizon.

Oliver Thomson took the stairs without visible haste, acknowledging the few colleagues he passed briefly but stopping to talk with none of them. When he reached the ground floor, he entered the flow of traffic to and from the exit and continued his steady progress. Human traffic was thicker here; it was nearing the end of the work day for most of the offices located in the Exchange Tower, and he was forced to slow his pace and excuse himself several times as he approached the rear door to the parking facility.

As he passed through the door, he felt something pinch his left arm. "Damn it!" he exclaimed in frustration. Rubbing his arm he looked down, expecting to see a snag in his coat sleeve, but there was nothing. Oliver shrugged in relief—this was a brand-new jacket—and continued on toward the private space designated for his car. The space for the car of the Assistant to the CEO of PETRO, he chuckled to himself. That's me! Oliver Thomson, best friend to the boss and jack of all trades—he was giggling like a child, weaving drunkenly as he reached his car. Confused, he braced his hand on the car door and looked down to fumble for the keys in his pocket, and suddenly he was on the ground between the cars, looking up in surprise. The keys fell from his nerveless fingers and slid under the car. Ollie lay on the pavement in the shadows as people passed by only yards away, but his muscles had ceased to function. He gave a strangled gasp as his throat closed, his eyes frozen wide in shock. It was over quickly. His heart stuttered...his body twitched once and was still.

A gloved hand reached into the coat pocket and removed a plain white envelope. Oliver Thomson, best friend and Assistant to the CEO of PETRO, remained on the ground next to his car, staring blindly into the grey Scottish sky. A single drop of water fell onto an unblinking eye and rolled down his cheek to be lost on the pavement. More rain was coming.

CHAPTER 9

SCOTLAND THE BRAVE

ubrey stood in the front garden of Nessie's house and looked out across the River Ness to the mist covered hills. Her imagination was doing a little dance, singing *the Highlands, those are the Highlands of Scotland!* They looked very much like the Appalachian Mountains back home in Pennsylvania, but so much more *Scottish.* She'd never given much thought to the Appalachians, they were just something that made the turnpike a nightmare in bad weather. But these hills! Rough men had hidden in their forests, camped upon their slopes. Fierce, ruthless clansmen, armed with claymores and dirks, fighting for the freedom to live the way they wished, living off the land as their forebears had done for hundreds of years, and laying siege to castles and keeps...and other clans' cattle. She smiled. Why did even thievery seem romantic here?

She shook her head and the image of a blue painted Mel Gibson faded. Well, she could stand here forever, or she could rein in her imagination and get going. The Owls had given her a new courage this morning, a balm to her battered self-esteem. People here cared about her, had her back. She was no longer alone. In fact, here in a foreign country she had already found more human compassion than she had experienced in eight months of half-life in Harrington, New Jersey. She realized with a jolt that, with the exception of three people, she had been a stranger there all that time. It was her own fault, she knew. Lost in a Marc-induced stupor, she had felt that no one else mattered. What a fool she had been!

Aubrey shook herself out of her reflection. It was time to explore her new home—Inverness was waiting. Armed with an impressive array of tour pamphlets and a walking map, she walked up the path to the very top of the ridge on which Nessie's house perched, and then down the other side into the city proper. Everywhere she looked was proof that Inverness, the Capital of the Highlands, was very, very old. The stately homes on the hill gazed at her from mullioned eyes, placid in their age and wisdom. *Aye, lass,* they said. *We've seen it all.* It was a comforting feeling.

The map took her to a square in the center of the city where, to her delight, she saw a mall, beaming at her in its benevolent normalcy. Although the air had warmed up a bit, Aubrey was reminded that she was woefully unprepared for the Scottish weather. She'd better buy a warmer raincoat than the one she had brought. And some "jumpers," she grinned to herself, thinking of Angus' terse warning. Deciding to shop on her way home, she turned to the first item marked on her map, a tall statue at the top of which reared a proud unicorn. Aubrey grinned. How could anyone resist a country which had selected a mythical creature as its national animal? *Fitz would love this*, she thought, and a sudden wave of loneliness seized her at the thought of her friends, thousands of miles away in another country.

Shrugging off the feeling, she continued down between ancient buildings to the High Street, a pedestrian walkway clogged with tourists on this Saturday morning. Passing the McDonald's on the corner and wondering if they made haggis burgers, she wandered down the street, soaking in the atmosphere. A bagpiper was settled in next to a Scottish souvenirs store. The young man, who couldn't be more than twelve or thirteen, puffed mightily at his pipes, emitting a sound that Aubrey would have recognized anywhere: *Scotland the Brave*. She sighed and dropped a pound coin into his case.

The music conjured a vision of Angus seated in his wonderin' chair smoking his pipe, and suddenly she felt another pang of homesickness, sharp and painful. She knew that she'd been avoiding calling him, knew she was putting off talk of the curse and the whole point of her being here. She could keep it all at bay as long as Angus kept his distance. That wasn't going to fly with him though, so she'd better call him this afternoon and let him yell at her for not checking in the minute she set foot in his homeland.

But first she needed to schedule that tour. Aubrey knew it for the procrastination it was, but she shrugged off the feeling and straightened her shoulders. She couldn't do anything about the damn curse until Angus gave her some marching orders anyway.

Nessie had told her that the visitor's center was in the middle of the High Street walkway, and there she found it, draped in the "Saltire," the national flag of Scotland. A tartaned display of history books at the front reached out and grabbed her, and she spent fifteen minutes lost in books covering Scottish landscapes, Highlands cooking, and tales of ghosts and supernatural beings. Leafing through this last, she noted that there was no mention of Rait Castle or its ghost. She wasn't sure if that was a good or bad omen, but at least none of these modern books hissed or buzzed or stank. Losing herself in stories of kelpies and selkies and hags—oh my!—she was started at the friendly voice at her side.

"May I help you?"

"Oh! Sorry, I got lost there for a minute," she said, blushing. "I tend to get carried away with books."

"Happens all the time. And what can I do for you today?" was the cheerful response.

"I just arrived in Inverness and I'm interested in a tour. What do you recommend for the raw beginner?"

"Well, for your first tour, you can't do better than Loch Ness and Urquhart Castle," the man told her. "It's a half day, with a self-guided tour of the castle and a lovely cruise down the loch. Maybe you'll even see our monster, Nessie!"

I've already seen Nessie, Aubrey thought, *and she's no monster.* But she kept her counsel.

"Our tour companies are all good," continued the agent, "but I personally recommend Dougie's Tours. Their guides are very knowledgeable, teachers and such, and they might give you some extra bits of history if that's what you're looking for."

"Sounds perfect." Aubrey bought a ticket for the half day Loch Ness cruise and castle visit on Monday, thanked the tour agent, and averted her eyes as she walked past the books on her way out. *I'll be back,* she promised them. *I have a feeling I'll be in here often.*

Back down the High Street, rearing into the grey sky on her left, Aubrey found Inverness Castle. She hiked up the long drive, marveling at the golden-bricked turrets and rounded facade. Standing before the statue of Flora MacDonald, she read the inscription, noting that it was engraved in both Gaelic and English. "The preserver of Prince Charles Edward Stewart will be mentioned in history, and if courage and fidelity be virtues, mentioned with honor." It was signed simply "Johnson." Wonder who Johnson was? she thought. Surely not someone who had ever watched *Outlander.* She grinned, remembering the effete, simpering portrayal of the bonnie prince on that show. Apparently the real Charles had found more favor with his Highlanders than she had realized.

Circling the castle, Aubrey found to her dismay that there was no entrance for the public. It was a working building, not a tourist attraction. A sign informed her that this was the location of the Inverness Sheriff Court, *thank you very much, and we do not care that you are looking at a medieval structure. This is the 21st Century and we are busy.* So unless she ran over a sheep during her travels or became drunk and disorderly, Aubrey was unlikely to gain entry. Shrugging, she decided that it probably wasn't worth breaking the law to see the insides of a castle. She bid Flora a fond goodbye and moved on.

Crossing the River Ness at the Young Street Bridge, she found herself gazing at a magnificent Gothic church whose spires soared majestically into the sky–or they would have, if there had been any spires on top of the twin towers. Odd, Aubrey thought, had they fallen off during a storm? She made a mental note to ask and entered the church.

Stepping into the dark nave, she was surprised to find that, although it was Saturday, the church was full. A boys' choir was singing *Highland Cathedral*, accompanied by a lone bagpiper who stood near her in the back of the church. As the young voices raised for the final verse, the piper began to walk up the aisle. He and his pipes seemed to float toward the choir, and Aubrey found gooseflesh rising on her arms at the power of the sound. This was not bagpipes as she had ever heard them before. Not the harsh squeal of air being forced unwilling into the world. This was the sound of history, the music that had cloaked the ancient Scots in courage as they rushed into battle. For the first time, she realized why the piper had been the heart of a Scottish fighting force, and she found herself in tears at the beauty and majesty of the ancient instrument.

With the magic of the pipes still resounding in her head, Aubrey retraced her steps up the High Street, past the souvenir stores and the seemingly endless number of kilt shops and tartan drapers. She stepped into one and bought a scarf in the Cumming tartan to wear on Monday for the cruise. Maybe Nessie—the monster—would appreciate the Scottish touch and come up for a wee chat. One could always hope. Aubrey giggled as she arrived back at the unicorn and the mall.

Two hours later, drooping with exhaustion, she let herself into the house and collapsed with her bags into a chair in the sitting room. Gladys was there, with the omnipresent Ronald, but no one else was in evidence.

"So, will you be going to find the Loch Ness monster, then?" Gladys looked up from her knitting. "I saw her once, you know!"

"Really?" Aubrey gave her a suspicious glance. "Is she that easy to find?"

"Oh, no! You have to know where to look, and most don't. Ask at the Loch Ness Centre, though, you might get lucky." She winked at Aubrey and glared at Ronald, who rolled his eyes.

Aubrey had a distinct feeling that these two were having a bit of sport with her, but she smiled and said, "I'll do that. Thanks, Gladys." She climbed the tartan carpeted stairs to her bedroom and unpacked her purchases, hanging the flannel-lined raincoat in the wardrobe and placing her new Aran sweater in the drawer. She couldn't afford "lots 'o jumpers," so she'd just have to layer when the weather went especially Scottish.

Flopping onto the bed, she hauled out her phone and checked the time. Eight o'clock in Harrington; she should be able to catch Kate before she left for work. Fitz rarely answered her phone, and she wasn't about to waste precious minutes on a voicemail. She'd save Angus for last, so he could get in a good grumble about her taking so long to call him.

Kate picked up on the second ring. "Aubrey! How do you like Scootland?"

"Awful weather, beautiful scenery. I miss you guys. I've met some real characters, listened to lots of bagpipes, and tried haggis. Oh, and I'm booked on a cruise tomorrow to see the Loch Ness monster!"

"Is that guaranteed in the cost?" Kate laughed.

"Yes, I think it is. One of my new housemates told me that there was a trick to seeing Nessie... the monster, that is, not Angus' friend Nessie. She's a sweetheart, nowhere near as grumpy as he is. I'm going to tell him that when I call him."

The line had gone silent.

"Kate?"

"Mmm, there's something you should know." Kate's voice sounded hesitant.

"What?"

"It's Angus."

The fear that clutched her heart was instant and searing, as her imagination supplied innumerable accidents and ailments that could have befallen the old man.

"He's...?"

"He's gone, Aubrey."

The room receded into a small dot on the horizon and a red haze filled her mind as the words sank into her consciousness. Nooo! She had just said goodbye to him on Friday! How could this be?

She managed to rasp out, voice gritty with pain, "H-how? What happened?" She couldn't breathe for the grief that was choking her.

"No, no, I don't mean that! I'm so sorry!" Kate gasped. "He's not dead...at least as far as I know. He's just *gone*. The shop is empty. Even the sign is missing."

"What?" Her heart restarted, stuttered back into a sort of rhythm. "That can't be! What about all the books?"

"Gone. It's as if he was never there."

Aubrey mumbled something, broke the connection and lay back on the pillow, shock and confusion blurring her thoughts. What the hell was going on? It was inconceivable that Angus could have moved himself and all his books out of that space without someone to do the heavy lifting, and he would never stoop to ask for help from anyone in Harrington. Anyway, why make such a move the minute she left town? Why hadn't he told her if he was planning to leave? Something was very wrong here. She dialed his number, listening in disbelief to the tinny voice informing her that this number was no longer in service.

Her mind flashed to the memory of that ancient book, buzzing and sizzling and reeking of death. Could Angus' disappearance have anything to do with the mystery invoked by that ominous volume? Not for the first time, she wondered about where her old Scot had been before he had appeared in Harrington. She wondered if he had sent her to Scotland so she wouldn't try to stop him from leaving. And she'd bet her new tartan scarf that his friend Nessie knew something about all this, she thought, as she ran down the old staircase and into the kitchen.

Nessie's blue eyes were wide and clear as she told Aubrey that she had no idea where her friend could be. Aubrey didn't believe her for a minute.

CHAPTER 10

TOUR DE FORCE

ubrey walked down the hill into town and, after a couple of wrong turns, found the bus station tucked behind the train depot. It was busy and chaotic; tour buses jostled with city coaches for the best positions at the curb, and gaggles of tourists milled about, looking confused but happy. The accents and languages were varied, as was the dress of the passengers. Locals bound for work wore business attire, an Indian couple stood apart dressed formally in the traditional sari and jacquard suit of their native land. She grimaced when she realized that the Americans could be told apart from the Scots by the fact that only the former were decked out in plaid.

Well, I *am* American, she thought, and restrained herself from taking off the tartan scarf. She handed the ticket agent her booking slip and was directed to a small bus third in line from the front. She boarded and settled in the second seat on the left-hand side, hoping that was where she might get the best view of the loch and the castle.

Three American teenagers boarded and took the seats directly in front of her, chittering like magpies, and after that the bus filled up quickly. An Asian couple, probably mother and daughter, an elderly American couple, and a group of several middle-aged women with English accents rounded out the tour. They shuffled their belongings, hauled out their cameras, and sat obediently. A placard on the back of the driver's seat read: "Dougie's Tours welcomes you! Your driver is Fionnlagh Cameron." *Well, that's Scottish enough*, thought Aubrey.

Time passed. "I hope we're on the right tour!" the elderly American said in a worried voice to her partner. She leaned up and tapped Aubrey on the shoulder. "Is this the Loch Ness tour?"

"Yes—at least I think so," Aubrey answered. Voices could be heard from various parts of the bus. "It is!" "That's what the agent told us." "Where's the driver?"

A young man bounded up the step and into the front of the bus, his kilt swinging about his knees. "Here I am, don't worry!" He beamed at his charges and launched into his talk. He looked familiar somehow, but Aubrey couldn't think of where she might have seen him before.

"So, you're the brave crew that's ready to meet Nessie, are ye?" They all nodded obediently. "Well, I'm to be your guide in this perilous adventure. And your driver, which is what makes it perilous!" He rolled the "r" in "'perilous" over his tongue and narrowed his eyes wickedly. Pointing to the placard, he added, "My name is Fionnlagh Cameron." He pronounced it *Finlay*. "But you can all just call me Finn."

"Oh my God!" one of the young Americans in the front seat whispered loudly into her friend's ear. "He looks like Tom Branson from *Downton Abbey*!" They all dissolved into giggles, eliciting a puzzled look from the guide, who shrugged and went back to his spiel. Americans, the shrug said. Aubrey leaned out to get a better look and had to agree. That was why he'd seemed familiar. He *did* look a bit like the Irish chauffeur from her beloved TV show. Sun-streaked brown hair falling into blue eyes, that lopsided grin...

She sat quickly back and stifled the laughter that threatened to burst out. Tom Branson in a kilt! And he was their chauffeur! Just wait till she told Kate and Fitz about this. She'd have to snap a picture to prove it, they'd never believe her otherwise. Now all she had to do was run into Jamie Fraser from *Outlander* and she could die happy.

Branson—Finn—climbed into the driver's seat, donning a headset with a microphone as he began to tell them what they could expect to experience on their trip, waxing poetic about the ancient beauty of Urquhart Castle and its enviable position on the loch.

"Is anybody here named Grant?" he asked them. "No? Well, if you were from Clan Grant, you could move right into the castle and take up residence. Urquhart was owned by the Grants for almost three hundred years, but they had to fight off the MacDonalds to keep it, and now you'd be fighting the Historic Environment Scotland people. Besides, it's a bit open to the lovely Scottish weather, now." He grinned at them. "Clan Grant was given the job of repairing the pile, but they didn't do a very good job, as you'll see!" He winked at his passengers in the rearview mirror.

He was certainly a charmer, Aubrey thought, and so did the girls in the seat in front, as evidenced by their lusty sighs and overly exuberant exclamations of delight at his wit.

Settle down, girls, she said to herself. *I'm sure he's used to being admired.* She remembered the agent back in Inverness telling her that Dougie's Tours employed teachers as tour guides. Finn Cameron's female students must work for straight As if he was their teacher! She felt her own heart quicken when his eyes made contact for a second in the mirror. *And you're not immune, either. Watch out!*

The bus pulled into a huge lot and parked in the designated space. Finn removed his headset and stood to face his group.

"We'll start in the visitors' center. It's quite lovely. You'll have two hours to roam around and visit the castle, and then I'll meet you at the dock for the cruise. I hope everyone has a warm jacket; it gets pretty cold out on the loch. Nessie likes it that way. And, of course, it being Scotland, it might rain at some point. Probably will." His smile was inclusive, taking them all in, but Aubrey thought his gaze might have lingered on her a second or two longer. Wishful thinking, she decided, but then she caught the baleful looks of the three young women who had sat in front of her on the bus.

You can have him. The last thing I need in my life right now is another handsome man. After all, he wasn't a Mackintosh, so he wasn't going to help with the curse. She sighed. Damn the curse. Damn Angus.

But she couldn't help the lift in her spirits or the quickening of her step as they trooped into the visitors' center. She might not want a man, but she was female, and breathing. She wasn't going to complain if one wanted to pay her a bit of attention.

The visitors' center was truly amazing. A huge, high-ceilinged building thronged with tourists, it offered every kind of Scottish souvenir one could want, as well as single malt whisky...and books. With a sigh of capitulation, Aubrey headed to the displays of history books and novels. The first table she encountered offered a display of *Outlander* books, mugs and scarves. She had all the novels at home, but just knowing that they were honored here warmed her heart toward the place.

A display of travel books caught her eye. *My Scotland* and *Wandering the Highlands* by Alastair MacGregor, with pictures of gorgeous scenery. She picked up a book on Robert the Bruce, the great King of Scotland. Against all odds, the book told her, the Bruce had defeated his Scottish challengers and booted out the British King Edward I, achieving independence for Scotland. He had ruled from 1313 until his death in 1338, a long time for a king in those times.

Her eye caught a name and she stopped to read in depth.

Robert was not universally welcomed by the Scots, a nation split by warrior factions and bellicose clans. In 1306 he agreed to meet with the head of the Comyn family, a man known as "Red Comyn," at Greyfriars Kirk in Dumfries. During their talks an argument broke out, which ended with Bruce stabbing the laird in front of the high altar. How much of this is true and how much historical embroidery, the fact remains that within six weeks Robert the Bruce was king of Scotland.

"You'll be a Cumming, then?" said a Scottish voice at her side. Aubrey jerked, coming out of her book fog to find Finn Cameron grinning at her.

"Oh...um...yeah. How did you know?"

He nodded at her scarf. "It's not one of the more popular clan tartans, you know. Most Americans buy the Stewart or the MacDonald." He glanced over his shoulder with a shrug. "Or the Mackenzie or Fraser, of course. Because of that *Outlander* nonsense."

"Nonsense?" Aubrey sputtered. "I'll have you know that *Outlander* is one of the greatest love stories ever written! Have you even read one of the books?"

Finn put his hands up in mock surrender. "Sorry! Fiction's not really my thing. Isn't it about time travel and such? I'm more into actual history." He added with a self-effacing smile, "I'm a professor of Scottish history, at the college." He gave her a penitent look.

Aubrey smiled at him; she couldn't help it. She was such a soft touch for a sad face. *And how has that worked out for you? Watch it, girl!*

"Anyway, I came to remind you that the cruise starts in one hour, so if you want to see the castle, you'd best be on your way."

Surprised, she looked at her watch. An hour gone, and she hadn't even left the visitors' center! Books always did this to her.

"Yes, thanks for dragging me out of the book. And, in my defense, this one," she brandished the book on Bruce, "is about *actual history*."She grinned and turned to leave, only to find him walking beside her down the path toward the castle.

"Do you mind if I keep you company on your tour? I could give you some bits that you won't find in the books." He smiled. "I usually charge tuition for this stuff."

Aubrey laughed. *Oh, what the hell!* He was pretty damn charming, and anyway she'd probably never see him again after today. She didn't have to fall in love with him or anything, she scolded herself. Finn was staring at her, an anxious look on his face. He was probably assuming that she was rejecting his company. "Is something wrong?"

"I'm sorry," she told him, a sheepish look on her face. "I'm a bit of a dreamer. One errant comment and I'm off in another world. It's not you." She held out her hand. "Aubrey Cumming," she stated formally. "Please do join me. I'm a sucker for history, in any form."

He looked relieved. "So, let's go find the secrets of Urquhart Castle."

An hour later they approached the small landing where two small launches were unloading passengers, and Finn left her to gather his small group in preparation for the next leg of their journey. She grabbed a seat near the window and was soon lost in the beauty of Scotland's famous loch. What was it about the hills and the water that called to her here? She gazed out onto the dark water, half expecting to see a huge, undulating body under the dark water. And wouldn't that be something to share with Gladys. She'd bet that even the taciturn Ronald would have something to say about that!

The cruise over, the group piled back onto the bus and headed for the Loch Ness Centre and Exhibition, in Drumnadrochit. "Drum-na-drrro-cchhhit", Finn pronounced it, drawing out the lovely Scottish word. As he pulled their chariot into the parking lot, they all gawked at the huge three-story grey stone building in awe. It was the perfect setting for a collection of memorabilia and research dedicated to Scotland's national treasure, the Loch Ness Monster.

"You might be surprised to find that Nessie's only been famous for about eighty years," said Finn, "which isn't much time in a country as old as Scotland. And her first sighting wasn't very noble, either. It seems a woman mistook a wee fish swimming in the lake for a monster, claiming that she had seen a huge creature with a long neck and gigantic fangs. After that, people began reporting all sorts of sightings, things that usually turned out to be a deer swimming with his antlers showing above the water, or large eels winding their way through the waves.

"But you'll have to decide for yourselves," he told them, releasing his charges into the huge exhibition center. He headed in Aubrey's direction, only to be cut off by the three teenage girls, who surrounded him and began asking a litany of questions about the truth of the legend. Aubrey passed alone into the building to find Nessie.

The exhibition was more like a National Geographic museum, with rooms dedicated to the scientific background and eventual debunking of the Nessie legend. Aubrey's romantic nature was miffed by the certainty displayed on the walls, although she normally had no problem with science. But what about magic? she asked the offending display of logic. Surely in a country as ancient as Scotland, there's room for magic! She thought of the book on the shelf at *Angus' Auld Books* and shivered. With a stubborn huff, she turned away from the display and passed out into the Scottish day. Little did they know!

Her tour over, Aubrey decided to wait for the others in the bus. As she made her way through the parking lot, a familiar Scottish voice hailed her, and she felt a frisson of pleasure as she turned to watch the approach of Finn Cameron. He had shaken off his admirers, she noted, and against her will her heart quickened.

"Wait!" He hurried to her. "Don't you want to see Nessie?" His expression was open and inviting.

"What?" She looked toward the loch, across the road. "Where?"

"Oh no, lass, not there. Come with me." He led her across the parking lot to a gate in the fence abutting the property. "Now, pay attention and you might have some luck! Go ahead, now." Finn stood back and waved her through the gate.

Aubrey looked askance at him, but his expression radiated innocence. Something is not quite right, she thought, remembering Gladys saying almost the same thing. She walked through the gate and along a wooden walkway that followed the fence to an opening about fifty feet further on, and then turned to look over the gap. And began to laugh.

There, across a small man-made pond, stood a gigantic dinosaur-like creature. It looked like a brontosaurus, with a long, sinuous reptilian neck and a small, beady-eyed head. It was staring at her...out of small, plastic eyes.

She turned back to find Finn laughing at her, and after giving him an evil look she joined in, snapping a picture to remember the joke before they walked back across the parking lot in companionable silence. Aubrey took her seat on the bus and Finn waited for the rest of the group outside. All in all, the day had been a wonderful introduction to Scotland. And she could always tell Kate and Fitz that she had seen the Loch Ness monster...in the "flesh."

On the way back to Inverness, their guide regaled his group with tales of Urquhart Castle's glory days, when the MacDonalds, the Lords of the Isles, swept in and carried off boats and guns in a series of raids. He must be everyone's favorite professor, Aubrey thought, delivering history through humor. And the good looks didn't hurt his cause either.

When they reached Inverness, Aubrey left the coach with her fellow passengers, noting that the three American girls lagged behind to gush to their guide about the wonderful trip. She walked toward the corner, deciding to pick up lunch at a lovely little cafe she'd spotted on her morning walk. She was grinning to herself, deciding how to tell Gladys about her discovery of Nessie, when she heard running footsteps and turned to see Finn bounding toward her. He came to a stop and stood before her, looking uncomfortable.

"Did I leave something on the bus?" Aubrey asked, puzzled.

"Yes," he said simply. "Me."

She stared at him. He held her gaze for a long minute. In a hesitant voice, he said, "What I mean is...I'd like to see you again. Would you have dinner with me tomorrow?"

It was a bad idea. She had sworn off men, unless of course they happened to be named Mackintosh, and she was too drawn to this one already. She had no business complicating her life right now.

"Yes," said a voice that just might have been her own.

His smile was brilliant. They exchanged numbers and he loped back to the bus station, leaving her staring after him.

Yes, a *very* bad idea.

*I'm beginning to feel as though
everything has happened before, that
our story has already been told.*

Helen Humphreys

SCOTLAND, 1442

e came awake in inky blackness. Pain knifed through his head, and he could not seem to move his arms. His memories were murky, lost in a dark void. Had they been hunting? Had he fallen? His face was wet...water or blood?

Rough hands gripped him, hauling him to his knees. The pain threatened to overwhelm his mind, and through a red haze he heard laughter, brittle and vicious.

Not alone, then. Not among friends. Where were his kinsmen? Fear began to seep into his consciousness, supplanting the pain.

"Bastard's alive." The rasping voice sounded disappointed. "Won't be for long, though." A bit more pleased. "The Comyn wants him well enough to talk before he joins his kin in Hell."

The Comyn? Fear seized his heart, squeezing. If he were in the hands of the Comyns, this pain was nothing. He was dead, or soon to be. A different kind of agony surged through his mind. His clansmen were all gone? It was too much. Coinneach Mackintosh went limp and collapsed onto the floor, and the welcome blackness closed in once more.

When he came awake again, warm hands were stroking his face. He felt an odd vibration course through him at the touch, making him shiver as though from an illness. Through bleary eyes he saw the face of an angel swimming above him in the dim light of his prison. So, it was over. He was dead, and soon he would be reunited with his kinsmen. He felt a sense of peace, allowed himself to drift.

"No!" said a soft voice. "Stay with me! I need you to remain awake if I am to help you." The angel was back...but why did he need help? Surely his struggles were over now. Then he felt the pain return, sharp and relentless, and knew the truth. He was still alive. Tears flowed unchecked down his cheeks. He was alive, and his clan was gone.

"P-please..." he managed a croak. "Let me go. Please. I just want to die."

"Well, I am not going to allow that," the angel said, a touch of vexation in her voice. "Come now...sit up. We have to plan. They will come for you soon, and you need to be gone. I will not let you go the way of the others!" Her voice was fierce.

Coinneach obeyed the angel, allowing her to assist him in sitting. He leaned against the hard stone wall, exhausted from the small effort.

"Who are you?" he said in a low voice, afraid to frighten her away in case she was real. "Where am I?" She did not answer, continuing to feel his body for injuries, pausing when he winced.

"Where am I?" he asked again, now with a touch of anger.

"Castle Raite."

Raite! The stronghold of clan Comyn, the keep that had been stolen from his people over a century ago! And now it all came flooding back. They had been on a scouting mission, he and six others of clan Mackintosh, sent to determine the strength of the castle's defenses.

Her words came back to him. "I will not let you go the way of the others." Pain ratcheted through him again. Gone! All of them—his brother Farlan, cousins Harald and Alasdair—all of them dead at the hand of their sworn enemy.

A flood of anger seared his mind. He no longer wanted to die. Not yet. First he had to avenge his family.

"Who are you?" he asked again.

"My name is Ailith," came the answer. "Ailith Comyn."

CHAPTER 11

SOMETHING AULD, SOMETHING NEW

"Your man is waitin' in the sittin' room," Nessie announced when Aubrey opened the door to her room.

"He's not my man!" she responded with more force than necessary. She was already having second thoughts about this date. *Why am I so easily subverted by a pretty face?* she thought, angry at herself. *I know next to nothing about this guy. I don't want to go through the aggravation. What if he's another Marc?* She was surprised to find that thinking about Marc no longer brought that biting surge of pain. Her emotional reaction to his name was evolving into disgust. Maybe someday it would disappear altogether and she'd be able to see his betrayal as just a learning experience, a step on the road to recovery. A cautionary tale.

Meanwhile, the next step on her road waited below, and she couldn't get out of it now. Aubrey checked her reflection in the old mirror in her bedroom. In spite of her misgivings, she had to admit that she'd spent an inordinate amount of time getting ready and she looked good, if she did say so herself. Her hair fell into a bob that ended at her chin, framing her heart shaped face and emphasizing full lips and large hazel eyes. Her smile was her best feature, she knew, straight teeth thanking her for the years spent in braces in junior high. In ordinary times she smiled a lot. She liked people and smiling came naturally.

But times hadn't been ordinary for a while now, and she realized with a shock that she had stopped smiling long before that text message. How had she been able to fool herself for so long? she wondered. She and Marc had had nothing much in common beyond lust, really. Perhaps her declining happiness had been apparent to him before she had realized it herself. She had stopped stoking his ego, and with someone like Marc that was akin to a mortal sin. She was remembering something Kate had asked months ago. "Are you sure that Harrington will be enough for you, Aubrey?" Maybe what she had really been saying was, "Are you sure that *Marc* will be enough for you?" Kate had no illusions about her cousin twenty times removed; Aubrey had just chosen to ignore the signs.

She had been blinded by the idea that such a paragon of manhood was in love with *her*, mesmerized by his interest. It hadn't been a level playing field at all. It was the fault of her damn imagination, she knew. She had created a fantasy lover and a magical world out of nothing. He had worked her into such a state that she was grateful for any attention he bestowed upon her. Honored.

Well, never again! She had a new rule. She would not allow herself to judge the worth of a man by his superficial qualities ever again. No! She would not get involved with any man, handsome or not, beyond a casual friendship. She would stuff her imagination deep into the recesses of her mind, where she kept the memory of the magical book, and leave it there to wither away. It just wasn't worth the heartache when she couldn't control it. With her new resolve firmly in place, Aubrey marched down the stairs and into the sitting room.

Finn Cameron was surrounded by her house-mates. Gladys had moved Ronald to a side chair and placed Finn beside her on the couch. Maxine sat on his other side, one graceful leg crossed, a ballet flat keeping time with music only she could hear. Harry was in his usual armchair, the ubiquitous newspaper held in front of him like a shield, but Aubrey knew he was missing nothing.

"And you teach Scottish history, love?" Gladys cooed. "Why, that is so interesting! Your students must fall over themselves to get into your class!" She gave a not-so-subtle wink at Aubrey in the doorway.

"My Ronnie loves history, you know," she gushed. "That's why we came here the first time, how long ago, Ronnie?" Ronald opened his mouth and closed it again as Gladys swept on, "And then we just loved the Highlands so much, now we come every summer for a month! We—"

"I came here with Ballet de l'Opéra national de Paris many years ago," interrupted Maxine. It seemed the only way to get a word in with Gladys. "It was a tour of the world, you see? And then, when I could no longer dance, I remembered Inverness as a place of such beauty. I now come in the summers for a visit."

Gladys reclaimed the conversation. "And Old Harry here, he is Scottish history!" She laughed at her own cleverness. The newspaper didn't move; Old Harry was used to Gladys.

Finn took advantage of the momentary break in conversation to leap to his feet, turning to face Aubrey. He was not in a kilt this evening. His khaki pants were pressed with a knife crease and he wore a navy blue sweater and tassel loafers. If it hadn't been for the tartan socks, she wouldn't have recognized him as a Scot, and certainly not from the tour yesterday. The socks, and the adorable lopsided grin, and the dimple, and....

She shook her weak, traitorous self. *Stop that!* she told herself. *Remember the rule!* But she couldn't help the smile that spread over her face at the scene before her. No one escaped her housemates when they had a new victim in their clutches. At least they'd given this one a seat! Finn must have passed muster for sure.

"Are you ready?" he asked, moving quickly to help her with her light jacket. She saw the approval in his eyes and was glad she'd taken the extra time with her appearance. Her smile grew, despite her resolve.

As they left the sitting room, Aubrey glanced back to see the Owls watching them. Old Harry was peering out from behind his newspaper, a curious expression on his face.

"Cameron, is it?" she heard him murmur. "Weel, noo. Ah wooldn't have expected *that*."

"I thought we'd walk," Finn said. "The weather is giving us a break, and I can point out some bits you might find interesting on the way. Of course, we can take the car if you'd rather."

"No, I'd love to walk," Aubrey assured him. "I just got here on Saturday, and only had the one tour so far. Other than the High Street, I haven't seen much of Inverness at all." She wrinkled her nose. "And that's so touristy."

Finn laughed. "Ach, and you're a local now?" he teased.

She flushed. "Sorry, that sounded snobbish, didn't it? But what I mean is, if I'm going to be here for a while, I want to see the really Scottish things. Where the locals go, you know?"

"And how long are you planning to be here?" he asked. Sneaking a sidelong glance at his face, she surprised a look of hope that set her heart fluttering. *Uh, oh.*

"I'm not sure," she answered after a moment. "It depends."

"Depends? On what?"

On whether I can end a curse and hear all the pipers in Scotland play at the same time, silly man! She wondered how fast he'd run away from her if she told him that!

"On whether I like it enough to stay, and if I can get a job," she said.

His face brightened. God, he was so handsome when he smiled!

"Weel, 'ats guid tae hear. We'll be sure tae make ye want tae bide," he said, putting on a heavy brogue that would have done Angus proud.

They walked in companionable silence until they reached the river, and then turned right on Castle Road, passing by Inverness Castle high on the rocky cliff to their right.

"Our castle isn't very old for Scotland," Finn said, assuming his professor voice. "It was built in 1836. But this one is only the last in a long line of castles that have stood on this site. The first one was built in 1057, and it had quite a story. Máel Coluim III supposedly burned the first one to the ground because Macbeth murdered his father, Donnchad I. You Americans do know about Macbeth, aye?" His eyes twinkled. "And then the castle that Coluim built was destroyed by Robert the Bruce."

Finn was warming to his subject. "And then, in 1428, James I was trying to make the Highlanders behave..." Hee paused. "Making the Highlanders behave is not an easy task. It took the Battle of Culloden to do that." Aubrey heard a sadness in his voice and wondered. She would have to take a tour to Culloden battlefield to see what caused that sort of reaction in a modern Scot, for an event that had taken place—what?—almost three hundred years ago. She wished she'd taken more time to read up on basic Scottish history.

"Anyway," Finn was back in 1428, "James called fifty clan chiefs to the castle, telling them it was to parley. When they got there, some were executed in front of their fellows, and others were put in chains. It didn't work, of course. Once they were let go, they came back and put the whole town to flame.

"One of the best stories of the castle was about Mary, Queen of Scots," Finn told her with relish. "Not all the Scots liked our Mary. When she came to visit in 1562, the castle gates were shut against her. The Munros weren't having that, though. They answered the insult by taking the castle for their queen. And the wee queen was so grateful that she hanged the governor who had refused her entry. Those were the good old days!" Finn chuckled.

Aubrey laughed. He was amazing, bringing the history of his country to life with passion and humor. Maybe she could get him to take her to Culloden. She was sure she'd understand the battle if he explained it to her.

Slow down, girl! You don't even know this guy. Don't go planning a life with him! Haven't you learned anything? Aubrey grabbed her imagination by the throat and shook it. It was *not* going to lead her into another disaster this time, not if she had anything to say about it. She steeled herself against Finn Cameron's brilliant smile.

In the distance, Aubrey could see a graceful pedestrian bridge, its lacy fretwork arching into the lowering evening sky.

"The Greig Street Bridge," Finn told her. "It's one of the wonders of Inverness." He winked at her but didn't elaborate. They reached the corner, and Aubrey noticed the sign: *Fraser St.* Finn heard her delighted intake of breath and rolled his eyes. "Yes, of course you know it was named after that famous," he intoned dramatically, "*fictional* character in your favorite books."

She laughed at him. "Of course I know it wasn't named after Jamie! But the setting of the books was this area, and it's–well, it's just exciting, that's all!" she finished, glaring at him.

He grinned at her. "Just messing with you. Here we are."

The sign on the old building read *The Mustard Seed.*

"Is it a very old restaurant?" Aubrey asked him.

"No, but it's in a very old building. Used to be a church and the architects kept some of the old touches when they made it into a restaurant. I wanted to bring you here because it's popular with locals as well as tourists and it has very good Scottish food. Have you had any Scottish food?"

"Oh, yes!" Aubrey said proudly. "I had a full Scottish breakfast on my first morning here!"

"Ahh. So, how did you like our haggis?"

"Um, I liked it a lot, until I found out what was in it!"

Finn laughed. "And you call yourself a Cumming! Well, if you're going to stay for any amount of time, you'd better practice eating haggis! Next time, I'll take you to a pub and introduce you to haggis, neeps and tatties!" He stopped, arrested by her odd expression.

Next time? Whoa, laddie! Aubrey thought. *Let's just get through the first time, why don't we?* But her heart, that imperfect, fallible organ, was singing. Next time! Whoo-hoo!

And then he took her hand to lead her into the restaurant. An electric current coursed through her at the touch, unlike anything she had ever felt before. It was as if every nerve in her body had begun to sing. She snatched her hand away in shock. What the hell? That had never happened before. She stared at Finn, speechless.

He looked surprised, and hurt. Aubrey cursed herself for her insensitivity, but there was nothing she could say that would make up for her violent reaction to his touch. *It's not what you think!* her mind cried out. *It's the very opposite of what you think!* But she said nothing, joining him in mutual embarrassment. They buried themselves in their menus, although Aubrey was not seeing anything on the page.

Finally, she spoke. "What amazing haggisy Scottish thing do you recommend?"

His eyes narrowed. "Are you making fun of me?"

"No!" she cried in distress. "Oh, no, Finn, never!" She sighed. "I'm just nervous, and I always try to cover anxiety with humor. I'm really enjoying myself! I am!" she said again, seeing the look of skepticism on his face.

"You're nervous? Why?"

"I don't know. I guess I'm not good at dating. I just got out of a relationship and I'm rusty." No way was she going to tell him about Marc, or about what his own touch had done to her.

He relaxed and the lovely smile, though guarded, came back. "Well, it's not as if I get around the dating scene all that much," he said easily, and they were okay again.

During dinner he regaled her with tales about the tours he'd done with Dougie's, and some of the eccentric customers he had dealt with.

"One lady," he said, waving his fork, "asked me 'how does it feel to have a Scottish accent?'"

Aubrey choked. "Bet she was American."

He bowed his head. "Wasn't going to mention it, but yes."

"And how often do they ask you what a Scotsman wears under his kilt?"

"Almost every time. If it's a young, rowdy bunch, I tell them 'the future of Scotland.'" He beamed.

"A Scottish friend of mine says his answer is 'me boots,'" she said, thinking of her own personal Scotsman. The wine and the laughter flowed. By the time the dessert menu arrived, any residual tension between them was long gone, and they had fallen into an easy comradery, as if they'd known each other for years.

"Weel, and who is this lovely lass?" said a voice.

Aubrey looked up and beheld the most gorgeous man she had ever seen in her life. At least six feet four, she guessed, with russet hair tied back in a queue, he had golden eyes and a smile that would melt butter. And he was in full Highland dress, from his lace jabot to his knee-high black boots. He wore a woolen waistcoat over a white shirt with turndown collar, and a wicked-looking dagger tucked into the garter of his argyle socks. Aubrey blinked when she realized that her eyes were level with his sporran, which seemed to be a little closer than necessary. He could give Jamie a run for his money, she thought. This guy belonged in Hollywood.

"MacConnach." Finn's voice was hard. "This is Aubrey Cumming, over from the States."

He bowed. The man actually bowed. "Connor MacConnach, lassie," he said solemnly. His voice was like the wind over the heather, honeyed and mellow. Beautiful. Everything she had told herself about handsome men went out the window at that voice. He was a god.

Finn signaled their waiter for the check. No dessert then? There was a history here, no doubt about it. These two did not like each other. When the check came, Finn signed it with a flourish and said, "I'm sorry, we were just leaving. See you around, MacConnach." And he hustled her out the door. When they stood on the pavement, he avoided her eyes, his mouth tight.

"Finn." He looked up, eyes wary. "Who was that man?"

"Connor MacConnach is the local playboy," he said shortly. "He works for the Mackenzies, sort of a man of all work, and does some modeling on the side." He spit out the word *modeling* as though he had eaten a bug by mistake.

"Does he always dress like that?" Aubrey asked.

"Usually. He has an image to uphold." He sounded petulant. Was he jealous? She found it somewhat endearing.

"Well, he does seem a bit over the top," she said, her voice carefully judicious. *Yeah, over the top beautiful!* Might be better to keep that thought to herself.

Somewhat mollified, Finn walked her back down to the High Street, pointing out the tartan shops geared to tourists, the Inverness Museum and Art Gallery, and the many kilt rental shops.

"People actually rent kilts?" Aubrey asked him, confused. "Why?"

"Well most of us don't actually wear the kilt all the time, or even much of the time," he told her. "I wear one when I do tours...for the visitors, aye? But usually we dress like you do in the States." He went on, "We wear them to weddings, or formal events like Rabbie Burns nights, so it's easier for most just to rent them when they're needed. I own mine, though. It's actually pretty comfortable. Air-conditioned, ye might say." He gave her a mischievous grin, his good humor restored. "You know, for the future of Scotland."

They walked homeward toward Nessie's, Aubrey thinking that this had been one of the nicest dates she'd ever been on. Except for that weird reaction to Finn's touch, and that was just confusing. He hadn't seemed to feel it.

"Wait!" she yelled. Finn stopped, alarmed.

"Is that a bookshop?" she gasped. The shop was huge, and very, very old. A sign on the stone building said "Mackintosh Bookshop."

"It's the oldest bookstore in the Highlands," Finn said. "Might still be open. Want to see?"

"Oh, yes!" she whispered. They pushed open the huge wooden door and went in. Aubrey gaped in awe at the largest display of books she had ever seen in one place. Books were stacked everywhere, from floor to ceiling, in wanton profusion. A circular staircase in the center of the cavernous space wound around to a second level filled with more books on shelves, tables, the floor.

"It's one of my favorite places in Inverness," said Finn. His voice was reverent. "Would you like to meet the owner? He's a personal friend, and he lets me have the run of the place to do my research." He led her around the huge book-piled desk to a clear spot where an old man sat, grinning an angelic, gap-toothed smile.

"Awrite, lass. Took yer time gettin' here, ye did," said Angus. "Hoors are on th' door. Ye start in th' mornin', dinna be late."

CHAPTER 12

DÉJÀ VU
ALL OVER AGAIN

"So, lass, whit have ye dain sae far," Angus asked her the next morning, "since ye didna hae th' time t' call me?" He glowered at her. "What have I *done*?" Aubrey shook her head in disbelief. "Well, let's see. I've traveled across the ocean at your command. I've been here three whole days, and in that time I've avoided killing any sheep with a car, I've met not one, but two Nessies, had a full Scottish breakfast...oh, and I've worried myself sick about you!" She finished with her hands on her hips.

And I kissed a gorgeous man who isn't a Mackintosh. She decided to keep that part to herself. Finn did not figure in Angus' plans, but she treasured the memory of that sizzle of energy that had passed between them when their bodies touched.

"Ach, sae nuthin' 'en."

"And that's another thing," she went on, hands on hips. "How did you manage that feat, anyway?"

Angus' look was pure innocence. "Ah dinna ken whit yoo're goin' on abit. Ah gang whaur Ah need t' be." He waddled around to stand behind the desk. "An' anyway, ahm here noo. Gie alang wi' ye, ye hae work t' do."

Aubrey threw up her hands in frustration. She should have known better; Angus always had the last word. And she was just so glad to see him.

"So what do you suggest I do next, oh Wise One?"

"Today yoo're goin on a train tae see a castle."

"Castle Rait? The one in the book?" Her pulse began to twitch, she wasn't sure if it was in anticipation or fear.

"Nae, yoo're no' ready fur 'at yit. Yoo're gon tae Dunrobin, home o' th' Sootherlands. They fought wi' th' Sassenach in th' forty-fife." His mouth drew down in a scowl and he hissed the last words. Aubrey knew that the Sassenach were the English, thanks to her favorite books, and the forty-five was the last Jacobite rising, in 1745, but she had never heard of the Sutherlands. It was obvious that Angus was not a fan.

"But...what about the curse? Isn't that what I'm supposed to be here for?"

"Yoo're—no—ready." He glared at her.

Aubrey sighed and gave it up as a lost cause. "So, if the Sutherlands were the bad guys, why do I want to see their castle?"

"Coz it's a verra fine castle," Angus said. "An' it'll help ye ken yer history a bit. Fur when ye meet th' ghost."

"The what?" Aubrey stared. "Is there a ghost at this Dunrobin Castle?"

Angus snorted. "Did Ah say 'at?" He handed her a ticket. "Yer train leaves a' eleven."

"But I—" Her protest was lost as Angus swished away. She sighed, knowing when she was beaten.

Aubrey found the train station without difficulty, tucked away behind the mall and the bus station. She'd been to both of those already; she was a real local now! Handing the agent her ticket, she sat in a metal chair between a family with two rambunctious children and an old man who hadn't had a bath in days, by the smell of him. He gave her a sweet smile and twinkled at her out of pale blue eyes, so she stayed put, not wanting to insult him by moving. As she waited for her train, she perused the book on Sutherland Castle that Angus had given her with her ticket.

The Sutherlands had backed the winning side during the Jacobite uprising of 1745, she learned. The book made a brief mention of Elizabeth Leveson-Gower, the nineteenth Countess of Sutherland, who had been instrumental in emptying northern Scotland of a huge number of its inhabitants during something called the Highland Clearances in order to farm sheep on the empty land. Those wooly little bastards had their hooves in everything in this country, Aubrey mused. Who'd have guessed they could make you so rich?

"Ah believe that th' train is here, lass," a soft voice broke into her reading. Aubrey looked up to see that her overripe friend was pointing toward the track.

"Ah see that ye'r interestit in the history o' our country." Aubrey looked over to see—and smell—that her waiting room companion was keeping pace with her as she hurried to the train. "Since Ah'm gang that way, Ah'll just keep ye company fur a bit, aye? Ah kin give ye some insider tips on the castle, so tae speak."

Why did she have to be cursed with a kind heart? Aubrey groaned. There was no way she was getting rid of him now; she'd been adopted. It could be a *very* long trip!

The train was quite modern. Pairs of double seats faced each other over rather sizeable tables. Her new friend took a seat across from her, which thankfully allowed her to breathe, and also to study his eccentric costume. He wore his dilapidated clothing in layers, like the homeless people back home on city corners. Perhaps he *was* homeless.

Long, thick grey hair straggled from under the brim of a leather hat that might once have belonged to a deer in another century. The hair wandered over the collar of a faded plaid shirt which was missing the third button down, and the belt on his corduroy trousers was a necktie. Over this he wore another shirt, denim, and over that a sweater—a jumper, Angus would call it—that might once have been blue but had faded to a questionable shade of brown. Grimy cuffs were folded back to expose the threadbare edges of the shirtsleeves.

And holding the collar proudly in place was a green bowtie. This last incongruous item gave the old man an air of surpassing dignity despite the worn, shabby ensemble. He reminded her of someone...but who?

Alastair MacGregor, she learned, was a wanderer. He had walked the length and breadth of his native land not once, but many times. Alastair explained that in Scotland anyone, resident or visitor, had the right to walk almost any mountain, moorland, forest or field, without regard for the owner's wishes, as long as he had respect for the land. It was called the "right to roam" and was a part of Scottish law.

Aubrey tried to visualize that happening in America and could not. Signs proclaiming "Trespassers will be prosecuted to the fullest extent of the law" sprouted like wildflowers in the land of the free. There were hundreds of old laws on the books defining the consequences for anyone daring to trespass on private property. "Roaming" was a suspicious word in the States, likely to earn the wanderer an overnight stay in the local jail.

When she shared her insights, Alastair defended her country by saying that much of Scotland was owned by about four hundred families, and many of those were not even Scottish! If the property laws of America were the rule in Scotland, he said, people would never see the beauty of the Highlands except in books or from the train. The government knew that.

"We like the tourists," he twinkled at her. "We need 'em." Still, he told her, he had never been one himself—had never left Scotland, and never would. His country had been good to him and he showed his gratitude by taking pictures and writing down his travels, sharing his experiences.

"Ye might see one or two o' my wee books in the visitor's centers," Alastair MacGregor told her. "I live in Forres, near t' Inverness, when I'm no' wanderin'. I've been on the trail for a week now, livin' in the same clothes, but I'll be home by the end o' the week. Lookin' forward to a nice bath, fur sure!"

So…not homeless. Not sad, or pathetic, or down-trodden at all. Just eccentric. There was a reason that "don't judge a book by its cover" had become a cliché. Aubrey felt shame at having fallen into the trap.

"I saw your books at Urquhart Castle!" she exclaimed suddenly. He dipped his head in acknowledgment.

"Aye, ye likely did."

"May I take your picture?" she asked him. "I want to remember meeting you."

"Aye, lass, it would be my pleasure. As long as yer in it with me," he added. "And then ye can text it t' me." They both laughed, Aubrey a bit red-faced at the knowledge that he had known what she was thinking all along and had forgiven her anyway. For a while they fell silent. Aubrey gazed out the window at rolling hills of purple heather standing sentry over a winding silver river…and sheep. There must be a sheep for every person in Scotland, she thought. The mountains in the distance were rounded, ground down by time until they resembled upside-down bowls—very much like the Appalachians back in Western Pennsylvania.

"Did ye ken that those wee mountains are the same ones ye have in the eastern part of yer own country?" Alastair MacGregor broke in. She blinked at him. That was spooky. Either she had the most open face on the planet, with all her thoughts parading across her forehead for anyone to see, or he could read minds. And suddenly she knew who the old man reminded her of. Angus had always been able to see what she was thinking, which was either comforting or annoying, depending on the situation.

"Pardon?"

"Scotland use t' be attached to yer own North America, way back before people came to the world. Then it broke off and meandered for a few million years, endin' up attached tae Europe for a while." He nodded at her. "Aye, but then the people came, and Scotland made the smart decision to break off with the mainland and go off north by herself. I think they were tryin' to break off from England, even then, but those people were hard t'get rid of!" He wheezed like an old bellows at his own humor.

"So, you see, the hills in yer country and the high-lands in Scotland are the same mountains. When the Highlanders got kicked off their land at th' time o' th' clearances, a lot of 'em emigrated to America and Canada. When they saw those mountains over there, they felt a connection t' their home, and they put down new roots."

Aubrey interrupted him to point out of the window. "Is that Dunrobin Castle? It's huge!"

Alastair squinted into the distance.

"Ach, no, that's really just a wee house. The Sutherlands built it t' get rid of a daughter-in-law they didn't like. It has a name, Carbisdale Castle, but the Highlanders back in th' day called it 'The Castle of Spite.'"

141

"Why?" Aubrey asked. This delightful old charac-ter was a walking compendium of odd facts. A real Guinness Book of Records, Scotland edition.

"Funny ye should ask," he said, settling back into his seat. "It's not even verra old, built in 1905. It was the last castle built in Scotland, in fact. After the Duke died, the family contested the will because they didn't like his wife. Nothin' they tried worked, so finally they agreed to give her a lot o' money and let her build herself a castle, as long as it was outside their lands. Since they owned most of the land in this part o' the Highlands, the Sutherlands thought they were pretty clever."

"But?" Aubrey sensed a punch-line.

"But the Duchess was verra smart, and she had her castle built just across the river over the property line, on a hill where they had to look at it from most places on their estate. See?" He clapped his hands in glee. "The Castle of Spite.

"And that's not all. Th' wee Duchess made sure that the clock tower was missin' a face on the side that looked toward her husband's family...because she didn't want t' give them the time o' day!" He broke up again, and Aubrey joined him.

"And here's yer stop," he told her, as the train began to slow. "Dunrobin has its own station. Benefits o' being a duke, ye ken?"

Alastair stayed seated as Aubrey stood up to leave the train.

"I'll be going on t' Thurso," he told her. "Got some wanderin' to do in the Orkneys. But I'm sure we'll meet again!"

As she descended the steps at the tiny train stop, she thought they just might. You never knew, in a magical place like Scotland.

Aubrey joined the other visitors passing through a massive stone gateway and down a shaded lane. The trees opened up and there was Dunrobin Castle, silhouetted against the sky. No wonder Alastair had laughed at her earlier; compared to this fortress, the Castle of Spite was a cottage! In the distance she could hear the faint sound of bagpipes.

She tendered her ticket in the grand foyer of the castle and began her self-guided tour. Marveling at the architectural detail of the grand public rooms, she passed through opulent halls into the wood-paneled dining room, the music room, a huge breakfast room, and a drawing room. Along the way she noted that the walls were almost completely covered in portraits of Gordons and Sutherlands, the earls and dukes who had lived on this site since William de Moravia started the whole thing in 1210. That anyone could call a place this size home boggled the mind, Aubrey thought in amazement. And then she found the enormous library and revised her thinking. Perhaps she could live here after all. Right here in this library.

Placards on stands positioned throughout the rooms told the history of the castle. My, Aubrey thought, these people were the movers and shakers of the country! One of the earls, she read, married the divorced ex-wife of the Earl of Bothwell, who had then married Mary, Queen of Scots. What a reality show that would have made!

The tour ended in a charming tea shop. Aubrey took a break to have a cup of tea and a sandwich before heading out for a walk about the grounds. Following a spacious stone balustered walkway along the outside of the building, she rounded the corner and her mouth fell open. The formal gardens of Dunrobin Castle stretched out for acres ahead of her, all the way to a huge body of water, a firth, she thought it was called.

The bagpipes were louder here. They made an eerie sound, as if calling from the mists of time to remind tourists that for centuries history had been made in this place. Battles had been fought here. These people had partied with kings and queens and had woven the tapestry that was Scotland. The guide book said that the Sutherland family still lived in a private part of the castle. Aubrey wondered if they ever visited their own library.

Continuing along the walkway, she rounded another corner and found the pipers. Four...and one of them was Finn Cameron. He was wearing his kilt again, with a more formal vest and jacket than the one he had worn on the tour. He saw her and stopped playing for a second, long enough to grin and signal her to wait.

Aubrey leaned up against the castle wall and watched him, remembering the end of their date the night before. He had walked her to Nessie's door, told her he'd call, and then he'd cupped her chin in his hand and kissed her. Her lips still sizzled with the memory of that kiss, of the vibration that had pulsed through her body and wrapped around her senses.

Nothing like that had ever happened to her before. Her reaction had been a mixture of shock and exhilaration, but this time she hadn't pushed him away. She didn't know what it meant, but she wanted to find out...very much. And here he was.

He looked very dashing in full regalia. Was there any pie this man didn't have his finger in? she wondered. He seemed to be a jack of all trades, and a master of them as well. Teacher, tour guide, book lover, piper, epicurean...almost too good to be true. She would have to watch her heart here. His eyes made contact as the quartet finished up their set, and he winked at her. She felt a trembling somewhere in the region of that heart and ignored it. *Later. I'll watch you later. Right now, I'm watching* him.

Finn finished packing up his instrument and came over to her, kilt swishing about his rather adorable knees.

"Well, what a nice surprise!" he said, as they walked back around the castle toward the parking lot. "Are you here by yourself?"

"Yes," she said, adding with pride, "I took the train!"

"Good for you, our rail system is pretty great. But do you have time to have a drink with me? I'll drive you home after. I dinna ken ye've had the chance t' meet our fine whisky noo yet, have ye?" he asked, thickening his brogue and leering at her.

"Well, I recently had a run in with one o' yer fine whiskies, right before I came over. It was called Talisker, and I ken they got it straight out of one o' yer fine peat bogs," Aubrey laughed, attempting to imitate his accent.

"Ach, that's sacrilege," he said sadly. "What you need is practice."

He helped her into a small grey Audi and drove them down the road to a charming pub called "The Naked Thistle." A chalkboard sign outside read "Sorry—no WiFi. Talk to each other and get drunk."

"This is one of the best pubs the tourists haven't found," Finn told her. "Just basic food and drink, no nonsense." He ushered her into a booth.

"Two Glenmorangie 10's, neat," he told the waiter.

"Just trust me," he admonished, catching Aubrey's wary eye. "It's a nice trainer scotch; you'll like it."

She did. She liked the first one, liked the second one better, and the third was fantastic. And they talked. She couldn't remember ever being with a man who asked her questions about herself and *listened* to the answers. It was beyond nice. He wasn't a Mackintosh, but who cared at this moment? Not her.

"Not like Marc at all," she said happily, through a whisky fog.

"Who's Marc?" he asked—had she said that out loud? She didn't want to talk about Marc. Not with Finn. "Just some guy I knew once," she hedged, and then all that lovely whisky betrayed her. "Have you ever been in love?"

He went still. "I have," he said at last. "Her name is Isla."

A dim warning bell went off in her muddled brain. Is? Not was? *Uh oh.* She felt herself beginning to slide backwards into the pattern she knew so well, inviting a handsome man to tell her about his heartbreak. She must be hard-wired for this.

"Tell me about her," she heard herself say.

"Isla Gordon," he said, his voice dull. "She's a distant relation to the Sutherlands at Dunrobin." And then it all came out...how they had been college sweethearts, but she was rich and her parents wanted her to marry well, and he wasn't in their plan, and how she had been unable to stand up to them in the end. It wasn't her fault, he insisted.

"It's over, but we're still friends," Finn said. "She volunteers at the castle sometimes as a tour guide for special groups. She got us the piping job. I owe her a lot." He gave Aubrey a wistful smile.

She put trembling fingers against her forehead. Her head felt as if it were full of wool, and there was a throbbing behind her eyes. Un-fucking-believable. It was happening to her all over again. Propping up a man's broken heart after another woman had trampled on it. "It's over," he had said. Right. She knew all about that one. She felt a helpless anger begin to build, and a threatening nausea. No! *It was not going to go that way, not this time!* She had not come halfway around the world just to repeat the same mistakes. She should have listened to her heart, should have heeded her own advice.

Well, she was listening now.

She managed to stand up. "I don't feel very well," she told him. "I think I'd like to go home."

CHAPTER 13

CALEDONIA

The air was stifling inside the gymnasium. There had been an attempt to place chairs, but the sheer numbers of people made it impossible to seat even half of those who had shown up for the rally. Everyone was standing now anyway, blocking the view of the makeshift stage. The noise was deafening. People vied with the ubiquitous bagpipes to be heard five feet away and failed. Tempers were rising; all that would be needed was a wrong word, a careless shove, and the crowd could turn ugly. It was a recipe for disaster.

Then the pipers stopped and a man stepped out onto the stage. He was an unimpressive man, average in height and build, wearing a navy blue suit and a white button down shirt. He was clean-shaven and his hair, cut short, was a medium brown. His only concession to fashion was a tartan tie.

He looked the epitome of ordinary. And yet, at his appearance, the room quieted, pushing and shoving ceased, and a respectful silence pervaded the room where chaos had ruled a moment ago. This man had a presence, an aura, and a reputation. His name was Lachlan Mackenzie, and he was the leader of the new *Caledonia First* campaign for Scottish Independence.

Mackenzie raised his hand in a simple greeting and began to speak. His voice was magical—fluid and resonant, at odds with his mild appearance.

"Welcome, all you who love Scotland! Fà, a tha dèidheil air Alba!" A great roar of approval went up from the crowd at the Gaelic words. Mackenzie waited for the noise to die down again, and then he began to speak.

"My brothers, in 2014 we had a chance to gain our independence from Britain. A referendum was held and we might have taken our country back. Not since the Bruce have we been so close to victory, but we were close then. So close...and then the British mounted an attack of immense proportions—an attack of propaganda, a war of words. The *Better Together* people used the media, and they asked, 'Can Scotland survive without us?' They told us that we would fail as a country without Britain. They instilled fear in good Scottish people, and they won. They thought we were finished, that our own people would never let go of the yoke.

"But they were arrogant, and they made a mistake. It was a mistake that will allow us to rise again from the ashes of that referendum, and this time we will win. Because this time they have shown their soft side...and its name is Brexit!"

Again the room erupted, until Lachlan Mackenzie raised his hand again.

"A new independence referendum is a surety now, brought about by the trickery and the lies that have marked the British Empire through the centuries, and the question now is no longer whether we can survive without them. The question has become... Can we survive *with* them? And the answer is no!

"Brexit proved what has been the truth throughout the ages—that the wishes and the needs of Scotland are unimportant to those in power in Britain. We have been shoved aside, made fun of, ignored, and yet we send billions to the rest of the UK. And what do we buy with this money raised by honest Scots? We buy lovely new things for London! And in return we are told that we could not exist without the financial decisions that Mother England so lovingly makes for us.

"But that is the greatest lie of all! Scotland must become independent so that our government can make decisions that benefit Scotland, choices that allow us to use our resources for our own people. The shame of Brexit is our shame, if we continue to allow ourselves to fall under the mantle of Britain, to be seduced by her lies.

"We have a proud heritage, an ancient culture that is ours alone, but until we are independent, that is also a lie. And so I ask you, are you willing to live yoked to a country that has abused us throughout time, or will we take back our proud nation? Will we be second to Britain, or will we be Caledonia, first, last and always? Is sinn Alba!"

The bagpipes began to play *Flower of Scotland* as Lachlan Mackenzie left the stage. The spell broken, the crowd broke into smaller groups, voices rising and falling as they talked about what they had just heard. Many of the discussions were in Gaelic, something that just a few years ago would not have been the case. It was another sign of the changing attitudes in the Highlands of Scotland.

Finn Cameron leaned against the back wall, wondering if he was witnessing a sea change in his country's history, or just another politician riding the wave of patriotism as far as it would take him. He hoped that Lachlan Mackenzie was the real thing. Finn believed in Scottish independence; what true student of Scottish history would not be stirred by the call to take back his country, once and for all, from England? But he also believed that politics made for strange alliances, not all of them honest. Some of those screaming for an independent Scotland were self-serving, deceitful, perhaps even evil, and he knew that it was best to keep a clear head when swimming in these currents.

"Fionnlagh Cameron!" came a voice he knew well. With a sigh, Finn turned to face Connor MacConnach. For once the man blended in with the crowd. Many of the attendees tonight wore kilts and clan badges, though Finn had chosen to attend in jeans and a corduroy jacket. False patriotism was not his thing. MacConnach, on the other hand, was the very definition of the Hollywood warrior. He was the embodiment of the fierce Highlander, and he worked hard to maintain that image.

Connor looked at him, a slight smile on his face as if reading his mind.

"Are you finally joining the cause?" he asked, his tone mocking. Finn tensed at the words, preparing to move away, but Connor put out a hand and clasped his arm. "I'm sorry, I didn't mean to come off like an arse. I know we have some history between us, but I'm glad to see you here. Truly. We're going to need every good Scot we can find if we're to make this thing happen."

Finn relaxed. MacConnach was making an effort; surely he could do the same? They did indeed have baggage, but the fault was not all on one side, if he were honest with himself. It took two to hold onto a grudge, and he didn't need to like the man to work with him. He extended his hand.

"You're right," he said. "We're all going to need to work together in this, what say we put our grievances aside, for Scotland?" And the two men walked out of the building, strange bedfellows united by a common purpose and a single goal.

❁

An hour later a phone was picked up in an office building in Edinburgh. Darius Sanderson listened, silenced his cell, and put it back in his pocket. He leaned back in his leather chair and stared at the ceiling. These *Caledonia First* people were idiots, but their numbers were growing. This latest rally had brought out more people than any of the previous attempts, and Sanderson knew how important good advertising could be in bringing people of similar mindsets together. Maybe *Better Together* needed a new name to go with the new battle looming on the horizon. He'd suggest the idea to his people. Change was critical to the game, and the right name could shift the balance in a political discussion. He was proof of that!

He frowned. This Mackenzie was going to be trouble. He was a first cousin to the Mackenzie clan chief and as such commanded respect in the Highlands. According to his operative inside the *Caledonia First* campaign, the man was a true orator. He had the voice of an Irish tenor; his words were simple and straightforward. He inspired people. He had had them in the palm of his hand tonight, his agent reported. Had them babbling in Gaelic like the barbarians from whom they were descended.

Sanderson could feel the rage building again. He was going to have to be careful. Ever since Oliver Thomson's death, he could feel his self-control eroding. Ollie had been the one who kept him centered. Darius had not realized how much he had depended on his friend for his advice and his unfailing loyalty. Darius Sanderson had never had many friends; in his business you could not afford to trust anyone. But he had trusted Ollie. He missed him.

No one would have thought that someone Ollie's age, in superior physical condition, would drop dead of a heart attack. Life was a crap shoot, and you never knew when it was your turn.

He shook himself back to the task at hand. Something was going to have to be done about this Lachlan Mackenzie before the Caledonia people got out of hand. He was pleased with the new operative he had planted in the organization. If this agent continued to gather information and carry out the tasks that had been assigned, there might be no limits to a future with PETRO. Darius needed an ally, now that Ollie was gone.

CHAPTER 14

RUINED GLORY

"'m so stupid!" wailed Aubrey into the phone. "I never learn! What's wrong with me?"

Kate listened quietly while her friend blubbered out her story, and then said, "Well, at least you wised up before this guy dragged you away from home like Marc did."

"But I *am* away from home. I'm halfway across the world! And that's part of the problem. What the hell am I doing here anyway? Angus won't even talk about the curse—says I'm not ready. What does that even mean?"

Kate's calm voice came down the line as if she were across town instead of an entire ocean away. "There's something very uncanny about Angus, you know that. The bookstore was there, and then it just wasn't. You'd think that in a town as small as Harrington an overnight disappearance like that would be the talk of the town. But nobody even seems to remember he was there! It's really strange, Aubrey. I think he's as ghoulish as that weird book that supposedly talked to you."

There was a pause on Kate's end of the line.

"But none of that has anything to do with this guy, does it, Bree? Why are you so upset about a guy you just met?" Her voice was gentle. "You'll probably never see him again."

"He's texted me three times, Kate! I feel terrible ignoring him, he's so sweet, but I just can't go through that again! He's not like Marc, not really. I don't even know if he realizes he's still in love with that girl! And that just makes it worse somehow! Why are men so damn dumb?"

"If he's not available you're just going to have to let it go and be glad you found out early on. Besides, you said this guy's name wasn't Mackintosh, so he's not the one you're supposed to find anyway."

"Well, that's another thing!" Aubrey's voice was low and raw. "I don't know if I trust Angus anymore either. His instincts were spot on about Marc; he knew him for what he was as soon as he met him. I just didn't listen. So couldn't he have warned me not to get involved with the wrong guy again? He seems to think Finn is the second coming, I get that, what with the history professor bit, but Angus was pushing Mackintoshes at me back in Jersey—why let me get involved with this un-Mackintosh without saying anything? What's he good for?" Her voice was petulant and childish; she could hear it and didn't care.

Kate laughed. "I don't think one date and an accidental meeting qualifies as 'getting involved,' Bree! And maybe Angus has more faith in you than you think. Maybe he knew you'd figure it out on your own. You know what a spooky old geezer he is—positively Machiavellian—but at the end of the day he has your best interests at heart. He loves you. He'd tell you if he thought you were going to get yourself into trouble."

Well, Angus couldn't know everything, Audrey thought stubbornly. She had been close to getting herself in trouble, closer than she wanted to let Kate know. She couldn't forget that electrical charge that had surged through her at the touch of Finn's hand. It had frightened and thrilled her at the same time. She had wanted to see if it would happen again in the pub...but then he'd ruined it all with his confession about his first love, which she had known immediately from her experience as a loser meant "my true love."

And Kate was wrong—she *was* going to have to see Finn again. She'd already caught a glimpse of him yesterday at the bookshop, head bent as he talked with Angus. She'd ducked behind the stacks and stayed there until he left, but how long was she going to be able to keep that up if she worked here? Angus obviously valued the man's company, and Finn had told her this was his favorite place in Inverness. He wasn't just going to disappear. Aubrey took a shuddering breath. She needed a heart transplant; this one was a lemon.

"I don't know, Kate," she said, her voice bleak. "I know I only just met him, but I really thought he was going to be different. I liked him—a lot. I'm tired of living with a lump in my throat. I think I should just come home."

Kate was silent. Aubrey could feel a tension coming through the line...a sort of sadness mixed with anger.

"What?"

"Marc and Angie are getting married." Kate's voice was flat. "They're not waiting. It's in three weeks, on Friday."

"Oh." Aubrey felt suddenly as if she were gasping for air that wouldn't come. Already! It was real, then. Marc was really gone. She'd known it, of course; in her saner moments she had known that she would never have taken him back, even if he had come crawling to her, crying about what a fool he'd been, begging her to come back to him. She had not really expected that. But couldn't he have felt a little remorse, a little shame, for the way he had ended things? It was proof that he had never loved her like she had loved him, but it didn't help with the pain.

She sighed. "I guess I'll stay over here and let Angus manipulate me for a little while longer then." Her voice sounded empty, drained of emotion. "But Kate?"

"What, darling?"

"I wish you were here. I need you and Fitz. I know that's impossible, but—"

"No. We'll be there as soon as we can work it out. Find us a room somewhere. We're coming as soon as we pack our wellies. I hear the Scottish weather is lovely."

After hanging up with Kate, Aubrey wandered down to the kitchen to look for coffee. Nessie was bustling about, feeding vast amounts of food into the AGA, but she looked up at Aubrey's approach.

"Ach, feeling better then, are ye?" she said.

"How did you know? Oh, never mind."

Nessie gave her an affectionate glance over the wheels of black pudding she was arranging on a tray. "Go sit, breakfast'll be ready in a minute."

"I don't want a big breakfast this morning. My stomach is still a little queasy from all the whisky I had yesterday." She felt a pang at the thought of the reason for all that whisky, and shook herself. *Don't go there*, her heart told her. *I warned you!*

"Just some tea, then. That'll fix ye right up. Angus says we're t' meet him at the shop. He says you're ready."

"Ready for what?"

"Ready t' meet the ghost, of course." Nessie returned to her cooking, pointedly ignoring her houseguest's astonished stare.

Aubrey wandered into the sitting room where Old Harry sat in his customary chair behind his newspaper and Gladys was placidly knitting something complicated and fluffy. "A muffler for my Ronnie," she told Aubrey, who nodded absently until her eyes fell on the pile of yarn. It was pink. Ronald's gaze met hers over his book and he grimaced behind his mother's back. Trying with the utmost difficulty to keep a straight face, Aubrey reflected that the Owls were always there when you needed them. They were good for a tortured soul.

Maxine glided into the room and sat on the arm of the sofa. "So," she said, "he is a very nice looking one, your young man. Ooh la la."

Aubrey blanched. Maybe *not* always so good for the soul. "I'd rather not talk about it, please. And he's not my young man."

Maxine looked at Gladys. "Have I missed something?" the look said. Gladys gave an exaggerated shrug, but for once had nothing to say. A small miracle, Aubrey thought. Maybe the glare she was giving them was sending the correct message.

Old Harry put his paper down and snorted, sounding exactly like Angus. He stared for a moment at Aubrey, and then put the paper back up and disappeared behind it. Somehow it seemed like a rebuke, but maybe she was feeling extra sensitive today.

"Breakfast!" announced Nessie, and they all trooped into the dining room.

After another full Scottish breakfast that she hadn't known she wanted, Aubrey dutifully followed Nessie into a battered old red Fiat. They stopped at the bookshop to pick up Angus and within minutes were on their way to Nairn. Aubrey felt swept along like flotsam in a flood, unable to change her fate. By himself, Angus was a force to be reckoned with, together he and Nessie were a juggernaut. It wasn't worth the effort to protest.

Following the A96, they wound their way eastward toward the coast through brush and trees and fields dotted with little white bushes that turned out to be sheep. Hills rose in the distance, covered with that low shrub-like growth that lent a lovely purple cast to the smooth hillsides. Heather, she remembered, recollecting her conversation with Alastair MacGregor.

"It's just startin' t' bloom," said Nessie, without taking her eyes off the road. "By August, the hills'll be covered with purple flowers. Verra bonnie, is heather."

"Hmmmph," was all Angus said on the topic of heather. Aubrey said nothing, every nerve ending on edge. Was she really supposed to be going to meet a ghost? This whole day was surreal.

They chugged into Nairn, an ancient resort town that sat on the edge of the ocean. Every town seemed ancient to Aubrey's American eyes. She felt as if she had lost control of her life, as if she were being carried along like so much driftwood, and today she just couldn't bring herself to care. The sea sparkled in the rare sunshine, challenging her to rise above her mood

"No' th' sea," said Angus, reading her mind again.

"This is the Moray Firth," Nessie broke in. "It's just a wee bit of water that sticks in from the ocean. Now, Nairn...Nairn has an interestin' history. A few miles to the east was the kingdom of Macbeth—Ah suppose ye've heard of Macbeth over there in the States, aye?" Nessie broke from her travelogue to slant a sly glance at her captive. Aubrey grimaced. It was the second time someone had tried that particular joke on her and it was losing its flavor. "An not far from here are the Clava Cairns, a burial ground from Neolithic times. Verra old, they are."

The little Fiat turned onto the A939 and wended its way south out of Nairn for only a few miles. They passed fields and hedgerows, but no people. The road narrowed and became a single lane.

"Lass, that's th' whisperin' stone." Angus nudged her, pointing across a field to where a huge boulder rose out of the pasture, incongruous in its solitary majesty. "Th' Comyn lassie an' 'er loover used th' stone tae send messages tae each oth'r. It was how she told heem abit th' massacre 'at was comin'." Aubrey craned her neck to see, and felt a cold sensation snake its way down her spine. It was real. At least this much of the legend in the old book was as real as that rock out there.

And then without warning, as they rounded a stand of trees, there it was. Emerging from the wildflowers and brush of the Scottish woods was the ruin of an ancient castle. Roofless, its turrets long gone, it was still a thing of beauty. Lovely arched windows, embellished with copper-colored stone fretwork, were set in grey stone walls, and the remains of an imposing tower graced the corner of the three-story hall. It stood as it had for centuries, ruined and yet somehow still noble.

Pride had gone into the building of this keep, Aubrey thought, and was entranced. There was nothing frightening about this place, nothing of the menace aroused by the book and its legend of doom. Surely such a peaceful place could not have been the site of so much betrayal and death! She was eager to explore, to see what the home of her ancestors had to share. Aubrey jumped from the car as it came to a stop.

"Be careful, lass. Rait Castle has its secrets. What ye see now is not what once was," cautioned Nessie. Angus said nothing, watching her. But Aubrey wasn't listening anyway. She moved forward, almost running, drawn by an unseen force to the imposing ruin of Rait Castle. Nessie looked at Angus and shook her head. He shrugged.

Aubrey circled the castle until she came to what must have been the front entrance—a huge arched opening into an inner space that yawned to the sky. She tried to remember the names of castle parts. Was it the bailey? No, that was outside the walls. The great hall? She stepped through the arch... and doubled over as pain gripped her stomach and nausea swept through her body. She heard the buzzing of a thousand bees, tasted burnt meat. And the smell! The dense, foul air that swarmed with maggots and decay. It was the reaction she had had to the ancient book, but so, so much worse. She bent over and lost the full Scottish breakfast that she had consumed an hour before, but the pain did not subside. The buzzing grew louder, the smell and taste more intense. Aubrey fell to her knees in the grass, helpless, and then hands gripped her arm and yanked her back through the opening, into the sunlit grass outside the walls of Rait Castle.

CHAPTER 15

WHISKY
AND OTHER SPIRITS

"Angus told me this might happen," Nessie muttered, as she knelt beside Aubrey and put her arm around her. "Shhh, it's all right, lass." She pulled out a handkerchief and handed it to Aubrey, who wiped at her mouth and then looked up, eyes bleary, to where Angus stood with his hands on sturdy hips.

"Ah telt ye tae be careful, didna Ah, lass? Ye canna juist go rushin' in when the castle isnae ready. Ye have tae be respectful. Ye have tae wait till ye're invited." He clucked at her like a mother hen.

"Are you kidding me?" Aubrey choked, fighting to catch her breath. "This pile of rubble has to invite me inside?" She glared at him. "It's connected to that book, isn't it? It's the same smell. Does this happen to everybody?" She heard the panic rising in her voice.

"Well," Angus said, "no' many people come this way. It's no' on the tours an no' many know aboot it. But no...th' castle doesnae act this way aften... juist one other time, Ah ken." He shrugged as if his words meant nothing but didn't take his eyes off Aubrey's face.

"Do you mean that it was the *castle* that made me sick? But that's impossible! It's just an old ruin!" She struggled to her feet and faced him, swaying, her face leached of color.

Angus looked sidelong at her. "Why dinna ye find oot for yerself? Gae slow this time, give it a chance tae remember ye." He nudged Aubrey toward the archway again.

She fought the urge to burst into tears. The very last thing she wanted to do was to *ever* go through that arch again. But something else was happening, warring with her fear. Her imagination was rioting, jumping up and down and screaming at her that anything could happen, that she had to find out the truth. The rational part of her brain was yelling back that this was stupid; ancient dead stones could not inflict pain or sickness. Neither could books speak and buzz...but she had felt the pain, smelled the rotting flesh, and the grass held the proof of her nausea. She wanted to run to the car, go back to Inverness and book a flight home. Forget about all of this. But unless she went forward, she'd never know the truth. And she had to know.

She took a deep breath, walked unsteadily to the castle's ruined opening, and stepped forward through the arch more slowly this time. And nothing happened. No, that was not true...*something* was happening. A feeling was building inside her—not nausea this time, but an *urgency*, an expectation. There was no reason for it, but it was there. A myriad of emotions welled up and began to swirl inside her mind—anxiety, fear, despair, and surrounding them all an inexplicable feeling of profound love. *I have to warn him!* she thought in desperation, and the thought was so strong that she turned in a circle, searching for someone who was in danger. But there was no one there. Slowly the sensations began to fade, sinking down through her body and dissipating into the ground. She was alone in the middle of a castle ruin, and she had never been so afraid for someone in her life. But who was it? Where had this feeling of love and need come from? What the hell was happening to her? She felt disconnected from herself, almost an observer of her own feelings and actions. *Possessed.*

She stumbled out to where Angus and Nessie waited, watching her closely. The look on their faces could only be described as satisfaction.

"You knew what was going to happen, didn't you?" Aubrey accused them. "What caused that? Please...I have to know why I felt those things!"

Angus shrugged and turned his back on her. Nessie gave her a sympathetic half-smile, and began following him to the car, Aubrey trailing behind in a daze. "Ye need to know a bit about the history of Rait Castle, then," Nessie said, turning to wait for her to catch up. "It was built by the Mackintosh about eight hundred years ago an passed to his son, whose name was," she paused, "Angus." She slanted a glance sideways

169

at Aubrey, and then continued, "But because Angus was but a wee bairn, the Comyns, who had wanted the lands for a long time, conspired to take over the castle for themselves. They supported the crown and fought against William Wallace and the Bruce, but despite standin' with the Sassenach they managed to hold the castle away from the Mackintoshes. That caused a mighty feud between the Mackintoshes and the Comyns that went on for two hundred years, until the Comyns invited the Mackintoshes to a feast to make a peace between them."

"The book!" Aubrey breathed. "The Mackintoshes came to the feast, but they weren't there for peace. The book said they rose up and killed all the Comyns in cold blood. And it was all the fault of the daughter of the castle. She planned it all, with her lover. She was a Comyn, and he was a Mackintosh. That's what the book said!" She stopped. "It's a very sad story, Nessie, but it's history! Maybe only a legend. It was so long ago, and the castle is a ruin. How can it think? How can it remember something? And what does it have to do with people now? None of it makes any sense at all!" She felt her control slipping again, hysteria threatening to overwhelm her.

Nessie reached into the glovebox and produced a flask. She unscrewed the cap and handed it to Aubrey without a word. Aubrey took a swig of whisky, thinking she had never tasted anything so wonderful in her life.

"Hush, child. There're more things in heaven and earth, Horatio, than are dreamt of in yer philosophy.

And that's Shakespeare. The one who wrote about Macbeth, ye ken?"

"Stop it," Aubrey said crossly, taking another swallow from the flask. "We do read Shakespeare in New Jersey, you know! You're just trying to distract me!" But she had to admit it was working—or perhaps it was the scotch working. Whatever, she already felt steadier.

"Well, aye. Ye do look a little peaked, to tell the truth. Of course, I dinna blame ye. It's a lot to take in, and I told Angus ye might not be ready, but he's a stubborn old coot for sure." Nessie glared at Angus, who stood on the other side of the car with his back turned, pretending to be deaf.

So they had been talking about her, discussing her behind her back. It made her feel like a child, helpless to understand what was going on or make decisions without her elders and betters. Well, she might be an idiot about love, but she was damned if she wasn't going to have some input into what happened with this irascible castle!

"So, what about the curse?" She decided to talk to Nessie, since Angus was ignoring her. She handed the flask back, remembering she was drinking on an empty stomach. Nessie gave her an innocent look that didn't fool her for a minute.

"What curse?"

"Come on now!" she exclaimed in exasperation. "The one about the Mackintoshes losing their home, and a Comyn having to fall in love with one to sort out all this clan nonsense." Aubrey tried to make her tone flippant, but it came out as a challenge.

171

"Ach, that's Angus' territory. Ye'll have to ask him about that." She opened the driver's door and plunked herself into the Fiat.

Aubrey looked over the top of the car at Angus, who was turned away, studying the trees nearest to the castle. She ground her teeth and leaned into the car. "I have, Nessie, but all Angus will say is what the book says, that a Comyn has to fall in love with a Mackintosh 'without guile', whatever the hell that means, and then the curse will be lifted and all the pipers in Scotland will start playing at the same time...or something like that." She knew Angus could hear her, but he remained with his back turned to the car, staring into the trees that surrounded Rait Castle. For his benefit, she added, "But I don't understand what it all has to do with an old pile of stones that's been moldering away for hundreds of years! Or how I'm expected to do anything about it."

Angus gave up his intent survey of the woods and turned to face Aubrey. "Th' stones o' th' castle remember everythin' that happened, lass, an' they ken th' story coz it's theirs. Yer a part o' the story, Aubrey Cumming. Ye'll juist have tae see whit part that is!" And he climbed into the car. Discussion over.

Aubrey walked slowly around to the other side of the car. She turned once more to look at the ruin of Rait Castle...and froze. In the topmost arched window of the tower, a woman was watching—staring directly at her. She blinked, and the woman was gone. A shudder went through her, and she felt the bile begin to rise again. She wrenched the door open and threw herself into the back seat, staring out at the field where, among the sheep and the grass, stood an innocent looking boulder called the whispering stone. A rock that, if all this could be believed, had acted as conspirator in one of the most vile acts of betrayal in history, perpetrated by her own ancestor.

Aubrey said nothing to Nessie about what she had seen...or imagined she had seen. Because it couldn't be. How could someone be standing at the tower window? There were no floors, no stairs. Rait Castle was a shell. And yet, unless she were losing her mind, she had seen something. A woman *had* been standing at that lonely window, a pale image dressed in clothes from another time, and she had been looking directly at Aubrey. In that flash of time something had passed between them, a sort of rippling in her mind. Aubrey had felt an *intrusion*, as if the woman was trying to tell her something. And in those few seconds she had been sure that she knew this person, that she had seen her somewhere before. She also knew somehow that the feeling was mutual. The woman had recognized her, and had spoken to her without words. Yet that was impossible.

They were silent on the way back to Inverness. Aubrey looked out of the window at the serene Scottish countryside and saw nothing. Nessie and Angus kept their eyes on the road, avoiding eye contact with each other and with her. Puzzling behavior, but maybe they understood her need to work through her experience at Rait Castle. If so, the joke was on them. She was going to need a hell of a lot more than mere time to work through what she had seen in that empty tower window, not to mention the castle's attack on her senses.

By unspoken agreement they didn't return to the bookshop. When the car pulled up to the house on the hill, Aubrey jumped out, intending to barricade herself in her room.

"Sae ye saw 'er then."

Aubrey turned slowly to face Angus. She should have known. He missed nothing.

"So you saw her too. Is she a ghost?"

"Aye, lass, she's th' castle's ghostie. Ah've seen her many times. No' minny do, but Ah've seen her, an' a few others hae seen 'er over th' years."

"What about that feeling I had when I went into the castle? The pain...the sickness? What about the smell, the buzzing? What about that horrible taste? Does that happen to others too?"

"It happened to Angus once," said Nessie, speaking for the first time since leaving the castle. "Never to me. But then, he's a Mackintosh." She shrugged, as if that explained everything.

"Tis th' castle tryin' tae protect itself... from th' massacre," Angus said, his voice soft. "Th' old keep's niver stopped tryin', even though 'twas too late."

Aubrey blinked at him. She started up the pathway to the front door of the house and then she turned back to face them again. "Thanks for taking me there. Even though it was sort of awful...thanks."

"You're welcome, lass," Nessie told her. Angus nodded.

"Angus?"

"Aye?"

"Who was the ghost?"

"Ach. 'At was th' daughter ay th' Comyn ye saw. 'At was wee Ailith."

Son, the greatest trick the Devil pulled was convincing the world there was only one of him.

David Wong

SCOTLAND, 1442

There was something wrong. He could not put a name to the feeling, but the darkness swirled with menace. The guard turned his head in every direction, listening, searching for the thing that had seemed out of place. Nothing. But something was wrong.

There was no wind tonight. Moy Hall rose behind him, stark and beautiful in its simplicity. Seat of the Mackintosh clan, the keep dominated the horizon, rising out of the heather and bracken, stoic and indifferent, to gaze with disdain on the humans who presumed to occupy its halls. It was over two hundred years old and impregnable, sitting on its own island in the center of the placid waters of the loch from which it had received its name.

He was probably imagining things again, Coinneach told himself. Since he had returned from the disastrous mission to Raite Castle six months ago, he had been prone to fantasies and phantasms. His wounds had healed, but his mind remembered the terror, the fear...

and the angel who had saved him from the enemies who had taken the lives of his clansmen that night.

Ailith. She had taken him from the dungeon to an abandoned stonecutter's cottage nearby, and there had nursed him back to health. He had no idea how she had managed to half-carry him in his condition, or how they had escaped discovery by her people, but she had come to him every night for a month, bringing food and wine, and as his mind and body grew stronger so did his feelings for the beautiful lass whose kinsmen had destroyed his own. When he was strong enough to leave, he had held her face in his hands and promised that he would return someday and take her away from Raite. Her tears had flowed over his fingers like the waters of the loch...

The loch! He looked down at his feet, where the water now lapped at the toes of his boots. It was higher—he was sure of it! Jerking himself to awareness, he saw that the level had risen at least a foot since he had been on duty. But how could that be, with no storm and no wind? Could something have blocked the neck of the loch?

He reported to the other guards and together they set out to investigate, following the Moy Water where it narrowed, until the muted sound of voices reached their ears.

"It's working! By morning, the dam will have done its job."

"I wish I could see the looks on those Mackintosh dog faces when they find themselves drowning in their beds!"

"That will put an end to them, for certain. The Comyn is a wily one."

The Comyn! The Mackintosh men stared at each other in astonishment. They had dammed the loch! If something was not done, the entire clan would drown by morning!

"I will go," said Coinneach. He had seen too many of his clansmen perish by Comyn hands. Enough was enough.

Silently he skirted the line, freezing in place when a head snapped up to listen. The going was hard, but he was grateful for the moonless night. It had aided the enemy; it would aid him as well. Creeping sometimes on hands and knees, he worked his way past the guards to the makeshift dam. It was shoddily constructed, logs and brush placed over the narrowest part of the Moy Water, but it was enough. It was not meant to last more than a night, after all.

Coinneach could barely see in the pitch darkness, but fortune was on his side this night. After working fruitlessly at the recalcitrant jam, a log shifted in his hand, and he was able to pull it out. The next was easier...and suddenly the dam broke and water began to gush through. He ran for his life then, rewarded with screams from the siege camp as water gushed forth, slowly at first and then with a great roar as the weakened barricade gave way and collapsed.

Exhausted, Coinneach made his way back to his men. He thought of Ailith and wondered. When would this treachery and enmity between their clans cease? Would they ever see peace? He wanted to believe so, but a dark foreboding filled his heart.

CHAPTER 16

DISCOVERIES

She couldn't see. The darkness was a blanket, foul and suffocating, robbing her of sensation. She extended both arms as far as she could reach and touched...nothing. But something was there in the dark with her. It was cold, and merciless, and evil. She cowered back and tried to scream as the thing grasped at her sweater, but no sound emerged from her frozen throat. She wrenched away and scraped her hand on rock. It was a wall. She had backed into a rough stone barricade. She felt flaking mortar and a dampness that brushed her fingers and seeped into her soul. The touch was frightening but it was not the source of the menace. That presence had dissipated. She was alone in the dark.

And then she wasn't. Seeming to rise from the ground itself, a substance took form, translucent, wavering, insubstantial. A human form, female. The specter had a face, black eyes in a visage etched in sorrow. The expression was twisted in agony and pain, yet somehow retained a semblance of beauty. It made no sound but held out its arms to her as if in supplication, and she recoiled in shock. *The apparition had no hands.* A scream forced its way out of her paralyzed throat—

Aubrey woke up clutching the sheets, her heart hammering wildly and her body drenched in sweat. She was alone in the darkness. She could make out the shapes of the wardrobe in the corner and the edges of the window where a faint light was trying to sneak into her room. Nessie's guest room in Inverness. She was in her own bedroom.

She took a few minutes to allow her senses to gather about her and her breathing to return to normal. Scotland is out to get me, she decided. Now I'm dreaming about ghosts! She lay quiet, examining the dream to banish its terror. Of course the ghost had been Ailith Comyn, the wild daughter of the overlord of Rait Castle, a girl who had died six hundred years ago. She had been a murderess, plotting with her Mackintosh lover to destroy her family, and she had died a traitor's death at the hands of her own father. And yet, the sense of threat and profound malevolence in her dream had not come from the wraith. The ghost had been reaching toward her for...what? Help? Warning? Impossible to tell. She had sensed nothing evil in the ghost herself, but the feeling of malignancy lingered. Aubrey shook herself and rubbed her eyes.

It was a dream. A nightmare brought on by too much whisky, and frustration, and a revival of an old heartache she'd begun to put behind her. *And that's on you, Fionnlagh Cameron! You with your smooth velvety brogue, and your translucent blue eyes, and your damn kilt! And your whisky.* She promised herself to watch out for handsome men bearing wee drams from now on.

She still squirmed when she thought of the return trip from Dunrobin on Tuesday. She and Finn had spent the hour-long drive in strained silence, and when he had pulled up to Nessie's and turned to face her she had steeled herself and told him that she thought it best if they didn't see each other again. It was the hardest thing she had ever done. Aubrey was never needlessly unkind, and she still felt the weight of her words, but her heart would never survive another man whose own lay with someone else. His answer, a flat "as you wish," was steeped in hurt and confusion, but he did not ask her why. The look in his eyes still haunted her two days later, but it had been the right thing to do. The only thing.

She needed to get up and do something. It was hours before she had to be at the bookshop, but going back to sleep was out of the question. What she needed was coffee. She threw on a pair of jeans and the t-shirt she'd bought at the mall her first day here. It was a cartoon depiction of cars backed up along a narrow road, blocked by a herd of cheerful sheep. The caption read "Rush hour in Scotland."

Bleary-eyed, she stumbled downstairs and into the sitting room. Old Harry Campbell sat in his customary chair, behind his ever present newspaper. He might never sleep, for all she knew.

He looked up, eyes sharp in his grizzled face. "So, ye met wee Ailith, did ye? She's a bonnie 'un, aye?" He leaned back in the worn armchair and speared Aubrey with a gimlet stare.

For heaven's sake, was she the only topic of conversation around here? She had to believe that there were actual current events that should be taking precedence. No wonder the Scots hadn't secured their independence yet if they insisted on living so much in the past! Well, she wasn't falling into a trap this time.

"Who's Ailith?" she countered, her tone light and questioning, the very picture of disinterested confusion. Naturally it didn't work. Old Harry narrowed his gaze even further. "Ach, lassie, Ah'd 'a kent you'd have a wee bit more respect fur a lass that's six hundred years auld, noo." He shook his head in dismay. "An' after everythin' she's bin thru, too!"

"Wait a minute!" Aubrey waggled a finger at him. "Just in case you think I haven't been paying attention, wasn't the massacre all her fault? So why are you so worried about what *she's* been through? Seems like she put a lot of people through hell herself, didn't she, plotting to get her own clan killed? And anyway, she's been dead for hundreds of years. I'm pretty sure she doesn't care anymore!"

"'There're more things in heaven an' earth, Horatio, than are dreamt o' in yer philosophy'," Harry said, his tone complacent.

Aubrey rolled her eyes in exasperation. "Oh, Lord!" She needed that coffee.

Three hours later she staggered into the Mackintosh Bookshop, wondering how she had been cajoled into another full Scottish breakfast. Between the haggis and the black pudding, she was going to go into carb overload. Kate and Fitz wouldn't recognize her when they came. And that wasn't even counting the whisky, for which she was developing a definite fondness. She was beginning to distinguish the "notes of caramel, cherry and brown sugar with hints of apple and roasted peat bog," or whatever. She needed to exercise, do some hiking in the bonnie hills—maybe gather some heather and frolic with the wee sheep.

"Whit ur ye gigglin' abit, lass? Have ye gain daftie?" Angus frowned at her.

"Och, let the lass be, Angus! She's all right," came a familiar voice from behind a pile of books.

"Mr. MacGregor!" Audrey exclaimed in delight. "How nice to see you again! You know Angus?"

Of course he did. Everyone with the slightest bit of eccentricity seemed to know Angus.

"It's Alastair, lass." He beamed at her. "So how did ye like Dunrobin Castle? A wee bit bigger than the castle o' spite, aye? Ach, what's wrong?" His smile disappeared. "Ye look like the kelpies took ye for a ride!"

"D'ye niver shut yer gob, man?" Angus barked at the surprised wanderer. "She's got 'er heart broke at Dunrobin! Have ye nae sense?"

Now Aubrey was staring at both of them. Was there any limit to what Angus knew?

"My heart's not broken," she insisted. "I just wised up and avoided a trap, that's all. I'm fine." She looked at the two old men. "Really."

Two identical Gaelic snorts rewarded her efforts.

"Anyway," she said, determined to change the subject, "what do you have me doing today, Master?" Angus glared at her. Humor was okay when it was *his*.

For the next few hours she worked in the stacks while her two wardens sat and talked in rapid Scots she couldn't understood and discussed things about which she had no clue. Customers wandered in, locals and tourists, and Angus engaged them all in conversation. He was very different here than he had been back in Harrington, she thought. There, he had hidden himself away in the workroom and let her handle most of the interaction with potential customers. Here he was in his element, waxing poetic on any number of subjects, aided and abetted by his wandering friend Alastair. It was good to see him home where he belonged, she thought with a surge of fondness. He *was* Scotland, and since he was hers, she guessed she belonged too. The thought warmed her frayed heart.

The rest of the week flew by, and Aubrey buried herself in the bookshop. Angus said nothing about the ghost or the curse, and she was happy to leave the subject. She didn't see Finn. He'd stopped texting after that first day and it was pretty obvious he was avoiding her. After her cold dismissal how could she blame him? Angus said nothing about his missing friend, so she returned to her work, determined to put the whole Finn Cameron episode behind her.

She was delighted to find several books by Alastair MacGregor. He was a talented writer, she found. His love for his country shone through his words and his photographs gave evidence of a true gift. His books would make lovely presents for Kate and Fitz, especially if they were signed by the author.

Her friends were coming next Friday and she was picking them up in Edinburgh. Although her driving skills had improved, she was more than a little nervous about negotiating the high-speed roads around the capital of Scotland and spent as much of her time practicing as she could.

On Wednesday, her day off, it rained. At loose ends, she remembered the Inverness Museum and Art Gallery, which was located just off the High Street behind a couple of tartan shops and an Italian Restaurant. The museum dedicated itself to the history of Scotland from its earliest days, when the Picts ruled a wild kingdom of rock and mountains and barbarous tribes.

Entering the museum, Aubrey was surprised to find that admission was free, although there was a large glass box filled with pound notes, euros, and dollar bills. On the first floor, she wandered happily through rooms dedicated to the geology and natural history of the Highlands, thrilled to find an exhibit representing the journey that the land known as Scotia had taken across the ocean to end up in the North Sea.

Upstairs was a section celebrating the more recent history of the Highlands. Aubrey was immediately drawn to the collection of Jacobite memorabilia, weapons and bagpipes. The doomed Jacobite uprising, "the 45," was a true testament to man's determination to dominate, and exterminate, his fellow man. Aubrey recalled Alastair MacGregor's mention of the Highland Clearances and complete subjugation of the Scottish people after the Battle of Culloden. Even from a standpoint more than two hundred years removed from that dismal time, she felt tears welling behind her eyes at the atrocities visited upon these proud Highlanders.

"'Twas a sad time for Caledonia, aye?" a soft voice said, and Aubrey spun around to find Connor MacConnach standing behind her.

"Oh!" she said, searching for breath. The man was even more imposing up close. Her previous estimate of his height hadn't been far off; he towered over her five foot six. Bursting with muscles in all the right places. Not her type, of course—and she could feel her insides shaking with laughter at that one. This guy was *everyone*'s type, as long as they were female and breathing, and he knew it. His amber eyes crinkled when he smiled, and was that a *dimple* at the corner of his mouth? Ah, hell, it was. The kilt stopped just above a lovely pair of male knees, and below it his legs were encased in soft black leather boots. She had never realized before how sexy boots were on a man. Or hair that fell to the shoulders in red-gold waves, for that matter. Wow, she thought. Just...wow.

She would have cast him as Jamie Fraser in *Outlander* in a minute. He was perfect.

Aubrey jerked herself back into the moment. "Wh-what's Caledonia?" she asked, fastening onto the last thing she could remember.

"Ah, Caledonia's the Latin name for Scotland, given to us by the Romans," he said seriously. "It used to mean just the part that's now the Highlands, but now it refers to the whole country. A true Scot takes great pride in the name, ye ken?"

"It's beautiful," Aubrey agreed.

"Aye. There's a lovely wee song by Dougie MacLean called *Caledonia*. It's by way of a national anthem for the Scots."

Aubrey couldn't help but notice that Connor MacConnach's brogue was softer and less pronounced than it had been when she had first met him at the restaurant. Had he been putting it on a bit, perhaps to irritate Finn? Again she wondered what the history was between the two men, but then shrugged. It didn't matter, *Finn* was history.

"Do you mind if I walk around with you, to give a bit of description to what you see?" he asked.

"Not at all, I'd appreciate the local input. Thank you." *I may be off men, but I'm not dead.*

They stopped before a display of bagpipes.

"One pipe makes the tune, ye ken? It's called the chanter and has finger holes like a flute or piccolo. The other three play single notes that are in tune with the chanter.

"It's a very hard instrument to play, but every Scottish lad, and many lassies, learn the pipes at a

191

young age. The good ones go on to perform in pipe bands that compete at festivals all over the world. Your friend Fionnlagh is one of the good ones," he added, glancing at her.

"He's not—" Aubrey started, and stopped. It was none of his business what Finn was or was not to her, after all.

"Hmm," he said, and moved on to the next display.

Over the next hour, Aubrey was forced to revise some of her earlier preconceptions about Connor MacConnach. He was a delightful companion, much less full of himself than she had been led to believe. He listened attentively to her questions about the artifacts and the displays and seemed quite well versed in the history of his country.

He worked for the Mackenzie, he told her. "Yes, the same one from the book that's been turned into a television series." He winked at her. "Have you any idea how many cars full of lassies come up the road to the castle every day looking for that Jamie Fraser fellow? It's on the tours, ye ken."

"You work at Castle Leoch? The real castle?" Aubrey stared at him in amazement.

"Well, the name is Castle Leod, but it is the real seat of the Mackenzie clan. Would you like to see it? It's not open most days because the family lives there, but I can give you a personal tour if you'd like." He reached out and closed her mouth for her, laughing at the glazed look in her eyes.

"Oh, my. Oh...*my*." This gorgeous man worked for the Mackenzie clan, he knew about *Outlander*, and he was offering to show her around? She just might be in heaven.

"You have no idea how much I want to take you up on that," she told him, "but my two best friends from the States are coming over and they would kill me if I saw Castle Leoch—Leod—without them."

"Well, now, since it's a matter of life and death, we'll just have to fit them into the tour," he laughed. "I can't have your death on my conscience. Now, what do you say to a bite of lunch, my fine lassie?" He offered his arm, and without allowing herself to over-analyze her reaction, she took it.

Over fish and chips, Aubrey asked Connor about his job.

"Oh, I'm just sort of a man of all work," he said. "Really just a glorified handyman. But a good one!" He shrugged. "MacConnach is a sept of clan Mackenzie, so the Mackenzie is by way of a cousin, ye ken? And I make ends meet with some modeling in Edinburgh." He seemed embarrassed about it. "So you like old castles and such, then?" he changed the subject.

"Love them! I've been to Dunrobin, and last week I visited an old ruined castle near Nairn. Really spooky place." She shuddered, remembering.

"Rait Castle?" he asked her, fork arrested midway to his mouth.

"Yes! Have you been there?"

"I should say I have! I'm the chairman of the Rait Castle Preservation Society!"

As she climbed into bed that evening, Aubrey reflected on the things life threw at you. It had started out as just another gloomy, rainy day in Inverness, and by the time it had ended she had learned about the Jacobites and bagpipes and met a gorgeous man who was going to take her to visit her dream castle, where he *worked*. To make a marvelous day perfect, he had offered to take her to Edinburgh on Friday to pick up Kate and Fitz so that she wouldn't have to threaten any sheep on the highway. Perfect.

He was also in charge of a group that wanted to preserve the castle of her nightmares. He hadn't mentioned the ghost and she hadn't shared her experience, but he had to know about Ailith. An errant thought whispered across her mind. Connor had said his clan was related to the Mackenzie. Was it possible that he could also be related to clan Mackintosh? She'd have to look into the clan system when she got back to the bookshop. And wouldn't *that* be something? As Maxine would say, ooh la la.

She fell asleep as soon as her head hit the pillow. In her dreams, a flock of sheep led by Jamie Fraser was marching down the High Street in kilts, playing *Caledonia* on the bagpipes, while a patient line of cars waited for them to pass. Not a ghost in sight.

CHAPTER 17

BAGGAGE CLAIM

"**D**amn it, their flight's been delayed an hour!" Aubrey came over to where Connor sat reading the newspaper. "I feel awful. You don't have to wait, I'm sure you have things to do. We can take the train back."

"Ach, no, it's no trouble at all," he said. "Although I do have a wee errand to do while I'm in town, so this is perfect. It's only just down the road, and I'll be back in plenty of time. Is that all right?"

"Of course," she answered, grateful that she wasn't putting him out, but at the same time disappointed that she would be deprived of his company. He really was charming. On the drive down to Edinburgh he had entertained her with stories of the Mackenzies and their problems fending off some of the more insistent tour groups. Tours were necessary for most people who owned ancient castle seats, he said. The great piles were difficult to maintain and impossible to heat, so even the wealthiest families were forced to open their homes to the public at least some of the time. Castle Leod had special hours for inside tours, but that didn't stop disappointed tourists from trying to peer in the windows at other times.

"It's only got worse with that television program of yours." He grinned at her.

She watched Connor hurry away, kilt swishing, oblivious to the fact that the eyes of every female and quite a few males were glued to his progress through the crowds. And he's with *me*, she marveled. Two weeks ago, if people had told her that a real life Jamie Fraser would have chosen to be her escort, she would have laughed and suggested that they were reading too many romance novels. But here they were.

Ordinarily Aubrey loved being alone in airports. She knew that not many shared her enjoyment of the noisy, chaotic spaces which attempted, with mixed success, to offer travelers a sampling of the regional culture. When she'd first landed in Scotland, Edinburgh Airport had been a disappointment—not enough tartan, no bagpipes. Now, after two weeks immersed in more tartan, pipes, and sheep than any tourist would ever need, she had changed her mind. The airport had a culture of its own; it was unashamed of its Scottishness, but didn't feel the need to shove it down everyone's throats. Connor MacConnach was probably the most Scottish thing the airport had seen in quite a while.

She checked the flight status board again to find that the flight Kate and Fitz were on was delayed another fifteen minutes. They were probably ready to kill each other by now, she laughed to herself. God, she missed those two!

True to his word, Connor was back in well under an hour, and the two spent the rest of the time people watching.

"Now, see that lad there." He pointed out a middle-aged man wearing more plaid than she had ever seen on a single human being. "He's not a Scot."

"How can you tell? It doesn't get much more Scottish!"

"Well, he's wearing the MacGregor kilt and the Campbell plaid. Those two clans are traditional enemies and were always at war with each other over some thing or other in the old times, like cattle stealing or land disputes. He'd have been killed for that in those days!"

"He should be killed for it now," Aubrey giggled. "He looks like he's at war with himself!"

Connor laughed. "Aye, and look at that bairn over there." He pointed out a small rambunctious child whose parents had lost control and didn't seem to care as he ran around between people's legs. He was wearing a Scottish tam and a tee shirt emblazoned with the words "Mammy's Wee Haggis" and he was brandishing a Star Wars light saber, which in his tiny hands seemed every bit as lethal as a claymore.

"The force is with him, aye?"

But Aubrey was no longer laughing. A chill was working its way down her spine, and she turned her head to see Finn Cameron staring at her with a hard expression. Connor spotted him at the same time and called him over with a cheerful wave. Trapped, Finn had no choice but to move in their direction, looking like a man going to his execution.

"Hullo," he mumbled to Aubrey. He nodded to Connor. "MacConnach."

"Hi, Finn," she said. The tension was so thick she wondered if she might be able to wrap it around herself like a blanket and disappear into its folds.

"What brings you here, then?" Finn asked. His voice sounded thick. Aubrey heard the words he did not speak as clearly as if he had shouted them...*with him?*

"She's meetin' her friends from the States," Connor volunteered, unfazed by the atmosphere. "Kate and— Fitz, isn't it? Their plane is late, so we've been gettin' t' know each other better." He winked at Aubrey.

How could he be so oblivious? Or was he? Was he being deliberately cruel? She knew the men did not hold each other in high esteem but come on! She had been with Finn the first time they had met, on a *date*. Could men really be that obtuse? Or was something more going on here?

"And who're ye meetin', Cameron?" Connor asked him. His brogue had thickened, dripping innocence.

For a moment it seemed as if Finn was not going to answer, but then he straightened his shoulders and said, in a tone straight off the chopping block, "Isla. She's back from London. Asked me to pick her up. Today. At the airport." He snapped his mouth shut and studied his boots. For a fleeting second Aubrey thought she saw a shadow cross Connor's face but then he grinned, enjoying Finn's discomfort.

Isla. The old girlfriend. Ah, thought Aubrey, so that's why the embarrassment. Well, this could be interesting. She felt a sudden urge to see this paragon who held Finn's heart in thrall. It was good that she had ended what hadn't even started; maybe this was just what she had needed.

"Fionnlagh!" A lilting voice rang across the waiting room. Aubrey looked up to see a figure coming down the escalator from the gates and her heart lurched. She had expected to see a pretty girl. She had not thought she would be a goddess. Isla Gordon was stunning. Tiny, she stood no more than five feet two, with elfin features and huge green eyes. Her hair fell over her shoulders in a glorious mass of auburn curls—*of course it did*—and her perfect figure was encased in white trousers and a simple black shirt that had to have cost a small kingdom. Oh, but that was right—her family *owned* a small kingdom. Even in her own mind, Aubrey sounded bitter. She felt big, and gawky, and poor. She had never stood a chance.

Isla hugged Finn and turned to Connor. "Well, and what poor lass are ye corrupting this time, dearie?" Her tone was light, but the words stung. *I'm not going to like her. I'm not going to like her even a little bit.* And that was ridiculous. She had barely met Finn Cameron; what on earth made her think she had some kind of grievance here? Thank God she had jettisoned him before she really fell for him...because she knew it had been a near thing.

"I'm Aubrey," she told the vision, trying for a light tone. "And how do you know I'm not the one corrupting *him*?" Connor roared with laughter. Finn winced but said nothing.

"Oh, I like this one!" Isla said in delight. She pushed Connor out of the seat next to Aubrey and sat down. "I'll let you in on all the secrets to taming this big lug," she said in a confidential tone. "We girls have to stick together, after all!"

Aubrey sensed that Isla was used to having everyone she met fall in love with her, male or female, and despite her resolve she felt herself falling under the Scottish girl's spell. She was enchanting and unaffected. *She* doesn't seem surprised that Connor wants to be here with me, she thought, so maybe it's not so far-fetched after all. She avoided looking at Finn, glad for Isla's charming prattle.

Despite herself Aubrey began to recover a bit of her self-esteem. If Isla had decided that she and Connor were a couple, why not go with the flow for now? She wasn't in danger of falling in love with him, and it was obvious that he enjoyed her company. *I might not be Highland royalty like Isla, but I do clean up pretty well.*

Again Aubrey wondered if Connor might be related somehow to the Mackintoshes, and she had to admit that fear was what was keeping her from asking Angus. She had tried to stop believing in the whole curse thing and her role in banishing it, although she knew it was why Angus kept sending her on these sightseeing missions. She hadn't seen that odious book since she'd arrived in Scotland, thank God, but it had to be here. She was even beginning to doubt her experience at Rait Castle. Connor was in charge of the preservation society for the castle and he hadn't even mentioned a ghost. This whole curse story could be just Angus and his cousin Nessie having a bit of fun at her expense.

You do know you're being stupid, right, her imagination whispered, and she squashed it like a bug. The ghost and the curse and the book were part of another life. Connor was here right now, in all his glory.

"Aubreeee!" She was jerked out of her riotous thoughts by loud squeals, and everyone turned to watch as two young women came down the escalator, dragging their carry-ons and trying to negotiate the moving stairway that was not getting them there fast enough. Their excitement was so contagious that everyone was grinning by the time they reached the bottom. Even Finn had relaxed his tight expression in the face of such happiness.

Aubrey jumped up to meet them, tears running down her face. The troops had arrived; everything was going to be all right. Until this moment, she had not realized how much she had been missing Kate and Fitz. Calling and texting were not enough, and her heart was bursting at the thought that they had dropped their lives at her call and crossed an ocean to be with her. No one ever had such friends. Maybe she should just go back with them and put an end to this nonsense. *And arrive just in time for Marc's wedding to the sainted Angie? Maybe not.*

She pulled them over to meet her Scottish contingent, not missing the exchange of looks at sight of the two hunky men she had managed to find so quickly, or their feminine reaction to the lovely Isla.

Introductions made, they all walked together toward baggage claim, the two new arrivals talking nonstop to Aubrey, words falling all over each other. Even Connor could not compete, and he knew when he was bested.

"So, you should have been there to see the kid behind us—"

"Did you know they serve complimentary wine in coach on international flights?"

"I hardly slept at all, I'm going to be so knack-ered—is that what they say over here?"

"I'm starving, what do they have besides haggis?"

And on and on. By the time they reached the baggage area, Aubrey was exhausted. She had been alone with her own thoughts for much of her two weeks in Scotland and was floundering in the sea of enthusiasm.

Finn left to collect Isla's luggage from her London flight, but returned in a few minutes to join the others in waiting for the transatlantic baggage. Isla excused herself to find the ladies' room, and Connor and Finn, ever gallant, waited at the baggage carousel to help Kate and Fitz with their suitcases. Aubrey was left alone to guard her friends' carry-ons and Isla's designer bag. It was taking a long time but neither of the girls seemed to mind, what with Connor's lovely brogue keeping them occupied while they waited. She watched her friends lapping up his attention and smiled.

"I need to talk with you, Aubrey," Finn said in a low voice at her side.

"Finn...I—"

"*Why are you with him?*"

Aubrey recoiled at the anger in his voice.

"I hardly think it's your place to tell me who I should be with!" she snapped.

"It's not what you think—" He never finished, as Isla returned and rejoined them.

"Darling, I really need to get home," she told Finn. She extended a hand to Aubrey. "We'll have to get together soon and have a real talk. Connor has my number. Bring your friends, aye?" She pulled at Finn's sleeve and he turned away, the hard look back on his face.

It's not what you think, Aubrey repeated to herself, watching as they walked away, Isla's hand latched onto his arm. *Darling, indeed. Not what I think! He's whipped—that's what I think!*

Kate and Fitz broke into her dark thoughts, reclaiming their carry-on bags and thanking Connor, who was pulling both large suitcases as if they weighed nothing while regaling them with some ridiculous story about the proper way to fold a kilt and what had once happened to his grandfather when he had tried to cut corners.

"It takes a long time to fold the pleats juist right," he was saying, brogue thicker than ever. "Then ye lie down on the floor and kinda roll up in it...an' if ye do it wrong, ye have t' start all over! Takes a real man to wear the kilt properly, ye ken!" He winked at them, knowing exactly what they were thinking. Aubrey was proud of her friends for not asking The Question, which was what he was waiting for, of course. They might be American, but they weren't stupid, their expressions told him, and his grin widened.

"So that other guy...is he the one you told me about, Bree?" Kate asked, her voice low. "And is that the girl?"

"Yeah. That's his Angie. Leave it, Kate. Please."

Kate gave her a sharp glance. "Too bad. He's cute. Reminds me of Tom Branson."

Nessie was waiting for them with tea and scones. When Aubrey had asked her if she knew of a room somewhere nearby for her friends, she had insisted that they stay in her third-floor attic room, which just happened to be empty, and had spent two days getting it ready. The room, with two dormer windows and a huge four poster bed, was larger than Aubrey's and had a gorgeous view out over the river to the Highlands beyond. If Kate and Fitz wanted Scotland, they couldn't do better than this!

"And they won't be payin'." Nessie had stared Aubrey down. Nessie's house had a definite *Alice in Wonderland* vibe, with its eclectic collection of odd characters. Aubrey was beginning to wonder if any of the odd assortment of guests here paid for their lodging.

After tea, Kate and Fitz were shooed into the sitting room to meet the Owls. Following the obligatory grilling as to their jobs... "Oh, a detective! We won't have to rely on Old Harry anymore to keep us safe," chortled Gladys. "A nurse! Maxine, you should ask this nice young nurse about your bunions..." Aubrey sat back, enjoying the show. It was fun to watch her friends run the gauntlet, but finally Nessie emerged from the kitchen and rescued them.

"Give th' poor lassies some peace, will ye?" she scolded. "They just got here, don't be scarin' them away now! They must be fair puggled from the long trip."

But puggled or not, no one was ready to sleep. Draped over Aubrey's bed, the three spent the next hour catching up. The space where *Angus' Auld Books* had been was now a laundromat, they told her. There was a fancy new supermarket that had opened its doors last week, but Fitz was sure it wouldn't make it. Oh, and another dollar store. Nothing new in Harrington, New Jersey.

Conversation wound down. In the end it was Kate who addressed the elephant in the room.

"So...Marc and Angie are going to live with Francine after they get married. Do you believe it, Bree? That could have been your fate!" They all shuddered.

"Can't wait to see how long the love affair between Angie and Marc's mother lasts," sniffed Fitz. She began to sing Miley Cyrus' *Fly on the Wall*. Tears began to run unchecked down Aubrey's cheeks.

"Oh, honey, don't cry! I shouldn't have brought Marc and Angie up...I'm such an idiot!" Kate exclaimed. "Colleen Fitzgerald, shut up with that stupid song!"

Fitz stopped singing and looked stricken. "I'm sorry, Aubrey! We didn't come over here to make you sad. We're just too tired to think straight! Wait! Are you *laughing*?"

Aubrey wiped the tears off her face. "I'm not sad. I just had a picture of Angie and Francine holding Marc down and stuffing pasta and gravy down his throat until he begs for mercy!"

"I give it two years," Kate said solemnly. "One year for them to get sick of each other, and another one because they're afraid of Francine. In fact, I want to be the detective on call when one of those three murders the other two!"

They collapsed on the bed laughing.

"Okay, Aubrey, dear." Kate had sat up and was looking at her through narrowed detective's eyes. "Tell us about this Scot of yours."

"Oh." For a moment she was silent. "Well, I really just met Connor two days ago, so the jury's out on him."

"The jury can sentence him to life with *me*," Fitz sighed. "He's delicious!"

"Well, if you're voting for him, then he's probably a bad choice," snorted Kate. "But I will have to side with Fitz this time. He seems like a great guy, and I think he's a lot smarter than he acts. All that 'tartans-in-the-heather' stuff seems a bit much, but I've only been here half a day. Maybe that's the norm in the Highlands."

"No," said Aubrey. "He's pretty unique. But I like him."

"And the other one?" asked Fitz. "The one with the la-di-da princess?"

A knock sounded on the door, saving Aubrey from the necessity of a reply, and she opened it to reveal Nessie, holding a tub of ice cream.

"I thought ye might like a treat from home, so I went shoppin' t'day. The *Cool Ness* shop in Castle Street had that Rocky Road stuff you lassies like." She handed the tub to Aubrey. "Enjoy it, lassies, cause tomorrow you're havin' a full Scottish breakfast!"

CHAPTER 18

PICK YOUR POISON

Darius Sanderson sat rigid, waves of rage washing through him. Hands fisted, he waited for his heartbeat to return to normal. Chief Inspector Alan Brown had been polite and respectful. He had remarked on the weather—always bad, on the price of oil—at a new low, and on the beauty of Darius' office. Mundane conversation. The detective's voice had been calm, his entire persona had projected boredom. His appearance matched his tone—grey suit, white shirt, blue tie. His thinning hair was grey, and so were his eyes, sunken in a sad face lined by experience and world-weariness. Everything about CI Brown, even his name, was bland. He reminded Darius of someone; he couldn't put his finger on it.

Darius Sanderson was a busy man, he didn't have time for this! Why couldn't the inspector get to the point? And then he had. The change was so subtle at first, Darius hadn't seen it coming. His assistant had died last week; how difficult it must be to carry on without him. And so young, too. It must be very hard. And then the questions. Sanderson had felt the anger begin to build, smoldering, and forced himself to smile, to sit still while the Chief Inspector questioned him about Ollie.

Brown had *questioned* him! How dare he presume to do so! How dare he suggest that his late assistant had died under suspicious circumstances? Ollie had had a heart attack. It was sad, but these things happened. There had been nothing in the autopsy to indicate anything other than the fact that his heart had seized in one of those unfortunate human anomalies that struck without warning. Death had been quick. It was tragic, shocking, and Darius still felt his loss every day, he told Brown, voice taut. But it couldn't have been foreseen.

No, sir, the Chief Inspector told him, his voice calm and soothing. Heart attacks in young people were not as common as one might imagine. Mr. Thomson had nothing in his health record to indicate a possible malfunction of his heart. And, his tone was apologetic at the need to contradict Mr. Sanderson, it was not quite true that the autopsy had shown nothing suspicious. The dead man had, in fact, had a small puncture wound on his arm, just above the left elbow. There had been nothing in his system to indicate a foreign substance, but there were several poisons that would not show readily in a postmortem examination. Because of the tiny puncture and the age of the victim, Oliver Thomson's death was being treated as suspicious. Further tests were being done.

The Chief Inspector had stood up and apologized again for intruding on Mr. Sanderson's grief. He had just wanted him to be aware, he said, in case anything should occur to him that seemed out of the ordinary. He had left his card on the desk, excused himself, and left, his rumpled trench coat flapping about his grey-clad legs. Darius sat at his desk trying to regain his equilibrium, waiting for his anger to dissipate. And suddenly he knew who the policeman reminded him of. That American television detective who pretended to know nothing, but whose shrewd mind forced the killer to give himself away in every episode. *Columbo*, he thought it was. His anger drained away, replaced by a cold apprehension that gnawed its way up his spine.

Darius stood up and began to pace. He had nothing to fear from the inspector, he had done nothing wrong. And he had more important things to worry about. Oil prices were at an all-time low, and the *Caledonia First* mob were ramping up their propaganda, galvanizing even people outside the Highlands and inspiring the fools with a misplaced sense of patriotism. If things kept up this way, there was a real chance that they could win a new referendum. And that would be a disaster for PETRO. It was a well-known fact that PETRO was heavily involved in UK oil interests, "in bed with the British," one headline had run. If independence became a reality, his company would be a pariah in Scotland. He could lose everything.

He recalled the conversation he had had this morning with his agent inside *Caledonia First*. The key lay in getting rid of Lachlan Mackenzie. The bastard was evangelistic in his zeal, and people were flocking to his meetings. He couldn't have him killed, although he would like nothing better. Killing Mackenzie would point the finger at those who were promoting continuing unity with England, and he had worked too hard to make sure that finger pointed in the other direction to allow that. He had thought of discrediting him, but that road was fraught with difficulty. Lachlan Mackenzie owned *Tulach Àrd*, one of the foremost distilleries in the Highlands. His whiskies had a brand and a stature that would be difficult, if not impossible, to undermine. Sabotage had worked well in other instances, but that would point the finger at Mackenzie's enemies, not at him. Therein lay the dilemma.

His agent had found the solution during their conversation this morning. The new assistant was turning out to be a much better choice than poor Ollie had ever been. Ollie's loyalty could not be questioned, but his intellect was not the highest. While he would have gone to hell and back for Sanderson, he had been that loose bolt in the works—an honest man. Hiding the truth behind his missions had been getting more and more difficult in the past months. Darius would always miss his friend, but he had become a liability. The unavoidable truth was, Ollie was not a schemer.

His new assistant was just that. Behind the polished mask lay the heart of a predator. The agent had never blinked at the idea of sabotage or murder; in fact, there seemed to be a fierce joy in the challenge. Clever and careful, the new factor blended in with the enemy, able to masquerade as one of them; and in fact this was true. Ruthless and cruel, the agent had no scruples, and Sanderson understood that taking this creature under his tutelage was akin to selling his soul to the devil. But this new talent was just what was needed to win this war.

War was nothing new for these people. Scotland had been at war forever, with the Vikings, the British, but most often with each other. The country's history was rife with examples of the barbarism of her people; this was no different. Wars were fought for religion, or land, or money, and money was always the best reason for killing.

This morning, his agent had proposed an audacious plan--one that would tie Lachlan Mackenzie's hands for the foreseeable future and put him out of the Scottish independence business permanently. *Tulach Àrd* whiskies were beyond reproach, but what about the distillery itself? What would happen if an accident were to occur at his distillery, the factor suggested, one that would point to an inexcusable carelessness? An accident that would show a criminal neglect in his safety procedures? One that would involve the tours that poured through his distillery's gates every day, disgorging happy vacationers eager to sample Scotland's famous single malt and see the process in action.

And what if such an accident resulted in the deaths of some of those eager tourists? It would be a tragedy of epic proportion, one that would shine a damning spotlight on the most revered symbol of Scottish identity—its whisky. It was brilliant. They didn't even have to lay a hand on Lachlan Mackenzie. He would be crippled, fighting legal battles that would hound him for years—long after the referendum for Scottish independence had failed. The *Caledonia First* movement, so closely associated with the distiller that had been at the center of the disaster, would collapse. The plan was beautiful in its simplicity.

It would not be difficult, the new agent assured him. There were so many dangers inherent in the distillation process: inhalation of the carbon dioxide produced by the fermentation process, explosions of ethanol gas, physical injuries caused by unsecured barrels and wet surfaces. Reputable distilleries kept fire extinguishers readily available, of course, and maintained adequate ventilation, but what if these safety precautions were removed or rendered useless? Darius Sanderson's new assistant had the means to make sure that it could never be traced back to the CEO of PETRO. It would be their biggest strike yet; they might not need another.

Sanderson shrugged away the residual annoyance caused by Chief Inspector Brown's visit. Let him concentrate on Ollie's mysterious puncture mark. It would keep the police busy, and it could never be connected to his grieving mentor and best friend, Darius Sanderson. The issue would go away in time, they just had to wait it out. They had more important things to plan for now.

CHAPTER 19

HOP ON, HOP OFF

"You eat that stuff every day?" Fitz muttered as they left the house the next morning. "*Every* day?"

Aubrey laughed. "You get used to it after a while. And in case you hadn't already noticed, Nessie is very much like Angus. There's no standing up to her when she's convinced you need something."

Fitz looked frightened. "Well, I have no intention of getting used to haggis! And what the hell was that round black cookie thing? More sheep guts?"

"No, not at all. Black pudding is mostly sheep's *blood*, mixed with suet and oatmeal." Fitz gagged and Kate patted her back.

"You're such a Jersey girl, Fitz!" she said. "What d'you think is in that awful scrapple you love?"

"I don't know. I just grew up eating scrapple. It's amazing!"

"Well," said Kate, with enthusiasm, "you might want to know it's made of pig guts mixed with corn-meal, you idiot!"

They continued down the path laughing, headed for the *Mackintosh Bookshop*.

"Hi, Angus!" they called out.

He beamed at them. "Sae th' troops have arrived. Glad tae see ye. I've gi'en the lass th' day off, so whit ur ye gonnae do?"

In truth, lately Angus didn't seem to care whether Aubrey showed up at work most days anyway. He'd stopped mentioning the curse or ghosts altogether, which was lovely but mysterious. So far the only Mackintosh she'd found in Inverness was Angus himself. Was she supposed to stumble on this paragon of manhood and recognize him by his haunted, lonely eyes, pining for her alone? It was puzzling in the extreme, but Aubrey had decided to leave it up to Angus. It was his show, and if she knew the old man half as well as she thought she did, he had something up his sleeve that he was bound to pull out at the most inconvenient time. For now he seemed to be giving her a lot of rope. Half the time when she arrived at the shop he would send her off to explore Inverness, telling her he didn't need her help that day.

And yet he paid her as if she worked for him full time. It was another in the list of odd things about Angus and his friend Nessie. No money ever seemed to exchange hands for either of them, yet they were the most generous two souls she'd ever met. They certainly didn't seem flush, but you never knew. She supposed she'd never understand Angus, but as long as she didn't lose him again, she didn't care.

"Thought we'd do the hop on, hop off bus." Aubrey had saved the most touristy attraction for their arrival, but she was looking forward to seeing parts of Inverness that were too far to walk. They wound their way down Castle Road, the river on their left and Inverness Castle looming above them on the cliff to their right.

"Finn says the Castle's had some pretty awesome visitors," said Aubrey. "Mary, Queen of Scots stayed here for a while, but she had to fight to get in. Finn says the current castle isn't very old, and it's been rebuilt many times."

They passed the High Street, arriving at the visitor's center. Buying their tickets, they settled in to wait for the bus.

"Look, there's a guy wading in the river!" exclaimed Fitz. "What's he fishing for?"

"Salmon," Aubrey answered her. "Finn says the Ness has some of the best salmon fishing in the Highlands."

Kate looked sideways at Fitz. "And what else does Finn say?" she asked, her voice even.

Aubrey's face closed up like the shutters on a window. The bus pulled in and she climbed aboard without a backward look.

Aubrey missed the eye contact between Kate and Fitz, and they followed her dutifully to the top deck, grateful that for once it wasn't drizzling. The tour guide, a short ruddy-cheeked woman with a fisherman's hat perched in precarious fashion on top of frizzy red hair, passed out the audio devices and ear buds and began her spiel without further ado. "Here we are at the first stop o' the tour. Ye can hop off any time if somethin' strikes yer fancy...as long as the bus has stopped, mind ye. We dinna want our visitors gettin' hurt, ye know. We need yer money!" She stopped to allow them time to enjoy her humor.

"Our next stop will be the Ness Bank. Ah recommend ye take a wee walk along the river here, an' maybe try one o' our bouncy bridges. They're no' for the faint-hearted!"

The girls decided to stay on the bus for the whole loop, and then return later to places they especially liked.

As the bus approached the Bank Street stop at the end of the loop, Fitz pointed. "Oh, look! That restaurant looks really old! We should try it some night. *The Mustard Seed*, what a cute name!"

"No!" Aubrey said, and then went silent.

"Bree?"

"I meant, no. It's not really old. It's just in an old church. I'd rather not go there, if you don't mind. Heard the food's not really that good."

"Well, I don't care where we go, as long as I don't have to eat haggis!" Fitz chirped, filling the awkward silence. Aubrey smiled at her, grateful. Filling breaches in conversation was one of Fitz's special talents, and as she had hoped, the tension was broken.

They walked back up the High Street to the Eastgate Shopping Centre. "Oh, look! An Italian restaurant!" Fitz pointed to a tiny cafe across the street from the mall entrance. "They should have normal food. Let's try that tonight."

"Darling, when in Rome..." Kate told her. "You're going to have to try Scottish food sometime, you know."

"I know, I know...just not so soon after that breakfast!" She shuddered.

Crossing the street to the shopping center, they spent two hours doing what women the world over do in malls. While Kate and Fitz meandered through the Tartan Shop looking for souvenirs, Aubrey wandered into a bookshop she'd found on her first day. Nothing like Angus' cavernous space, this one was typical of its kind. Every book was new, no magic in sight. Still, books.

Aubrey found herself gravitating to a section labeled "Scotland" and began to peruse the titles. *Lochs and Rivers of Scotland, Highland Clans Then and Now, Ghosts and Legends of the Highlands.* This last seemed to leap into her hand, and she ran her finger down the table of contents, then the index. Cawdor Castle, Dunebrae Castle, Eileen Donan, Stirling. There were so many castles in Scotland! Many of them were ruins, most of them had ghosts, but there was no mention of Rait Castle.

She put the book back and took out the one about Scottish Clans. Under Mackintosh, Aubrey read that one of the clan's strongest allies had been clan Mackenzie. Did that mean that they were related? Did allies count as relatives? Did that make Connor a candidate for Mackintosh-ness? She felt her heart begin to do a silly dance. Angus would know. She'd just have to suck it up and ask.

Kate and Fitz came in, carrying small bags.

"Look what I bought Eddie!" Kate said, pulling out a flat cap with the words "Harris Tweed" on the inside band. "Won't he look great in this? I was thinking of getting him a kilt, but he'd never wear it, and they're *expensive!*"

"I bought an Aran hat!" Fitz said, showing them a wool hat with a distinctive cable pattern. "Very Scottish."

Aubrey looked at the label inside the hat and laughed. "Fitz! You're such an idiot. Trust you to come to Scotland and buy something from Ireland!"

Trading insults, they left the mall. Aubrey led them down Hamilton Street and around the corner to an arched wooden doorway which boasted an old-fashioned clock and the words "Victorian Market" above its double doors. "It's an indoor shopping market that runs all the way through to the next street," she told them. "Very quaint and very Scottish. There's even a bagpipe workshop."

"Oh, look!" Kate's tone was reverent. "Knives!" She was staring into the window of a kilt shop which displayed a large number of short, single-bladed daggers with wicked looking blades and beautifully ornate hilts. Kate sighed in admiration; where others gravitated to jewelry or clothes, Kate's passion was weapons—especially knives. Guns were what you wore to work, she told them, knives were for fun.

"Those are sgian dubhs," said Aubrey. "The men wear them with kilts, tucked into their stockings or boots. They're very cool. Connor had one. Did you notice?"

"I wasn't looking at Connor's boots," said Fitz. "There were much more interesting things to look at on Connor." She gave an exaggerated leer. "And speak of the devil..."

The man himself was just emerging from the kilt shop. In spite of Fitz's silliness, Aubrey had to admit that Connor did indeed cut a fine figure. His bright russet hair was pulled back in a ponytail today, framing the strong bones of his face and highlighting those lovely amber eyes and ridiculously long lashes. Why was it that men always got the long lashes? Aubrey thought. He treated them to one of his brilliant smiles, his eyes lingering just a bit longer on hers. *He's good*, she thought...*he's damn good! He's wearing down my resistance...and I'm letting him.*

"What are ye fine lassies up to t'day?" he asked, falling into step with them.

"Just tourist stuff," said Aubrey. "And shopping."

"Well, can you make time on Friday for that tour of Castle Leod? I've permission to show you around a bit. The castle is closed to the public so we'll have a private tour, aye?"

A chorus of exuberant "Ayes!" greeted this invitation. The time was set up, and Connor gave Aubrey directions to the Mackenzie keep.

"And while ye're touristin', be sure to save space for the Games," he ordered them.

"Games?"

"Aye, the Highland Games. They're held all over Scotland during the summer, and Inverness is having them Saturday next. They're more contests than games, in truth, tests of strength and manliness, ye ken?" He gave Aubrey a sidelong look and a wink.

"And I suppose," she said in a dry tone, "you'll be competing in these games?"

"Well, and aren't you the clever lass!" Connor laughed. "As a matter of fact, I just might be at that. I hold the record in the hammer throw, so I'm bound to defend it. And if three lovely lassies are there to cheer me on, I canna lose!"

"We wouldn't miss it, would we, Bree?" Fitz's elbow made sharp contact with Aubrey's ribs.

"Ouch! Oh, no, of course we wouldn't. It would be a tragedy to pass up such a display of athletic prowess as we are likely to see, despite the admirable show of modesty from our friend Connor here."

He burst out laughing. "I dinna ken what you mean, but I'm glad you're coming. I'll get your tickets and leave them at the gate. And now I'd best be going, I've got work to do at the castle." And he was off, his long stride carrying him out of the market.

Fitz sighed. "He's lovely, Aubrey, and he likes you, I can tell. I'm never wrong about men."

Kate and Aubrey choked.

"Wha-at?"

That evening, as they sat in a tiny Italian restaurant on the High Street sipping complimentary limoncellos after a wonderful dinner, they sketched out the rest of the time Kate and Fitz would be in Scotland.

"We'll do the walking tour of the city, and if I'm brave enough to drive that far we should go to the Isle of Skye next week. Nessie told me that's a must.

We *have* to tour a whisky distillery—oh! And we must go to Culloden!"

"Our itinerary is filling up fast," Kate said. "I wish we had more than two weeks, but work calls, and Harrington just wouldn't know what to do without us if we stayed longer. Besides, I'd miss Eddie."

"I'm surprised he could stand you being gone this long," Fitz grinned. "He's probably sleeping with your picture next to him on the pillow."

"Absence makes the heart grow fonder, you know." Kate's deep brown eyes were soft. Some people had all the luck when it came to romance, Aubrey thought, wincing at the flash of jealousy that coursed through her.

Fitz, who was facing the window, looked suddenly startled.

"Hey! Isn't that Connor?" The others craned to look. A tall man with russet hair pulled back in a ponytail stood in the shadow of a doorway. His back was to them, and he seemed to be in deep conversation with someone. He was leaning forward, his head bent close to a much smaller man who was blocked by his body. As they watched, he turned and scanned both directions of the High Street, and then hurried away.

Two things stood out to the three girls in the restaurant. He wasn't wearing his kilt. And the smaller man wasn't a man. It was Isla Gordon. *Finn's* Isla Gordon.

CHAPTER 20

A MAN'S HOME
IS HIS CASTLE

On Friday morning, they all piled into Aubrey's little rental car and set out for Castle Leod. Giving Kate her cell phone, Aubrey said, "You're the navigator. Our lives are in your hands."

"Just don't hit any sheep," Kate responded, bringing up the GPS app. "OK, turn right here. Now left. And now we spend about fifteen minutes on the A9. This is easy."

Aubrey's hands were clenched on the wheel as she tried to remember not to cross lanes every time she came to a roundabout. "Speak for yourself," she muttered.

The girls exclaimed over the scenery as it flew past. "Is that heather?" Kate asked. "It makes all the hills look purple, like a carpet. Gorgeous, isn't it?"

"Look!" said Fitz. "I think that's a Highland Cow! Oh, it looks just like the pictures! Needs a haircut, poor thing."

Signs flashed by, pointing off the road to castles and small towns with odd names. Strathpeffer, Dingwall, Knockfarrel, Fodderty. Kate began a limerick, "There once was a man from Strathpeffer, whose wife looked a bit like a heifer..."

"Stop it!" Aubrey choked. "You're going to make me crash!"

Another sign flashed by. "Oh, look," said Fitz. "There's a distillery. *Tulach Àrd*, sounds lovely. Maybe they run tours."

"Well, we'll have to check at the visitor's center, because I sure as hell won't be driving if there's whisky on offer!" Aubrey proclaimed. "I have enough trouble negotiating these roads sober."

Despite her fears, they arrived at the car park for the castle in little over a half hour, parked, and presented themselves at the ticket booth just ahead of a huge tour bus.

"You lassies must be special," the ticket agent told them. "The castle's closed today for tours. All these other folks'll just be walking around the grounds and looking at the outside." He handed them their tickets. "Walk right up the lane, there. Someone'll be waiting for you." They walked past the horde of tourists disgorging from the bus, curious glances following their passage.

"This is so cool!" whispered Fitz. "I feel like royalty!"

Connor met them at the front door, resplendent in his Highland garb. Somehow, in this setting, he looked as if he belonged to the place, much more than they did in their jeans and polo shirts.

"I'm gonna pretend he's Jamie," Fitz whispered as he led them into the castle. "You two can do whatever makes you happy."

"Well, it's not much of a stretch," Kate said out of the side of her mouth. "He does remind me of an actor. Kind of fake."

"You're just jealous because he has eyes only for Aubrey," Fitz told her.

"Like I'm here for romance," snorted Kate. "Although, I do think Eddie would look pretty amazing in a kilt. Maybe I *will* buy him one. He'll have to learn to strut, though, like this guy."

"Shut up, you two!" Aubrey hissed. "He'll hear you!"

"Oh, I think he'd love it," muttered Kate under her breath.

Connor, if he heard any of their conversation, was gracious enough to ignore it, and for the next hour he took them through the Mackenzie seat, evidencing a surprising knowledge of Scottish history in his discussion of the paintings and artifacts that graced the ancient keep.

"How old is this place?" Aubrey asked him.

"Well, they think the castle was built over an ancient fort that was here sometime in the twelfth century," Connor said. "Not so old for Scotland, ye ken?" He winked at her. "Of course, it wasn't always this pretty. In 1746 the third earl lost the whole lot because he followed the Bonnie Prince. That part's in your wee telly program, aye? They got it back about a hundred years later, and it's gotten a few face lifts since then." He paused to judge his effect on his audience, then asked, "Would you like to meet the current earl?"

Three pairs of eyes goggled at him.

"Th-the earl" Aubrey could barely speak for excitement.

Pleased with the impact of his words, Connor led them through a door marked "No Admittance," and they found themselves in a much less ostentatious area of the castle. A silver-haired gentleman sat in a leather armchair with a huge dog at his feet, reading the newspaper. Dressed in simple black trousers and a green sweater, he nevertheless radiated power and privilege. When he saw the Americans, he beamed and stood up to shake their hands.

"Connor told me about you. Come all the way across the pond to see our wee castle, have you? Very pleased to make your acquaintance." His faded blue eyes twinkled in a face that said he was quite aware that he was one of the lucky ones, and that he was grateful. He seems a very nice man, Aubrey thought. Content and not pretentious.

"And how did you entice these lovely ladies into your lair, John?" said a mellifluous voice, and another man entered the room through a side door, carrying a cup of tea. "I leave the room for one minute and you have a bevy of beauties at your feet!" The man was of average height and had a mild, friendly face. He could have been any age from forty-five to sixty. Everything about him was unremarkable—everything but his voice. Caramel, thought Aubrey. With tones of chocolate. Awed, she stared at him, wanting to beg him to speak again—recite the alphabet, count to one hundred, anything.

"This humorous gentleman is my cousin, Lachlan Mackenzie," the earl said, smiling. Seeing Aubrey's expression, he smiled. "He has rather a way about him, doesn't he? Should have been Irish," he added with affection. "Has the gift of the gab. Used to talking to crowds, has them eating out of his hands."

He could sell me anything, Aubrey thought.

"But my cousin's greatest achievement is his whisky," the earl went on. "*Tulach Àrd* whisky is the best in Scotland. Of course, I may be a bit biased."

"Oh, we saw the sign to your distillery on the road here from Inverness!" Kate told the earl and his cousin. "We were hoping to take a tour before we have to leave next week."

Lachlan Mackenzie smiled at them. "We'd be honored to have you," he said. "The distillery runs tours every day of the week, but you'd better book early. They fill up quickly."

A few minutes later, Connor excused the group and they went back out to the front entrance. "I'll leave you here," he told them. "I have to get back to work. You're welcome to walk around the grounds before you go, though. Maybe attach yourselves to a tour group and hear about the sheep and the rowan."

Aubrey pulled Connor aside as Kate and Fitz stepped outside. "Thank you so much, Connor, really. That was wonderful! My friends will never forget this. And it was so special meeting the earl. I think that was my favorite part. His cousin is rather amazing, isn't he?"

Connor gave her a steady gaze, his amber eyes warm. "Ach, he is that. But you're rather amazing yourself, Aubrey," he added, his voice soft and oddly shy. "I'd like to see you again. I enjoy your company, lass, very much."

"Oh." Aubrey felt her face warming. "Well, we'll be seeing you on Saturday at the Games, right?"

"I don't mean in a crowd, or with your friends," he said, keeping his eyes on her. "I mean just the two of us. And I think you know it." He noted the flush creeping up on Aubrey's face and said, "We can talk about it at the Games, aye?" He brushed a lock of hair off her face, making the simple gesture a caress. His hand was warm and intimate, and for a moment she forgot where she was.

Aubrey was in a bit of a daze as they walked back down the path. When had she turned into a femme fatale? she wondered. Had the air of Scotland somehow changed her? Whatever the cause, she thought she might just ride this magic moonbeam as far as it wanted to take her.

There were more tour buses in the car park now, and Aubrey noted with a sudden pang that one of them was a Dougie's Tours van. Her heart quickened as they passed, but the van was empty. Dougie's probably had lots of guides, she told herself. Exasperated with herself, she grabbed her imagination by the throat and shook it. *Stop that!*

They wandered near enough to a tour group gathered in the field to hear the guide's recitation.

"The earl has several rowan trees planted around the property," the guide was saying. "In early times, the rowan was thought to carry magic, and was special to the Faeries. The wee folk thanked the owners of a house for planting rowan by offering protection from witchcraft and enchantment."

Wonder how the tree would get along with Angus's mad book? Aubrey thought, and a shiver went through her. *Bet the Faeries would have something to say about the curse.* Maybe she should buy a rowan sapling and plant it at Nessie's.

"Aubrey!" said a low voice at her elbow, and she turned to find Finn Cameron standing next to her. A thrill that was completely unbidden coursed through her at the sight of him, and she tried to pull herself together so he wouldn't notice. What was wrong with her?

"Please, come over here," he said, his voice sounding urgent. Aubrey turned to her friends.

"We'll meet you at the car," Kate said in a brisk tone, and grabbed Fitz's arm to hurry her off.

Finn reached for her arm, and then thought better of it. *He's remembering what happened last time he touched me. He's afraid of touching me.* He pulled his hand back and gestured for her to follow him a short distance away from the group of tourists. For a moment the two stood facing each other, neither saying anything. The silence lengthened and began to be awkward.

"What did I do wrong?" he asked finally, his voice low and hoarse.

"Nothing, Finn, really," she said, trying to keep her voice steady. "Nothing. I just...it wasn't going anywhere, and I—"

"That's not true!" he exclaimed, frustration darkening his eyes to a stormy blue. "It *was* going somewhere! At least for me it was! And I think it was for you, too. We made a connection, you know we did! Then something changed, all at once, and I'd like to know what it was. It can't have been *him*." The last word was a hiss.

"N-no." Why was her throat so dry and scratchy? She was having difficulty forming words.

He stared her down, daring her to explain.

"I-I can't explain, Finn. It's not your fault. It's me. I'm just a bit confused right now, and—"

"Is it about Isla?" The question caught her off guard and her eyes snapped up. "It is, isn't it?" He took a deep breath. "I told you we were close once, but that's over. It is!" Aubrey was shaking her head, and Finn's shoulders slumped. "All right. I can't make you change your mind about Isla....and I won't push, but can we at least be friends? I like talking to you. It doesn't have to be any more than that." His anger was gone, replaced by a look of hope. Staring into those eyes, she was lost.

"Yes, Finn. Of course we can be friends. I like... talking...to you, too."

His entire demeanor changed, lighting his face and bringing back the lovely smile she remembered. She realized that she had missed that smile. She was playing with fire here, but she just didn't care at this precise moment. Friendship was fine. Friendship was good.

"All right, then. It's a start." He grinned again and walked away from her and back to his group, kilt flapping about his knees.

Men in kilts. She sighed. For some reason, as she walked back to the car, Aubrey felt happiness spreading through her heart, as if the sun had been hiding behind a cloud and had decided to come out and warm the world. As she walked, she began to hum "*Scotland the Brave.*"

The sun was going down over the hills as the three girls dragged themselves into the front hallway at Nessie's, after another Italian dinner at Fitz's new favorite place. Kate had insisted that they stop for something at the supermarket on the way home, but she wouldn't tell Aubrey what it was. As soon as they walked through the door she and Fitz disappeared in the direction of the kitchen.

"How was the castle?" Gladys called, beckoning Aubrey into the sitting room. "Did you meet the earl?"

"Yes, and he was lovely," Aubrey told her, squeezing herself into a space between Maxine and Ronald. "Connor took us on the grand tour and we met the earl's cousin. He owns a distillery and we're going to visit it next week, if we can find a tour. We heard about the fairies and the rowan trees, and the real history of the Mackenzie clan." *And I'm friends with Finn again.*

"Well, that's wonderful." Gladys beamed at her. "I think that Scotland has been just the thing you needed to get yourself right again. You seem so much happier. Doesn't she, Ronnie?"

Kate came into the sitting room carrying a tray on which eight wine glasses jingled as they tapped into each other. Fitz and Nessie followed, each bearing a bottle of wine.

"She's going to be even happier when she gets this one last thing out of her system," Kate announced. "You are all cordially invited to the celebration."

"Celebration?" Aubrey said, puzzled. The Owls accepted their wine with barely suppressed excitement. They loved secrets.

Kate raised her glass.

"I would like to make a toast to Aubrey's freedom from the worst mistake she ever almost made," she announced. She looked at her watch. "Just a few minutes ago, Harrington time, the inestimable Marco Russo tied the knot with the sainted Angela Ferrari. Long may they live in boredom and mutual selfishness. To Marc and Angie!"

For a moment time stood still. Everyone stared at Aubrey as they waited for her reaction, wondering if this time Kate had gone too far. A maelstrom of emotions swirled through Aubrey's mind, buffeting her senses. She could feel something fighting to get out, to burst free, but panic held her in a vise.

Old Harry put down his newspaper and raised his wine glass.

"Slàinte!" he said, and took a long gulp.

Aubrey dissolved into laughter, recognizing the gift she had been given. It was freedom.

The world is full of magic things, patiently waiting for our senses to grow sharper.

W.B. Yeats

SCOTLAND, 1442

ilith Comyn was careful as she picked her way down the hall. The castle was her conspirator, aiding her passage, allowing moonlight to shine on her path down the huge staircase, through the rushes strewn across the Great Hall, and out the door to the kitchens and beyond...to freedom...to him.

She was a wraith in the moonlight, dancing through the garden and the bailey, feet barely touching the ground in her eagerness to be gone. Reaching the stable yard, she stopped for a moment and listened. A low whinny greeted her soft breathing. Corbel, her favorite. Like the castle he was her ally tonight, as always.

"Shhh, be still," she chided the horse in a gentle voice. He had been hers since her fifteenth birthday, and together they had explored the countryside about her home and learned to trust one another as she could trust no other. He did not know it, but one day very soon Corbel would carry her away from her childhood *home and the violent men who stood in her way. She ached for that day with every fiber of her being.*

Continuing around the stable, Ailith crossed to a path long unused by any but her and found her way to the stonecutter's cottage where her life had begun so many months ago. She opened the door and entered, standing for a moment in silence as her eyes adjusted to the gloom within.

He was waiting, standing proud and tall, his love reaching out to gather her in. His eyes gleamed in the moonlight as she came into his arms and he held her tight. He had spread a blanket and brought wine and bread, but she saw none of it as she drank in the sight of his beautiful face. It had been a month this time, and she had thought to die with the waiting...but he was here now, as she had known he would be. This was the third time he had come to her, and always their meeting was much too short—only a few precious hours in the dead of night. She knew how dangerous this was. If he were caught here it would mean his death, and hers as well. Her father cared little enough for her except for what she could buy him, and if she were discovered to have lain with another she would be of no use.

Not just another. The enemy. The younger son of the clan chieftain who was her father's greatest foe. He had cheated death once at the hands of her clan, had been given back his life in an act of pity that had turned to love during the long weeks she had hidden him and tended to his wounds in this cottage. It had become their refuge, and now it was their hope for the future, as she had news for him. But not yet. She sank to the floor of the cottage and lost herself once again in his love, feeling again that odd vibration that flowed through her at his touch.

It was curious, she thought later, as they lay together in the stillness listening to each other's breathing that all their meetings were in darkness, and yet she could have drawn his face, his body, his soul, and never faltered in the memory of it. She knew that their time was nearing its end, and so she turned to him and told him.

Coinneach Mackintosh walked back in the darkness to his tethered horse, mounted and rode the long trail home, never knowing how he got there. His mind was flooded with the news she had given him, with the joy of knowing.

He was to be a father.

CHAPTER 21

HIGHLAND MAGIC

ubrey could hear the bagpipes from Nessie's front porch. She felt her excitement building as she listened to the ancient music. It was easy to understand how the pipers had brought the clans together over the centuries, calling them to battle, to celebrations, to funerals. She had read that sometimes a piper had been killed in the midst of a battle, and another would step in and take his place so that the music never faltered. She looked out over the Highlands and thought of the thousands of pipers who had stood on those hills and played the same music that she now heard emanating from the park where the Highland Games were beginning. She wondered if Finn was down there with his pipe band. Connor had said he was "one of the good ones," so maybe.

She had not seen or spoken to either man since the visit to Castle Leod yesterday, and she had no idea how she was going to handle seeing them again. Juggling two men was not a problem Aubrey was familiar with; this was uncharted territory. She was glad that she and Finn were friends again, even though there was pain with that friendship. She and Connor...well, she wasn't sure what she and Connor were, but he had made his interest clear, and he seemed the persistent type.

Oh, poor me! Two gorgeous Scottish men! Whatever shall I do? She laughed at herself and went back inside to haul Kate and Fitz out of the bathroom.

Gladys came out of the sitting room, Ronald in tow. As she passed Aubrey she cocked her head and said, "Keep the one who makes you sing." She continued up the stairs without missing a step. Ronald looked at Aubrey and shrugged, as always keeping his counsel.

"Thanks, Gladys!" she called after her, though for what she wasn't sure. Nessie's boarders were quirky at the very least, but they seemed to have her best interests at heart, and she could use all the help she could get.

Kate and Fitz were no help. Since their visit to the Mackenzie Castle their antennae had been out and quivering, and like two feuding advice columnists they had determined to help Aubrey move on with her love life, dissecting it incessantly and giving her tips that from anyone else would be invasive. The problem was, Fitz was firmly in Camp Connor and Kate, while insisting that she was staying out of it altogether, admitted that she rather preferred

Finn. If their own love lives were anything to go by, she should run as fast and as far from Connor MacConnach as she could, because Fitz's track record was abysmal. Connor was the village playboy and Finn had the lovely Isla, and neither of them was a Mackintosh. So why not just enjoy what was being dangled in front of her while it lasted?

Because you are not good at this. Because you are going to get hurt. Well, nothing new there, she told her heart, and maybe I won't. Maybe I'll just have a little fun and go home.

Humph, said her heart. *Sure. You just keep telling yourself that.*

The weather was kind today, which meant not raining and only a light jacket needed. They walked down the hill to the river and turned left toward the city park and fairgrounds. As they drew closer, a suspension bridge came into view. "That must be one of the 'bouncy bridges' the hop on hop off lady was talking about!" Kate exclaimed. "The park's on the other side. Let's cross and see."

They started across the pedestrian bridge, and halfway over had to grab the railings with both hands as the bridge began to bounce up and down in alarming fashion. In a moment it had subsided, but as soon as they began walking the bouncing started again. Laughing like children, they bounced their way across the bridge to solid ground.

"Well!" said Kate. "I guess we know what she was talking about, don't we? Cross 'bouncy bridges of Inverness' off the bucket list!"

Having retrieved their tickets as promised by Connor, they proceeded into the park. The fairgrounds had been divided into sections, with large grassy areas set aside for the athletic events. In front of a huge amphitheater burly men, many in kilts and tee shirts, were throwing heavy objects around: logs, disks, and heavy metal balls attached to a wire of some sort. It all looked rather silly to Aubrey, but this wasn't her country so she wouldn't judge. She wondered which of these "manly" implements was the hammer that Connor had said he was so adept at throwing.

Across the field were tents with signs advertising crafts and food for sale, and on the right was a stage where presumably there was to be some sort of dancing. To the left, next to the athletic fields, a large group of bagpipers began a new song. Aubrey was pleased to note that she was beginning to recognize many of the traditional tunes. This one, she was sure, was *Flower of Scotland.* It was all somewhat confusing, but exciting in a chaotic kind of way.

"Let's go find Connor!" yelled Fitz, and headed for the athletic fields. "Shouldn't be hard, he should be the biggest guy here!" she threw over her shoulder.

He wasn't. Not by a long shot. There were men here who were monsters in size. Most of it was muscle, but some of them had been eating a *lot* of haggis to get into that weight class, thought Aubrey. They found Connor by the yells of "MacConnach!" from a group of spectators lined up along the field. As they watched, he began to swing a metal ball which was attached to a wire about four feet long. As he picked up speed, his body spun in ever-faster gyrations until at last, when it seemed that he must lose his balance, he stopped and hurled the object across the field, where it landed near a painted marker. It must have been a good throw, because the cheers from the crowd of spectators were thunderous. Connor grinned and lifted his arms to more hoots from his fans, and then, spotting the three girls, he trotted over.

"That was actually quite impressive!" Aubrey congratulated him. "Did you win?"

He laughed. "Ach, no, lass, that was just the first round. There are four rounds, and the longest single throw wins. That'll be me, of course." He winked at them.

"Of course," said Aubrey, grinning. He was just so irrepressible.

"Go have some fun," he told them. "It'll be awhile before I go again."

"I'm for the craft tent," Kate announced.

"Me too," said Fitz. "Coming, Bree?"

"In a few. I'm going to check out the bagpipes first."

Left alone, Aubrey wandered over to the large group of musicians, surprised to see that several of them carried drums instead of bagpipes. All of them wore identical kilts in a soft green tartan pattern.

"Fancy pipers, do ye?" a familiar voice teased behind her, and she spun to find Finn Cameron grinning at her. He was wearing jeans and a grey tee shirt that read: "Whisky and Bagpipes Gang Together."

"Oh, I'd hoped you were performing," Aubrey said, disappointed.

"No, not this time. This is the *Spirit of Scotland* band. Ours is the *Inver Caledonia*. We have one of the bigger pipe bands; the group you saw at Dunrobin was just a few of us. There'll be others here, but our band leader is away for a family emergency so we're off today. Are you having fun? What've you done so far?"

"I'm meeting Kate and Fitz in the craft tent in a few minutes. We just watched Connor do the hammer throw." At the name, Finn frowned.

"Um, Aubrey, I know I don't have the right to tell you what to do, but I wish you would stay away from that guy."

"You're right, Finn. You don't have the right." She softened her voice. "If we're going to be friends, you have to respect my choices...as I respect yours."

"My—" Finn exhaled in resignation. "You're right. Truce. Mind if I walk with you to the tent? Some friends of mine from the college run a genealogy booth here every year."

"Of course," she said, "I'd like to check that out myself." They walked in companionable silence. Aubrey spied Kate and Fitz having their pictures taken with a life-size cardboard cutout of Jamie Fraser from *Outlander*. Fitz had her arm around the cardboard figure and was leaning in with her head on its shoulder. Aubrey waved to them. "They'll be busy for a while," she laughed.

Finn's friends Dave and Alex worked in the history department with him. They had a no-nonsense display of charts and books offering ancestry searches and clan information and seemed quite happy to meet Aubrey. She was introduced as "my good friend Aubrey, a prodigal Scot who got lost and has found her way back to her homeland."

"Ah, so this is the Yank you've been rattling on about," said Dave. Finn gave them a furious look and his friends laughed, enjoying his discomfiture.

"Well, lass, you've come to the right place if you want to learn anything at all about your roots. Verra smart, you are."

"They're quite modest," said Finn, with a dark look at his friends. They ignored him.

"Here's the starting place for the Cummings," Alex told her, turning to a section in one of the books. "A sad tale, for sure. They used to pretty much own the north of Scotland, back in the days before the Bruce. "Very warlike, the Comyns—that's what they called themselves then—are you a warrior, lass?" He broke off and eyed her with exaggerated trepidation. "Are you planning to break our lad's heart, now, and steal his castle?"

"Shut *up!*" Finn warned, his color deepening.

They took pity on him and continued, Dave taking over the story. "The Comyns weren't always called by that name, ye ken. They were Norman knights, so when they stole land from the Mackintoshes and built a great hall on it, they took the French name de Rait."

"Rait Castle!" Aubrey breathed. "I've been there. Go on!"

"Well, it was Gervaise de Rait who built the castle in the fourteenth century. It had a curtain wall that surrounded a courtyard, and probably a ditch, like the moats you see in fairy tale castles. Only the one tower, but it's a beauty, and still standing."

"Well," Alex took over again. "The trouble for the de Raits started when they decided to swear fealty to Edward I—he was called Longshanks and Hammer o' th' Scots'—not a nice man, our Edward—in 1292. They were calling themselves Comyn again by then, and by supporting the king they made themselves enemies of William Wallace and Robert the Bruce. You've seen *Braveheart*, I suppose?"

"Of course! William Wallace was the bravest man in Scotland!"

"Well, he might have been. He was the hero of the common people, and a fierce enemy of Longshanks. Wallace supported the Bruce, who brought independence to Scotland and became king."

"Wish we had him now," muttered Dave. "Wouldn't be dealing with all these unionist bastards if those two were here."

"Well, we've got Lachlan Mackenzie," Alex interjected. "He's sort of like our Wallace now."

"Oh! I met him! With a smooth voice that covers you like hot fudge sauce on ice cream."

The men laughed. "That's our Lachlan," Dave said. "He could talk you into marching into England and taking over Windsor Castle, I think. And his whisky's just as smooth." All three men stared into the middle distance for a minute, no doubt lost in thoughts of good whisky. *Scots!* Aubrey shook her head.

"The Comyns?" she prompted after a minute, and they snapped back to reality.

"Where was I? Oh," said Alex, "somehow, even though they backed the wrong team, the Comyns managed to hold onto Rait Castle, and that made the Mackintoshes *verra* mad. Battles were fought back and forth until 1442, when the Comyns decided it was time to make peace. Guess they were losing too many men, and they didn't have that many left to begin with."

"Let me tell this part," Dave jumped in with enthusiasm. "So the Comyns invited the Mackintoshes to Rait Castle to have a great banquet and bury the hatchet, so to speak. And the Mackintoshes came. The Comyns should've suspected something; after all, they weren't giving back the land that clan Mackintosh knew was rightfully theirs, so what would they be celebrating? It was more like rubbing it in their enemies' faces, and if that was the idea, it was a bad one. The Mackintosh chief decided that this was their chance to get rid of their enemies once and for all. But it wasn't his idea. Look here." He pointed to an inscription on the crest displayed on the Cumming ancestry page. "*Fhad's a bhios maide sa choill, cha bhi foill an Cuimeineach.*"

"What does it mean?" asked Aubrey.

"*As long as there is wood in the forest, there will be no deceit from Clan Cumming,*" Finn translated. "It's the clan Cumming war cry."

Aubrey hadn't the heart to tell them she already knew this part—too well. Besides, they told it so well.

"But there *was* deceit in one Cumming," Dave took over again. "The daughter of old Malcolm had taken the son of the Mackintosh as her lover. History isn't clear on how they even met, or whether she really loved him. There're a lot of missing pieces and it was a long time ago, but it seems clear she hated her family and wanted to be rid of them. She concocted a plot like that *Game of Thrones* red wedding, ye ken? The Mackintoshes were to attend the feast, and at a signal from the lass they were to rise up and pull out the dirks they had hidden in their cloaks and slaughter the Comyns in their own hall. And that's what happened. The Mackintoshes surrendered their swords as custom demanded, all meek and mild, but kept their daggers hidden. And it worked. All the Comyns were cut down with their drinks still in their hands."

"My turn!" said Alex with relish. "The lass's treachery caught up with her in the end. Her father was mortally wounded, but he looked to his daughter, maybe to warn her to flee, and he saw from her face she was guilty. So he chased her up to the top of the tower, and when she tried to go out the window he cut off her hands!" He made a chopping motion with his arm. "And now folks say the castle is haunted by the ghost of a woman with no hands. *I've* never seen her, but—"

"Aubrey, what's wrong?" She heard Finn's terrified voice as if from a great distance, but she couldn't breathe. Her vision clouded and all sound receded as the grass floor of the tent rushed up to meet her...and then he grabbed her around the waist to stop her fall, and the electricity rushed through her body again at his touch. It was gone as quickly as before, but Finn continued to hold her tight as her breathing slowly returned to normal and the color came back into her face. Then he stepped away, a look of shock on his face. He had felt it too, she was sure of it this time.

"I-I'm okay," she stammered. "I don't know what that was about. I've never fainted before in my life! Must be something I ate." But it wasn't, and she knew it. Fainting might be considered a natural reaction, after all, when a ghost story turned into reality. She had *seen* the ghost! It was all real. Nessie wasn't spinning her a yarn, the book had been right—and suddenly the chill was back. Did that mean that the rest of it was real, too? The curse? The pipers?

In the distance the sound of bagpipes rose on the air as the pipe band resumed playing. It leant the whole episode an eerie touch, as if all Scotland was in on the joke at her expense. And there was something else—something not related at all to the story of Rait Castle and her ancestors.

What the hell, she wondered, was that surge of power that went through her when Finn Cameron touched her? And, although it had never happened with anyone else—certainly not with Marc—why did her body *recognize* it? She spotted her friends crossing the tent to join her and felt a flush of relief. If you were going to go insane, she decided, it was best to do it in the company of your best friends.

CHAPTER 22

OUT OF KILTER

e'd better get back to the Games," Fitz said. "Connor's going to be back on soon."

Connor! She'd forgotten all about him. She turned in time to see Finn striding away, looking as if he wanted to put as much distance as possible between her and him. It had been the mention of Connor, she knew. And so what? He had no claim, no right at all to be angry at her. She wasn't sure she could maintain a friendship with a man who was so easily irritated by her choices when his were elsewhere. It wasn't fair.

Aubrey said goodbye to Alex and Dave and thanked them for the history lesson, and the three girls walked back toward the athletic field. In the distance she could see Connor surrounded by well-wishers, lapping up the attention.

Maybe he was just the ticket right now. In spite of the kilt and the ridiculous good looks, he was so *normal*, and normal was what she needed. She made a deliberate attempt to shake off the memories of the tent and its revelations, and for the next two hours they watched Connor beat his rivals at the hammer throw.

"There'll be no living with him now, you know that, right?" she muttered. But he seemed to be practicing modesty now that he had won and was the perfect escort as they took in the Highland Dancing and munched on hamburgers and fries—chips, Aubrey told Fitz.

"Chips come in a bag, Aubrey," was her friend's stubborn response.

"When in Scotland—"

"I don't care. It's American food, whatever they call it here! Nice, unhealthy, wonderful American carbs!"

Aubrey laughed. Fitz had the right of it. While it was great fun to make fun of her friend and her haggis phobia, it was nice to eat something once in a while that tasted of home.

She didn't see Finn again. She didn't know what to make of that touch, that visceral reaction when he was near. Again she wondered if she should have agreed that they be friends. He wasn't available for anything else, and she knew that her feelings for him were outside the lines of friendship. She was playing with fire, but she didn't care. She didn't want to lose him. She'd just have to let it go its own way and take what she could get. If that was friendship, so be it. Besides, maybe that ship had sailed. Maybe he'd decided that he no longer wanted to be her friend if she was with Connor. Well, screw him, then. It was her life!

No one seemed to notice Aubrey's preoccupation. Connor walked back with them to Nessie's front walkway, teasing Fitz with tantalizing descriptions of Scottish food. When the girls began to walk up the winding path, though, he held Aubrey back. "Have dinner with me tonight?" he asked, in a voice that was surprisingly tentative. And that was what did it. Aubrey could have withstood the self-assurance, the cockiness, the muscles and all the rest; yes, the package was beautiful, but that wasn't her Achilles heel. No, it was when a man looked hopeful, unsure, when he held his breath waiting for her answer. She hadn't thought the Playboy of Inverness was capable of such humility and it toppled her over the edge.

"Yes," she said, and was rewarded for that one word with a smile that lit his whole face.

"I'll pick you up at seven," he told her. "Dress casual. It's not a fancy place, but I think you'll like it." And he swished away, taking long strides back toward Castle Road and the river.

I wonder where he lives. Castle Leod? Does he have a walk-in closet full of kilts? A mirror on every wall? She watched him disappear around the corner. *There's a lot I don't know about Connor MacConnach.* Of one thing she was certain, though. What you saw was what you got. He didn't have a mysterious bone in his body, and that was just what she needed right now.

Kate, Fitz, and all the Owls were waiting for her when she reached the sitting room.

"He's asked you out, hasn't he?" Fitz demanded. "You lucky dog! I am so envious."

"Are you sure about this?" Kate asked, her voice concerned. "Make sure you text us where you are so we can come get you if it goes south."

"Yes, he's asked me out. We're going to have dinner. I don't know where. Yes, I will text the location when I get there. And thank you, Kate, for assuming that I will be murdered over dessert or sold into slavery to work on some peat farm in the Outer Hebrides. I think I can tell when a man is sincere." She replayed that last comment in her mind and burst out laughing. "Oh, yeah. Not a great argument coming from me, is it?"

Gladys said nothing, which was more than odd. Old Harry stayed hidden behind his newspaper, and Maxine launched into a story about the young dancer she had known who had gone to some Arab country and never returned, presumably because she had been kidnapped and forced to become a concubine for the local sheik. Ronald patted Aubrey on the arm and said helpfully, "There's not a lot of slavery in Scotland. You'll probably be all right." As if surprised to hear himself speak, he clamped his mouth shut and turned on the television.

Nessie came into the room and announced, "There'll be some o' that rocky ice cream if ye need it later," and turned on her heel and left. Aubrey was almost sure she heard something Gaelic caught in Nessie's throat.

What's wrong with all of them? she wondered. *It's almost as if they don't want me to be happy.* But she knew that couldn't be true. She knew they all cared. *I don't understand it a bit.* She gave up thinking about it and went upstairs to take a nap, expecting to dream about ghost girls with no hands, but the minute her head hit the pillow she was asleep.

Kate and Fitz sat on her bed while she got ready later that evening, offering unsolicited advice about what to wear and how she should do her hair. Aubrey tuned them out, choosing from her limited wardrobe a simple green sweater—jumper—that brought out the green in her hazel eyes and hugged her in all the right places, and her favorite pair of skinny jeans. At the last minute, she pulled out the Cumming scarf that she'd bought on her first day in Scotland and draped it around her neck for a little added color. She left her hair down in the usual bob—it wouldn't do to look as if she were trying too hard—and stood in the center of the room for inspection.

"Oh, Bree, you look so beautiful! He's going to fall right in love with you and carry you off to live in Castle Leod! I'm so jealous!" Fitz threw herself on the bed in mock despair.

"Shut up, Fitz! Do I really look all right?" She felt like the awkward kid she had been in high school, trying to find the courage she needed to get through her first date. If she remembered correctly, it hadn't gone well, the first in a long series of only dates. *Well, I've improved since then. At least I can carry on a conversation now!* And then she remembered that it was Connor—laughing, funny, *talkative* Connor—and decided that she didn't have to worry about carrying the conversation. She'd be lucky to get a word in edgewise.

He was there at six fifty-five. Points for prompt-ness. Aubrey came downstairs to find him in the sitting room surrounded by the Owls. Tonight he was dressed in light grey cotton pants and a black V-neck sweater that set off his red-gold hair, again tied back at the nape of his neck. She stood for a minute admiring him. When he looked up in panic she took pity on him and rescued him from their clutches, pulling him out the door and down the pathway.

"Those people are scary!" Connor told her. "Only the Sassanach lady talked, and she asked me more questions than my mother! The rest didn't say anything, just stared at me like a lot of ghouls. You put up with that every day?" He shook his head. "You are a verra brave woman, lassie!"

She laughed at him. "They're a little odd, I'll give you that, but they're harmless."

"Humph."

He folded her into a little BMW convertible. Aubrey knew less than nothing about cars, but she knew an expensive sports model when she saw one. Either the Mackintoshes paid their handyman better than most, or the modeling was a lot higher-end than he had let on!

"You look lovely, lass." Connor was looking at her with frank admiration that sent a shiver of pleasure down her spine. She couldn't tell how serious all this attention was, but he knew all the right words, and she was beginning to think he was just what her battered heart needed right now. He was still staring and she felt as if she'd better say something soon.

"So do you. In fact, you look just as good out of a kilt as..." She stumbled to a stop, face assuming the color of a ripe tomato. Had she just said...*Oh God.*

A low rumble filled the car. "don't worry. I know what you mean, lass." And suddenly they were both laughing, dispelling the tension.

They didn't drive far, just into the center of town. With great skill, Connor backed the little car into one of the few parking spots left on the street and escorted her into a charming restaurant called *The Fig and Thistle.* Doesn't get more Scottish than that, she thought. Nice.

"Gets a lot of tourists in the summer," Connor told her. "But they know how to treat the locals, and the food is the best around."

It was. Connor ordered wine for both of them, and Aubrey was surprised to find that he knew his way around a wine list very well. She would have thought him a whisky man, or maybe beer. He was a constant surprise, this one. As a starter they had haggis bon bons, which she considered slipping into her purse to take home to Fitz. These would change her opinion on haggis, for sure. But then she decided that Fitz didn't deserve them.

Over coconut ice cream, Connor asked her where her next adventure was taking her, and Aubrey told him that they had hoped to get to the Isle of Skye early next week.

"Kate and Fitz are only here one more week, and we have to fit in Culloden and a distillery tour so it's getting tight. Also, I'm a bit nervous to drive all the way to Skye," she admitted. "And I'm sure the sheep are petrified."

"I'll take you," he said, nodding his head as if it were a done deal.

"That's very sweet of you, Connor, but I don't think Kate and Fitz will agree to be strapped on top," she said.

"Ach, lass, you underestimate my abilities! I'll get the castle's van for the day. The Mackenzie won't mind. Is Tuesday all right?"

"Really? Are you sure? Oh, Connor, that would be fantastic! Thank you so much!" Her relief at not having to drive surged through her and she wanted to kiss him, right here, right now. Even Kate would have to show the man some appreciation for this!

They pulled up to Nessie's and he walked her to the porch door.

"Thanks for the lovely dinner and the wonderful company," she told him.

Without warning, he pulled her into his arms and kissed her. It was sweet, and nice. Verra nice. The kiss deepened and she let herself be carried away. *Damn it*, she thought, *he's a great kisser too! This guy really could give Jamie Fraser a run for his money.* And for once her heart kept silent as she leaned into the kiss and just enjoyed it. There'd be time later to worry that he wasn't a Mackintosh.

CHAPTER 23

OUR MAN
IN INVERNESS

"I don't think I can do this anymore!"

Chief Inspector Alan Brown maintained his disinterested expression. He had been expecting this for some time now. It was nothing new. He sighed. Everyone thought spies were highly trained, ruthless machines, like James Bond. Tuxedos, beautiful women, champagne and caviar.

The reality could not be more different. Police departments were not funded like the spy tanks in the movies. There were no pens that turned into guns, no spike-throwing umbrellas, no flamethrowers masquerading as bagpipes. Although that last might be quite useful in Scotland, where bagpipes vied with people for supremacy.

The police were often forced to utilize the civilian population to help them in their quest for answers.

Some were mere informants, criminal types themselves, who traded information for a reduced sentence. Some were simply people who felt the importance of right and wrong, people who could not be seduced by money or power—like this man. This one had a unique perspective on their suspect, a reason for them to be seen together. At one point in their history they had been close friends.

And there was something else that was unique to the man who sat across from him. He had a conscience. He cared about people, about truth, and about morality. Above all, he loved his country, and hated those who raped her for gain. Too compassionate to be the perfect spy in the eyes of the movie directors.

And therein lay the problem. It was the reason for today's meeting, and he had known it was coming. That moral compass, that conscience, was beginning to bother him, to cripple his desire. It was not the danger, Brown knew, although there was danger in what they had asked him to do. It was the deceit. Honest people simply did not like leading double lives. And the man who sat before him, pain etched on his face, was above all an honest man.

"You can." Brown steepled his hands and looked at his agent. "I don't think you realize how much is depending on you, or how well you're doing." The man shook his head in frustration.

Brown changed tack. "Do you trust me?"

The man was surprised at the question. He sat for a moment, thinking. Then he said, his tone quiet but firm, "Yes. But that's not the problem!"

CI Brown took a deep breath. "I understand. The problem is that you're too close to the situation, that you feel pain at the idea of stalking people you know. But know this...your country is in mortal danger. There are those who will use anything at their command to get what they want. They are driven by greed and self-interest, and no one who stands in their way is safe."

"I know, but I can't accept that—"

Brown interrupted. "We believe that the CEO of PETRO, Darius Sanderson, is the brain behind the sabotage that has plagued Scotland for the last six months. He is frightened by the *Caledonia First* movement, afraid that it will destroy the empire he has built on the shoulders of the Scottish people. We believe that he has orchestrated the violence and destruction directed at his own oil platforms and others, for the simple purpose of pointing blame at those who want an independent Scotland. We believe that he had his own assistant killed, even though our investigation has told us that the man was the closest thing he had to family.

"We believe that he has now targeted the leadership of *Caledonia First*. We do not yet know his next steps, but our information points to a definitive strike very soon. The specter of a Scottish Independence referendum is anathema to Sanderson, because an independent Scotland would destroy his stranglehold on the oil business. Are you with me so far?"

The man nodded, his face still tense.

"Someone has gone to a great deal of trouble to point the finger at *Caledonia First* for the sabotage.

The newspapers have taken his bait and run with it, and the movement has lost some support as a result. But not enough. If the referendum were to be held today, we believe that the results would be too close to call, and that is not good enough for Sanderson.

"Sanderson has, throughout his endeavors, utilized others. First, it was Oliver Thomson, the assistant. For some reason he found Thomson unsuitable and had him eliminated. Then it was a series of others, almost as if he were auditioning a replacement for his friend. We think he has found that person, and it is someone you know well. That is why we need you. I am not asking you to spy on this person, merely to note any odd movements or meetings that are out of the ordinary. You will, of course, need to maintain a certain level of contact in order to do this."

The man's face twitched. Ah, thought Brown. This contact is what is bothering my man here. Something has caused him to wish to avoid the connection he has had in the past with our suspect. He thought of asking about it, then demurred. The man had the right to a personal life, after all. He had not chosen this job. And Brown regretted the need to cause him pain. But he had to know what failure to bring this to a close would cost. Not only to him, but to his friends, his colleagues...his country.

"I have spoken with Darius Sanderson," he said. "He is arrogant and self-important, and he thinks he is untouchable. But he has a weakness."

The man seated across from him looked up but did not speak. He waited. Brown respected him for his patience.

"Mr. Sanderson was angry at the very idea that the police would have the temerity to question him. He thinks he should be exempt from the dirt that clings to the shoes of lesser men. His weakness is his vanity, his need to keep his own hands clean," Brown said. "He does not do his own dirty work; he believes himself above all that. So he must rely on the services of others. His minions, if you will. And your acquaintance..."

His guest was staring at him. His face had changed. The pain was still there, but there was something else. A new determination, perhaps. Brown sensed that it had to do with this acquaintance from his past. Was that what was driving this new reticence?

"Your acquaintance is the best candidate that he has ever found. We believe that this agent has been working for him for some time but has now moved up to the position of second in command. Sanderson believes that he needs but to dictate his wishes to this person and they will be carried out. We believe, in fact, that it was this one who killed Oliver Thomson. It is this individual who will be in charge of the ultimate action, and because this agent is from the Highlands, we believe that the strike will happen here.

"I will continue to visit Mr. Sanderson in Edinburgh, and I will keep asking him questions. I want to rattle him, to make him feel insecure. Possibly, in his efforts to convince the police of their stupidity, he will make a mistake. Right now I have angered him. Perhaps I have begun to unsettle him as well. But that is all I can do, for now.

"You are my contact here in the Highlands. I cannot be here on a regular basis. I cannot state strongly enough how much I need you to continue to do what you're doing. If we stay the course, follow this to its inevitable conclusion, I do not think that this will go on for much longer, and then you will be free to pursue your life, to go back to what makes you happy." He paused, wondering what it would be like to have a simple life, to live and love as you wished. He envied the man his opportunity to do so. If he could stay the course, if he managed to keep from giving himself away. If he could stay alive.

"So," CI Alan Brown asked, when the silence had gone long enough, "can you do it? Are you willing to be my man in Inverness?"

The man across from him sighed.

"Yes," he said.

CHAPTER 24

BLOOD
ON THE THISTLE

Aubrey woke disoriented, wondering if she had been transported to a different world. Something was different, but her sleep-fuddled brain could not wrap itself around the new feeling. She lay still and let the fog clear—and there it was. She had been kissed last night, and kissed well. She could not remember the last time a man had kissed her and meant it. Marc had stopped being romantic long before the Text, she realized now. And Marc had never been as good as he thought he was, at anything. Last night was proof.

Her phone buzzed. She groped for it on the end table, pressing the button and yawning as she answered, "Hello?"

"Hi, Aubrey, it's Finn." With a whoosh, the fog lifted and her senses went on alert. Was he calling to tell her to stay away from Connor again? Had he found out about their dinner date?

"Finn." To her own ears, her voice sounded wary, devoid of emotion. Just how she wanted it to.

"I hope I didn't wake you," his smooth brogue came over the phone. "I wanted to see if you'd like to bring your friends on a wee trip to Culloden tomorrow. I'm doing a tour for Dougie's and I thought it was high time you paid homage to the saddest place in Scotland."

"Are you kidding? I've been saving that one." She was wide awake now. "Oh, Finn, that's perfect! The girls are going to love you. They already think you look good in a kilt!" she added. His answering chuckle was warm.

"Right, then. Be at the bus station at ten, your tickets'll be waiting for you."

She hung up and lay back in the bed. Apparently he was over his snit, and they were still friends. Good. But she'd have to be careful not to mention Connor—that seemed to be a trigger. If Finn only knew what she'd been doing last night...ooh, that didn't bear thinking. She certainly wouldn't be headed to Culloden, that was for sure!

Three eager Americans joined the group boarding Dougie's tour bus the next morning. Aubrey sat back and let the girls enjoy Finn's humorous anecdotes during the ride to the famous battlefield. She thought of asking him what it felt like to have a Scottish accent but stopped herself in time. "He's really fun!" Fitz whispered. "I thought he was kind of an old stick, he always acts so gloomy around you, but he's actually pretty adorable, isn't he?"

He is, she thought, and felt a surge of affection tinged with sadness. *Adorable.*

The bus pulled into the car park of the huge modern visitors' center and Finn gathered his group around him.

"First, I need to remind you that this is a grave-yard as well as a battlefield. Most of the Scots who were killed here on April 16, 1746 were buried right where they fell, and the English dead are here as well. So we ask that you keep your voices low to show respect. Everyone ready?" He pointed out at the field of heather and thistle, toward where two rows of flags flew, one red and one blue. "The blue flags show where the clans were lined up, along the ridge line there, and the red is for the British troops.

"We'll walk out onto the field first, and I'll give you some history of the clans who fought here on Drumossie Moor that day." He thickened his brogue. "Then any o' ye who are lucky enough t' have some Scots hangin' in yer family tree," he winked at them, "can look for the stones that mark where they fell." His voice took on a somber tone, and his audience leaned closer to catch every word. "That day marked the end of the Highland culture forever. The English banned the wearing of clan tartan, and the playing of bagpipes, and even the speaking of the Highlanders' language, Gaelic, on penalty of death." His expression saddened, almost as if he remembered the day from personal experience.

Was the battle still this real for all Scots? Aubrey wondered, and thought again that he must keep his students enthralled; his descriptions were so vivid. She gazed out upon the moor, so innocent in its cloak of summer heather, and it changed before her eyes. The field was covered in smoke from the cannons, the noise sucking all other sound from the world. The man next to her screamed as a bullet pierced his throat, nearly ripping his head away from his body. Another clansman stepped into the space he had occupied a moment before, charging past Aubrey with a howl of defiance and fury. She lifted her target, tried to focus on the enemy in front of her. If only she weren't so tired! If only she had had more training before being set on this impossible course! She could not see, she could not hear for the deafening roar of the relentless artillery...

With an effort she pulled herself back to the present to hear Finn saying, "We'll meet back at the visitor's center in one hour. I'll give you some time to spend all your money in the wonderful gift shop, don't worry." Some of the group peeled away to explore on their own, but most followed Finn like acolytes. No one seemed to notice where Aubrey had been. Lost in her imagination again.

Her friends stood beside her, bickering as usual.

"Wonder where the Fitzgeralds fell?" whispered Fitz.

"Somewhere in Ireland, I'm guessing," snorted Kate. "You're such a nitwit!"

"Well, I don't think you'll find any Bianchis here," she retorted.

"Because I'm not dumb enough to look for them, and besides, that's Eddie's family!"

"Are they always like that?" Finn had circled back to walk beside Aubrey.

"Usually. They like sparring, keeps them amused— and I think it's just habit now. They love each other like sisters, and fight like sisters too."

"And where do you fit in?" he asked. "Let me guess, you're the peacemaker of the group. You're the most sensitive, the most empathetic." He was studying his boots as he walked.

"That's very sweet, Finn. But actually it evens out in the end. I keep them from killing each other, and they keep me from letting my imagination run away with me. Their job's much harder."

"You're different, Aubrey. Strong. I knew that the moment I met you. Your imagination makes you even more special." His voice was low and seemed congested. "It—it's one of the things I love about you." He turned from her then, walking rapidly away to resume his place at the head of the group. Aubrey was left staring after him in shock.

"This is the Cameron stone," Finn was saying as she rejoined the group. "My own ancestors fell hereabouts, as they charged across the swampy ground through the thistle and the heather to meet the might of the English." He did not look at her as he continued his talk, his professor voice back in place as he resumed the story of the doomed Highlanders and their last effort to free their country from the grip of England.

The group gathered around the monument in the center of the battlefield and took turns reading the words in hushed tones. "The Battle of Culloden was fought on this moor 16th April 1746. The graves of the gallant Highlanders who fought for Scotland and Prince Charlie are marked by the names of their clans." Simple, like the men who had died here. And from the news, she had gathered that the Scots were still to this day trying to win their independence from Britain. Did it never end for these courageous people? She felt a surge of pride to be a Scot, to share a kinship with this war-weary country whose people never gave up in their quest for freedom.

A large group, mostly women, was clustered around a small boulder inscribed with the name "Fraser." Several offerings of roses and other flowers rested on top of the stone, and the women were whispering in excitement. Aubrey caught Finn's glance and he rolled his eyes. She giggled at the look but joined her friends in taking a picture of Jamie Fraser's clan stone. Couldn't be helped.

On the way back they passed a tiny hut standing alone in the huge field of heather and gorse.

"Leanach Cottage," Finn told them. "It stood right between the two lines, and was probably used as a field hospital by the English. You're lucky today—it's being thatched, just the way they did it back then." He indicated the men on the roof tying bundles of heather to the roof using old fashioned tools.

In the visitor's center, Finn pointed out a huge book which detailed all the Highland clans who had fought in the battle and what had happened to the survivors. Aubrey found the Mackintosh page and, as often happened when she and books found each other, she became lost in the amazing story of Angus's ancestors.

In February of 1746, the book told her, Charles Stewart was in retreat from the British army. When he reached Moy Hall, the seat of the Mackintoshes, he was welcomed by Lady Anne Mackintosh, who had raised the clan for the Jacobite army. But the government commander gathered fifteen hundred men and chased him down. The prince was warned and fled into the fields to hide. The Mackintoshes had only twelve men, but they conceived a desperate plan. As the British drew close, the Jacobites began to make a horrendous noise, banging their shields and shouting orders to regiments that did not exist. The enemy believed that they were facing a great horde of the enemy and retreated in panic. The ruse was forever after known as "The Rout of Moy," a battle in which fifteen hundred men were defeated by twelve.

Aubrey turned the pages, attempting to find the Cummings, but they were not listed. So they hadn't fought at Culloden. Did they support the prince or side with the English government? Or were there simply not enough of them to matter? Had they been destroyed as a clan in 1442, as Angus' book and Finn's historian friends had said? Sad, if so. It was hard to believe that one young girl had caused the virtual extinction of a once proud Scottish clan, but all indications were that this girl Ailith had been truly evil. And poetic justice had her haunting the ruins of Rait Castle to this day.

Something about the whole thing didn't feel right, however. The emanation of evil that Aubrey had felt inside that ruin had not come from the ghost. She didn't know how she knew that, but she was sure of it. The ghost had been trying to *tell* her something, something just beyond the reach of her senses. Besides, if this Ailith was so bad, why was Old Harry defending her? He was a spooky as Angus; he *knew* things. There was just too much here that didn't make sense.

Aubrey decided to stop thinking about all of it for now and spent the next half hour engrossed in another wonderful gift shop. Scotland really knows how to do souvenirs right, she thought. None of those shot glasses with "I left my sporran on the battlefield," or salt and pepper shakers in the shape of Highland Cows. There were tartans, and whisky flasks...and books. Aubrey set the alarm on her phone for fifteen minutes and lost herself in the stories of the battle.

When her phone's alarm pulled her back to the present, she sighed and stepped outside into the bracing Scottish air. She walked to the corner of the building, intending to find a patch of sunshine in which to purge the shadows of the past from her mind. But as she reached the corner, she saw two men standing in the shadow of the building's eaves and froze in place. Finn...and Lachlan Mackenzie.

They were deep in conversation, and it was obvious from their body language that the two men knew each other well. Mackenzie turned and saw Aubrey at the corner of the building, said something to Finn, and quickly turned and walked in the opposite direction without acknowledging her. *That was odd*, she thought. He'd been so friendly when she'd met him at the castle. Today his actions seemed almost furtive. Perhaps he hadn't recognized her from her trip to Castle Leod.

Finn walked over to where she stood and gave her a distracted smile.

"Well, it's about time to join the others, aye?" Without another word he turned and walked toward the bus, seeming almost in a hurry to get away from her.

"There are more things in heaven and earth, Horatio..." she muttered to herself, as she followed in his wake. Hamlet might not have been a Scot, but he had the right of it. Odd things were piling up.

CHAPTER 25

LEGENDS

onnor drove the Mackintosh van up to Nessie's gate at nine on Tuesday morning to collect his three charges. They piled in and began their trek out of Inverness, winding their way northwest toward the Isle of Skye. Connor took the scenic route, although to their New Jersey eyes everything in Scotland was the scenic route. The van headed out on the A82, with Loch Ness on the left and high, shadowed cliffs to the right. As they passed through Morriston, they could see wind farms on the hillsides and Scots pines left standing in magnificent isolation.

The van slowed and the scenery changed again. Connor pulled over at a sign with crossed swords and invited them to read about one of the minor Jacobite uprisings in 1717.

"That's right," Aubrey said. "There were two risings, I read about them before I came. Bonnie Prince Charlie's father was supposed to be the king. James, wasn't he?"

"Aye, lass, but there were lots of risings besides the two you know about. The Highlanders wanted to return James to the throne. He would've been king of both countries, not just Scotland—James II of England and VII of Scotland. And he almost did it, but in the end the rebellion just fizzled out, and James turned tail and ran away." His look was bleak. "Running away was something the Stewarts did verra well."

They continued on, the road twisting and turning in and out of the mountains. Much of their journey was on single track roadways, the road in some sections so narrow that when they encountered oncoming traffic, one of the vehicles had to make use of the strategically placed turn-out areas which stuck to the sides of the roads like warts. Sometimes Connor pulled over, other times it was the oncoming driver who gave way.

"How do the drivers know when to pull over?" Aubrey asked him the third time this had happened. "In the States, it would be a free-for-all. Don't you have road rage here?"

"Road rage?" He looked puzzled. "Do you mean people who get mad at each other on the road? Well, most o' the people on the road up here are tourists, and it's not their country, so perhaps they leave their rage at home, aye?" He was quiet, thinking. "It's the code of the Highlands," he said after a moment. "Scottish people know that if you see a car coming and your turn-out comes up first, you should pull in, because the other driver will likely not stop. People take turns, but the rule is that the one closest to the turn-out has to use it, even if it's behind him." He shrugged. "It works."

Aubrey thanked the gods again that it was Connor who was driving. The only good thing about single track roads was that you didn't have to worry about which side to drive on!

Because it was summer, traffic was rather heavy, and not only with cars. Several times they had to stop and wait for a flock of sheep to meander across the road. *I wonder if sheep ever have road rage*, Aubrey thought. She remembered something Alastair MacGregor had said while on the train to Dunrobin. No, she thought, sheep have the Right to Roam, like everyone else in Scotland. No road rage to get their wool in a bother.

As they crossed the Skye Bridge, Kate pointed to a ruin on the headland to their left. "What's that? An old fort?"

"That's Castle Maol, the historic seat of clan MacKinnon. It was built in the twelfth century, and once stood alone to mark the passage through the narrow part between the mainland and the island. Ever hear of Saucy Mary?" he asked them. Three pairs of curious eyes gazed at him, waiting. "Well, legend has it that round about the year 900 there was a Norse princess who married Findanus, the chief of the MacKinnons, and they lived in a castle even older than Maol, called Dunakin, on the same spot. Like all rich people, they always thought they needed more money, so they kept themselves in coin by stringing a chain of boats across the narrows and charging a toll on ships that wanted to pass through. After they paid, the princess would come out and lift up her shirt and flash 'em her...you know...anyway, it was a pretty saucy move, aye?" He chortled with laughter at their faces.

"So," he continued, "Castle Maol is a grand part of Highlands' history, but it's been allowed to fall into ruin." His voice was suddenly sad. "That's what's happening to so many of our national treasures."

"Like Castle Rait?" Aubrey touched his arm in sympathy. She remembered the desolation of that once glorious old pile. It had been sad to see the ancient castle losing its battle to the elements, trees growing inside its walls and grass taking over everything. Unless man intervened to keep up the battle against nature, his greatest achievements would always be fated to return to the earth in time.

"Aye, lass. Rait Castle is a national monument and a fine example of a historic hall castle, only one of five or so still standing. But it costs money to keep a castle standing, and so far the Historic Environment Scotland people don't seem too interested in helping. That's what our group does. We're trying to get Parliament to pass a law that forces the owners of these fine buildings to act to keep them from falling down." He shook his head. "It's a battle, for sure, but we won't give up!"

His voice had risen during this speech, and Aubrey caught a glimpse of the passion that lurked behind the devil-may-care facade he presented to the world. There were depths to Connor MacConnach; she wondered why he took such pains to hide them from the world. He glanced over at her then, and in his golden eyes she saw that he had read her mind, and that her thoughts pleased him. Depths, indeed!

They started their tour of Skye by cruising through Portree, the largest town on the island. "We won't waste our time in Portree, lassies, we only have the one day and there's lots to see."

Aubrey saluted him. "Yes, boss. You're in charge."

He grinned. "As it should be," and she felt bold enough to give his arm a light punch.

"The first place we're going to see is The Old Man of Storr, coming up on the left," he announced. "Anybody see it yet?"

"Wow!" Fitz exclaimed. "Is that a standing stone?"

"Well, it's a stone, and it's standing, so I suppose so," he answered, "but the Old Man is a natural formation, not put there by people. There is a legend, though."

"Of course there is," said Aubrey. "Isn't there always?"

Connor glared at her in mock annoyance. "Who'd ye say was in charge, again?" She put a hand over her mouth, and he laughed. "So, the legend is that the Old Man was a giant who lived nearby. When he died, they buried him, but because he was so big his finger was left sticking out. And there it is." Ahead of them they saw a huge pinnacle standing by itself on the hillside, looking like a petrified fir tree, but one over one hundred fifty feet high.

They continued around the narrow coastal road until Connor announced, "Kilt Rock!" And indeed, the cliff face before them looked much like a giant folded kilt, standing against the sea.

"Is there a legend about that?" asked Kate, her tone innocent.

"Aye, lass, of course there is!"

"Oh, do tell!"

"Well," he began, "it's about a giant."

"What's with the obsession about giants?" Aubrey interrupted.

"Hush, lass," he admonished. "As I was saying, there was a giant. He lived on the coast and he watched out for the people of Skye for hundreds of years. Finally, he got tired so he just sat down and turned into rock. He's still sitting there in his kilt today, guarding the island."

"Oh, that's a nice one!" Fitz purred. Connor beamed.

"I wouldn't ask *him* what he wears under his kilt!" exclaimed Kate. Connor looked at her with surprise, and then doubled over with laughter.

"Next stop, the Quiraing." At their puzzled looks, he told them, "It means 'land fold', and it's a land slip... kind of like a slow avalanche, that's been going on for thousands of years. It's still moving, and they have to keep fixing the road because it's sliding into it."

As they marveled at the undulating folds of green before them, Aubrey asked, "And what's the legend?"

"What's with the obsession about legends?" he asked, with a dangerous look, and then grinned at her. They walked for a way along the trail, and when Connor took her hand, she didn't remove it.

"Almost forgot," he said. "Wee Isla wants to invite you and your friends for drinks when we get back, if that suits ye," Connor said suddenly. Kate and Fitz turned around at the words.

Aubrey's hand trembled and she pulled it out of Connor's warm grip.

"Just Isla?" she said carefully.

"Aye. I'm to drop you all off and pick you up when you're done," he said. "She said girls only."

Aubrey sighed. "Okay. I guess that's all right." She had to face Finn's girl sometime, she supposed, might as well get it over with. But somehow the warmth had gone out of the day. Connor didn't seem to notice, taking her hand again in his as they walked back to the car.

Isla Gordon lived in the most exquisite flat Aubrey had ever seen, high on a hill overlooking the river and the mountains. She welcomed the girls as if they were long lost friends, her manner so natural and unaffected that, despite her determination to hate the girl, Aubrey felt herself pulled under Isla's spell again. *How can I blame Finn for loving her, when she makes me want to love her too? She's adorable, damn her!* She glanced at her friends and saw that Fitz too had been ensorcelled by the tiny enchantress. Kate alone seemed unaffected by Isla's charms, and the knowledge steadied Aubrey.

A maid served them drinks in etched fluted glasses. "Pink gin," Isla told them, "with sugar syrup, lemon juice, and champagne. I hope you like it."

"Lovely," Kate said. "And how do you know Connor?" She threw the question out as if it had just occurred to her, but Aubrey hid a smile behind her glass. Kate was being a detective.

"Oh, I've known Connor all my life," Isla said. "He's like my brother."

"Mmm." Kate sipped her drink. "And Finn?"

Aubrey felt as if the air had been sucked from the room. She wanted to kick Kate under the exquisite coffee table, but she couldn't move.

"Ahh, my Fionnlagh. He's just...special." She winked at the girls and smiled her beautiful smile. Aubrey felt her world narrow to a thin spear of agony, shocked at the intensity of her reaction.

"But I'll tell you something," Isla continued, "Connor is the one you need to watch, Aubrey. He really likes you. I've never seen him like this." She clapped a dainty hand over her mouth. "Oh," she moaned, "he's going to kill me for telling you! You won't tell him, will you?" She put a finger over her lips.

Aubrey spent the rest of the visit in a daze, barely taking part in the conversation. Her thoughts were whirling. Connor liked her? *Really* liked her? She searched her memory for signs and realized that he'd been sending signals for some time. She had just put them down to his natural tendency to flirt with any woman he was with. But maybe that wasn't true either. She had only Finn's word for that, and he was jealous of Connor.

A knock on the door announced the return of the man himself, and Aubrey found herself looking at him with new eyes. Softer eyes. His own smiled back at her, warm and golden. On the drive back to Nessie's Aubrey studied his profile. When he looked over at her he smiled that sweet smile, but now she saw a vulnerability that she hadn't noticed before. She smiled back and he took her hand again and held it, caressing her palm gently as he drove.

Kate and Fitz, the perfect friends, piled out of the van with a hurried, "Thanks so much, Connor," and almost ran up the path, leaving Aubrey to say her own goodbye. Without a word Connor pulled her close and kissed her, his lips warm and trembling on her own.

"It was a wonderful day, Connor. Thanks so much." Aubrey's voice was husky.

"Aye, lass, it was." His brogue was like smoke, warm and thick. "It was a privilege to take ye."

Aubrey watched him pull away down the drive. It had been a perfect day in the Scottish Highlands. Incredible beauty, a little magic, and a hint of romance.

The Owls were in the sitting room but Aubrey was too tired to fall into their clutches for the inevitable grilling, so she waved and smiled at them, and the three started up the stairs to their rooms.

Expecting to fall asleep immediately, she was surprised to find herself staring at the ceiling wide awake, nerves tingling. She tried to empty her mind, but her rebellious imagination refused to cooperate, replaying everything that had happened the last few days, searching out the corners and crevices of her memories for little nuggets of torture.

Since she had come to Scotland, her imagination had not needed much help in its effort to create chaos. Reality was doing quite a fine job of that itself. Who needed to rely on imagination when there were real ghosts lurking about—springing out of books, or hovering at upper windows of castles with no floors? Or when one man's touch sent sparks of electricity racing through her body, and another's kiss made her feel warm and wanted? Aubrey knew that, as much as she told herself she wanted a normal, rational life, there was that part of her ruled by fantasy, and that part wanted more. It wanted excitement, and wonder, and...yes...maybe even a bit of danger.

She had felt the danger ever since she'd touched the old book in Angus' shop, back in New Jersey. It danced at the edge of her senses, teasing her with what ifs. *What if all this is real?* it asked. *What if there's more out there? What if Scotland truly is the place you're meant to be?*

She had no answers. Two days ago she had been thinking of going back with Kate and Fitz when they left on Saturday, but she had said nothing to them about it. Why hadn't she? Because she knew they would try to talk her into it, she realized. They had flown all the way over here because she had needed them, and she loved them for it. But when they left, she would be all right. She would stay right here, in Inverness, and research her family tree. Or maybe she'd take up the bagpipes and join a pipe band. She chuckled softly in the dark at the image of herself standing on the corner of the High Street, decked out in Cumming tartan, blowing air in and out of a sheep's stomach.

Her phone lit as a call came through. Connor. "Wondered if ye were still up," he said, his brogue thick. "Did ye have a good time today?"

"You know I did. It was lovely. Skye is lovely." *You're rather lovely.*

He was silent for a time.

"This has never happened to me," he said finally. "I think I'm fallin' for you, lass." His voice was low, his words a caress. "I don't need you to say anything. I just wanted you to know. Good night." And he hung up, leaving her staring at the blank screen on her phone, hearing two different voices replaying their message over and over.

"I think I'm falling for you."

"It's one of the things I love about you."

Two men, very different, and both of them wanted something from her that she wasn't sure she could give. She wasn't ready! She needed time, and time was moving too fast. Connor was sweet, delicious, like a big cake with sprinkles and whipped cream. Finn was like one of those chocolate lava cakes, intense, deep, with a hidden center that waited patiently to be discovered.

She got up and put on her robe, padding silently downstairs to the kitchen. The AGA watched without comment as she got out a bowl and a spoon and opened the freezer door. Carrying her bowl into the empty sitting room she sat by the window, staring out at the Highlands shrouded in the evening mist. The ice cream melted on her tongue, easing her anxiety and calming her imagination as it always did. Some things were constants.

I hope that real love and truth are stronger in the end than any evil or misfortune in the world.

Charles Dickens

SCOTLAND, 1442

She stood swaying in the corridor, her mind unable to comprehend the evil she had just heard. They were going to kill them all! Entice them here, serve them wine under the guise of friendship...and then kill them, cut their throats where they sat.

She had known that her father was cold, unloving. Now she knew that he was a monster. Ever ready with his fists, he had seemed unable to find his heart. Even his sons, raised in his image, had not received the affection that a parent should bestow upon his child. They had striven for his attention, and received only beatings and harsh words for their trouble. They had become just like him. She had been the lucky one, beneath his notice, a girl. He was not cruel to her for the simple reason that to him she did not exist.

His special target had been her mother. Sweet and kind, she lavished her love on her daughter, and Ailith Comyn responded with everything in her being. Her mother had taught her to love. She barely knew she had a father, until she grew old enough to hear the moans, to notice the bruises, to understand the pain and sadness in her mother's eyes.

He had killed her, Ailith knew it. Her mother had wasted away, had lost her grip on reality, had stopped eating, and one day she had just ceased to breathe. Her father had caused her death as surely as if he had raised the sword himself. And then he had finally noticed his daughter.

He had come to her room a month after her mother's death...drunk and slobbering, and tried to force himself upon her. He had punched her when she resisted, but when he would have taken her the drink had overcome him, and he had fallen on her bed, snoring. After that she had barred her door. She knew he was waiting.

But tonight was the night she would gain her freedom. Coinneach was coming for her, and after the feast she would ride away with him on her beloved Corbel, to live with his people.

She started in terror. Coinneach! She had to warn him! His clan was camped outside the castle, awaiting the feast, but she knew how to reach him. Pulling a dark cloak over her day dress, she hurried out the side door and past the stables to the praying stone. Once there had been a chapel, but her father saw no purpose in religion, and now all that was left was the corner-stone. It was their special place. It was how they communicated when they could not touch, through notes left in the cleft of the stone. She left her note now, and prayed that he would find it before tonight.

The feast was in full swing when Ailith, in her best gown, descended into the hall. Almost too terrified to stand, her eyes sought Coinneach among the boisterous, cheering men. She could not find him, and she smiled. He was safe, and he would come for her.

She stood in the shadows, unnoticed, barely able to contain her fear. And then, at a signal from her father, the Comyn men rose up and pulled the knives from their boots. But the Mackintosh were ready for them. Their daggers were already out, and as if they too had been waiting for the signal, each man rose and plunged his weapon into the breast of the man to his left. Caught by surprise, the murderers were themselves cut down by their victims, and blood flowed like wine into the rushes.

Ailith had closed her eyes, unable to witness the slaughter, but now she opened them...to look into the face of her father. His tunic was red from a terrible wound to his stomach, but he staggered toward her... and she fled.

❄

She ran blindly.

She stumbled, nearly fell, forced herself up and continued her desperate flight. Up the curving stone staircase to the next floor, down countless corridors until the tower door loomed before her out of the darkness. She was breathing heavily now, hampered by her heavy gown, faltering.

At long last she reached the top, gained the empty circular chamber. Her heart caught as she heard stumbling footsteps on the tower staircase, and she melted back into the shadows of the wall. The door opened, and she saw her death in her father's eyes. He raised his sword. "Traitorous bitch!" he spat.

She heard a faint cry from outside the tower. "Ailith! I am here! Come to me, love!" He was waiting for her. Forcing herself through the aperture, she clung desperately to the window's outer edge, knowing that he would catch her, yet afraid to let go. The next moment the sword came down, severing her hands at the wrists and plunging her downward to the rocks below. She made not a sound as she fell.

Her last thought was of him.

CHAPTER 26

TULACH ÀRD

"Your friends are going home at the end of the week and they haven't done a distillery tour yet. Which means they haven't done Scotland! There's one tomorrow and you need to be on it!"

"Stop wheedling!" Aubrey laughed through the phone at Finn. "All right, we'll go! You didn't have to work so hard, you know. A distillery tour was on the bucket list...and you're a half-decent tour guide, after all."

"*Half*-decent? I'll have you know that I get the most star reviews of any guide on the website!"

"Probably because they want to know what you wear under that skirt!"

Choking sounds came from the other end of the phone. It was good to be laughing and joking with Finn again. Things had been strained between them after the Culloden trip, but now they seemed to have achieved a sort of peace with each other. She had missed the easy comradery. She knew he wasn't pleased that she had spent Tuesday on Skye with Connor, but she wasn't pleased about a few things either. So there.

She had seen him with Isla again yesterday. She wasn't surprised, but she *was* surprised at the pain that knifed through her at the sight. It hadn't looked romantic, but it was clear that Isla still had a hold on him. He'd said it was over between them, and she thought he'd meant it. But when something was over, you didn't keep seeing each other, right? She had to face it, he was still in love with her. He just didn't know it.

And it was okay. Really. They were friends, and anyway she had Connor for romance. Dependable, lovable, *free* Connor. He didn't have any old girlfriends in his kilt closet; she'd swear it on a dram of whisky. There was something relaxing about dating the Playboy of Inverness—no female baggage.

Kate and Fitz were going home in three days. They had packed in so much during the two weeks they'd been in Scotland, and their very presence had been a balm to Aubrey's soul. But she knew she didn't need them to keep her on track anymore. She'd be fine. She left them to do some last minute souvenir shopping and decided to go down to the bookshop. She had hardly seen Angus since Kate and Fitz had arrived and she wanted to hear his voice. Even though he was the most mysterious character she had ever met, he was also somehow the most grounded. She trusted him.

"Angus, you know Connor MacConnach, and I know you know Finn Cameron. What do you think of them? As people, I mean."

"Is one o' them a Mackintosh, Ah wunder?" he said, looking at the ceiling. She should have known better.

"Um...Angus?" This time she was treated to a dour look that was as impenetrable as a stone wall. But she tried anyway.

"Aye, lass?"

"Do you have that book? You know, the one with the smells and stuff? Is it here?"

"Aye." He stared her down, refusing to elaborate, and after a moment she left, defeated.

Kate and Fitz met her on Thursday at the bus station, and together they boarded Dougie's tour bus, taking seats at the front where they could enjoy Finn's presentation. He grinned at them but said nothing, launching into his talk as soon as the bus pulled away.

"I can tell I've got a wild bunch here today," he told them. "You're all here for the whisky, aren't you? Aye, I thought so. Well, you're in for a treat. We're going to the place where God gets his own whisky.

"Now, who are the lucky souls on my trip today?" The group numbered twelve, and Finn spent time learning their names and places of origin. He's so good at this, Aubrey thought. A natural teacher.

Edith and Fred Johnson were from Kentucky, their rich southern accents an amusing counterpoint to Finn's brogue. It was their first trip to Scotland, and Fred wanted to test Scotch against his own beloved bourbon, Edith told the group. "It'll be a hard sell," she warned. "Fred does love his bourbon!"

A French couple, Emíle and Marie Deyeax, were making their second trip. "Marie is the drinker in our family," Emíle told them, his voice affectionate. "She would like to skip the tour and go right to the tasting. What can I do? I love my wife." He gave a Gallic shrug that reminded Aubrey of Maxine.

"No skipping the tour," Finn warned with mock severity. "You have to *earn* the tasting."

There was a group of three young girls from Canada who were in Scotland to trace their family heritage. An elderly English couple from Cornwall, and a German couple and their daughter. By the time they reached the *Tulach Àrd* car park, they had all bonded. People on vacation are basically friendly, thought Aubrey, but it's Finn who brings them together. It's his gift.

They disembarked from the bus, and Finn gathered them around. "Now, here are your nametags. We give you these in case I have to come and find you after the tasting." He winked. "And if you *really* enjoy the whisky, I might let ye drive the bus home. Emíle, are you okay with Marie driving?" Emíle's look of horror had them all laughing.

Finn released them then, and they joined the line waiting for the tour.

Aubrey looked at the distillery. Long, low buildings painted a clean white, with *Tulach Àrd* blazoned on the side of the largest in the whisky's distinctive font. They were met just outside the door by their guide, Jim Thompson, who told them in a low, conspiratorial voice that he had been born in London. "Don't let the kilt fool you," he said. "It's a disguise. If these Scots found out, they'd throw me into the wash tub and be done with me. I take the risk because the whisky's so good." He winked at them.

"Now, before we start, you should know a little bit about our fine whisky. This distillery is the beloved child of Lachlan Mackenzie, who is the cousin of the current clan chief. The name *Tulach Àrd*, means 'the high hill,' and it's the slogan of clan Mackenzie. It's a Speyside single malt, because we're located near the River Spey. Speyside is home to a couple of malts you might have heard of, *The Macallan* and *The Glenfiddich*, which are almost as good as *Tulach Àrd*...but not quite. They keep trying, though."

Aubrey had stopped listening, her attention caught by the sight of a familiar kilted figure near the side of the building. Connor MacConnach was in deep conversation with Finn, and by the looks of it the discussion was not a pleasant one. Connor was gesturing wildly, his head bent close to Finn's. Those two, she thought, and wondered again where all the animosity came from. Neither had seemed inclined to talk about it with her, but it was clear that this was not simple dislike.

The group moved into the distillery and Aubrey lost sight of the two men. Oh well, she thought, they're grownups, they can handle their own problems.

"Here we are in the grist mill," announced Jim Thompson. "Like most distilleries, we get our barley from a malting house. The malted barley comes here, to the grist mill, where it's crushed by these giant rollers you see here into a sort of flour, called grist. This makes it easier to extract the sugars from the barley."

He paused. "There are hazards in whisky making, as in most industries. For example," he continued, "the rolling process creates dust which can be extremely flammable. Our electrical equipment has to comply with very strict regulations. In the washback room, the danger is carbon dioxide, which can build up and cause dizziness, or worse. So our ventilation system is constantly checked.

"Once the wash is transferred to the pot stills, which you'll see a little later, flammability becomes an issue again, but *Tulach Àrd* uses indirect heating steam coils to protect against any danger there." He stopped and eyed them. Some of his group were looking uncomfortably around, as if expecting to be blown up at any moment. "Don't worry, you're in no danger. *Tulach Àrd*, I'm proud to say, has the highest safety rating possible, and we take the safety of our workers and our guests very seriously." He grinned at them. "Over sixty thousand tourists come through our facility each year, and that's a lot of drunks wandering around." They all laughed, reassured.

Thompson led them into another room, containing huge wooden containers that looked like giant barrels with pipes extending into them. Through the pipes a clear liquid was pouring into the tubs. The air in the room smelled sweet. "These are the wash tubs," he told his group. "Here the grist comes to be mixed with hot water to dissolve the sugars. The mix that results is called wort."

Kate leaned over and spoke into Aubrey's ear. "Look at Marie. She looks as if she might jump out of her skin waiting for the alcohol part of the tour!" They giggled. The Frenchwoman was squirming, moving from foot to foot as if preparing for a race.

"I can't wait to see her in the tasting room," Aubrey laughed. "Poor Emíle's going to have to carry her to the bus!"

Finn Cameron paced back and forth beside his bus, fuming. This altercation with MacConnach had been worse than usual. Well, usually there *was* no altercation, he thought, because he avoided the other man like the plague. But lately he seemed to run into the big lug everywhere he went, and the reason was plain. Aubrey Cumming. MacConnach felt threatened by her friendship with Finn. He thought that the American girl was his. It was that simple.

And it seemed as if he might be right about that, he admitted to himself. Since that damned trip to Skye, they had become a couple—or so it looked to Finn's jealous eye. Because yes, he was jealous. How could he compete with the glory of Connor MacConnach, when the big kilted wonder was everything a woman could want? He had charm, the rugged good looks of a Highland warrior, and that damn kilt. He had thought Aubrey too smart to be sucked in by superficial glory, but he supposed she couldn't be blamed for falling for such a perfect package. And anyway, he had had his chance, and he'd blown it.

He had gone over and over that moment when everything had gone wrong. It was in the pub in Sutherland. One minute they had been laughing, getting along as if they'd known and liked each other for years—or at least that's what he'd thought—and the next she had shut down like the power in an electrical storm. He cringed, remembering the ride home. Yes, she had had a bit too much to drink, but that didn't explain the hostile silence or the complete turn-off.

He wasn't MacConnach, but he scrubbed up pretty well if he did say so himself, and he had never had that kind of reaction from a woman. He'd been stunned, afraid to ask what the problem was. And then she'd told him that she didn't want to see him again, and he'd just sat there like an idiot and let her go.

He'd been over it again and again in his mind, and finally figured it had something to do with his confession that he and Isla had once been an item. Well, she'd *asked*, hadn't she? And they had, but so what? Everybody had a history, but then they moved on. It probably hadn't helped that he'd been picking Isla up at the airport the next time he'd seen Aubrey. He'd wanted to sink into the floor at the look on her face. But again...so what? He'd bet *she* had an old boyfriend or two that she regretted; she was too beautiful to have gone through life without attracting male attention. Had some bastard hurt her?

She *was* beautiful. And kind, and funny, and... and there was that weird electrical charge that had surged through him when he had touched her. It had been out of the blue, and extraordinary, and wonderful. And then that kiss! The third time he had wanted to grab her and pull her to him and kiss her senseless, and he might have, had it not been for the fact that she would likely slap him in the face in front of Alex and Dave. So he had let her go and agreed to her terms, and now they were just friends, while Connor MacConnach—

No! He stopped himself. It didn't have to be this way. Not without him giving it one more try. You didn't let someone you loved go that easily, unless you were a fool and a coward.

His brain snapped back onto one word. He loved her. The blinders came off, and he admitted to himself what he had always known—he was in love with Aubrey Cumming. And in fact, he had slipped and almost told her so at Culloden battlefield. He'd run away from her then, like Bonnie Prince Charlie deserting his army, before he could see the look on her face.

He stopped pacing and began to jog toward the distillery. He was going to find his group and join them for the rest of the tour. And then somehow he was going to let Aubrey Cumming know that he didn't want to be her friend. Not for a minute longer. What did he have to lose?

Jim Thompson ushered his group into a large room containing four large wooden vessels.

"This is the washback room," he told them. "Smells like a bakery, doesn't it? After the wort cools, it's pumped into these large tubs called washbacks, and yeast is added to convert the sugars into alcohol."

Marie stopped fidgeting and perked up. "Does anyone want to look into the inspection hatches to watch the process?" Marie was the first, but Fred Johnson was close behind her.

"Not for me!" said Fitz. "I think those two might run me down if I tried to get in front of them!"

Aubrey and Kate decided to forego the experience as well.

"I think I can miss looking at a pot of mush," Aubrey told them. "Not something on my bucket list."

Then she stopped talking, her attention diverted by something she saw out of the corner of her eye. Turning, she looked. There was nothing there, the image gone before her brain could recognize what she had seen. But there had been *something, something that was out of place...*

Aubrey wandered toward the place. She stood still, trying to recall what it had been. A what... or a who? Her thoughts were fuzzy and her head was beginning to ache. Maybe she should just stop worrying about it. Weird, she was having trouble catching her breath. She felt lethargic and wondered if she were getting sick.

Suddenly a scream went up from near the washbacks. "Marie! Somebody help her!" Emíle's panicked voice filled the room. Marie Deyeaux had slumped to the floor, her face beginning to turn blue. A minute later, Fred collapsed beside her.

Jim Thompson was struggling to be heard. He was struggling just to breathe, but he knew instantly what was happening. "Get out of here!" he managed. "Everyone! Get out, now!"

Those who could helped to drag the unconscious forms of their tour companions out the emergency door and Fitz, all silliness gone, snapped into professional mode. "I'm a nurse. Bring them over here!" The others did so, recovering quickly as fresh air began to circulate around them.

❁

Finn appeared, his face pale. "What happened?"

"Carbon dioxide poisoning," Jim Thompson gasped. "Had to be over 100 ppm for them to be affected so fast. I don't understand how that could happen. The ventilation—"

"Where's Aubrey?" Finn suddenly demanded. "Where is she?" At Kate's horrified expression, he charged back into the room, holding his breath. He saw her immediately, slumped in a heap on the floor near one of the tubs.

"No!" he gasped, crossing and picking her up. Staggering, he carried her to the emergency door where Kate was waiting, her face a mask of anxiety. She helped him carry Aubrey outside into the air and then stepped back as Finn laid her on the grass, fear for her friend paralyzing her in place. Finn forgot about Kate, sinking to his knees and feeling for a pulse. Weak. But she wasn't breathing. *She wasn't breathing!*

He placed his lips on hers and began CPR, wracked with anxiety. He felt her body shudder, and then she gasped and began to breathe. He was so grateful that he gathered her up and kissed her, crying in relief. The electricity that went through him was intense, more powerful than ever before, but he couldn't stop. He paid no attention to Kate, who was watching him in shock. Aubrey was still unconscious, but she was alive. She was alive.

Aubrey was running. There was a shadow stalking her. She was racing for her life, but her feet were mired in something sticky—was it *blood*? The shadow was gaining on her. It was going to catch her and she knew that if it did, she would be dead. She reached the top of a tower and knew she was trapped. She would never see him again. It was over. She turned to face the shadow, and suddenly it was inside her, stopping her breath. Despairing, she allowed it to take her. She could feel his kisses, felt his arms around her, but it was too late for them. The shadow had her, would never let her escape now. It was almost a relief.

CHAPTER 27

RAIT CASTLE

Aubrey came awake slowly in a bright room with sky blue walls. Her brain was muddy, as if she had fallen into a vat of—wait! The distillery! This wasn't the distillery! Where was she?

"Good afternoon, dearie," the nurse said, her voice cheerful. "Glad to see you're awake. Your friends are making quite the nuisance of themselves. Seem to think we can't take proper care of you." She smiled. "Would you like to see them?" Aubrey nodded. Her mouth felt like cotton and she didn't trust herself to speak. The nurse left, and seconds later Kate and Fitz rushed into the room.

"Thank God!" Kate breathed. "Fitz said you'd be all right, but you know what a crappy nurse she is, so I had to see you to be sure."

"Oh, get out of the way, Kate Bianchi!" Fitz shoved her aside and looked Aubrey in the eye. "How do you feel, sweetie?"

"Fine...I think. Wh—what happened?"

"There was a failure of some kind in the ventilation system at the distillery. Thank God that guide knew what the symptoms he was experiencing meant or we'd all have died!" Fitz shook her head. "It was carbon dioxide poisoning. He yelled at everyone to get out, and we all took off for the emergency exit."

"Except you, you fool." Kate's voice was harsh, roughened by the memory of watching her friend struggling to breathe. "For some reason, you had wandered away from the group, and no one knew you were missing until it was almost too late!"

Aubrey tried to cast her mind back, to remember anything about the tour, but the memories were jumbled, confusing images of fear, and blood, and running. She had been dying. The fear was so real she could almost touch it. A demonic shadow had stalked her through cold stone passages, and she had known that if it reached her it would kill her. And then someone was there, protecting her, kissing her with a passion she had never before experienced in her life. The memories surged, and faded, and she was back at the distillery, looking for...what?

"I don't know," she said. "When I try to think, my head hurts."

"Don't try, then," Fitz cautioned her. "The memories will come. Just rest. They want to watch you for a bit to make sure there was no damage. Of course, we told them that you weren't very smart to begin with, which was probably why you thought it a good idea to wander around by yourself!" Fitz grinned at her, giddy in her relief.

"That's it!" Aubrey said suddenly, and then grabbed her head. "Ow."

"Careful, darling," Kate admonished her.

"No! I saw something. Something that shouldn't have been there. I wish I could remember—"

"Well, how's my fine lass?" Connor's voice boomed from the doorway. He crossed quickly to the bed, taking her hand in his. "I was verra worrit about ye." His golden eyes had darkened to amber and his brogue had thickened. "I shoulda been there, I shoulda protected you."

"But you *were* there." Aubrey looked at him in confusion. "You were talking to Finn before we went in for the tour. You were arguing about something."

"Oh...aye...well." He seemed embarrassed. "Well. That was just a conversation we were having. I was up seeing Lachlan, and when I went back out there he was. Ye ken I don't like the wee man much, aye? We just don't get on. But I left right after, so I wasna there when it happened."

"What did happen? Something with the ventilation system?"

"Aye, seems there was something clogging the works. Lachlan's going to be right pissit, for sure. This'll ruin his reputation." Connor shook his head. "It's a damn shame."

Then he brightened. "But the important bit is, you're all right. I don't know what I would've done, lass..." He paused and cleared his throat. "You mean a lot to me.

"Well, I'd best be going. I'll leave you to the tender mercies of your friends." He turned to Kate and Fitz. "Take care of my lass, aye? Aubrey, I'll call you later." With a swish of his kilt, he was gone.

Fitz sighed. "Aubrey, you are sooo lucky! That gorgeous hunk of Scotland really likes you. I think we're leaving you in good hands."

"Oh my God, you're leaving in two days! I have to get out of here! We need to go have some haggis!"

"Ah, I can tell she feels better," Fitz muttered. "She's being funny."

Later she sat propped up in Nessie's sitting room, with the Owls ministering to her every need. Nessie bustled in with a plate of scones and a pot of tea. "Angus is in a rage that ye put yerself in danger, lass. He never wanted this tae happen. Angus is upsit when he loses control, an' he loves ye. There's no livin' with 'im now."

"I'm sorry, Nessie. I didn't plan to be overcome with carbon dioxide gas, you know. It was an accident."

Nessie looked at her through narrowed eyes. "Try tellin' Angus that, lassie. See how it works."

"I get your point," said Aubrey, shivering. She was not looking forward to facing Angus when he was "upsit."

The next day was spent with Kate and Fitz. She felt normal again, and it was their last day in Scotland. Connor had agreed to drive them to the airport, and then he said he had something special planned to celebrate her narrow escape from whisky poisoning.

Something *very* special, he said, with a meaningful look.

She hadn't heard a word from Finn. Kate had said he had been checking regularly on her condition, which was nice, but it would seem that a *friend* might have at least come to see her in person. It hurt.

Aubrey had tried many times to put a face on the image she had seen in the distillery. It was a person, someone who shouldn't have been there. But try as she might, the figure remained dark and evasive. For some reason she knew it was important, but she guessed she'd just have to wait until it came to her. It had been on the edge of her memory in the hospital, just before Connor had come in, but his arrival had driven it out again. Maybe it meant nothing after all.

The three girls stood at security, hugging and crying. Aubrey didn't know when she'd see them again, and it left her feeling bereft. Connor had gone off to find a newspaper, sensitive enough to leave them to their farewells.

"He's a keeper," said Fitz. "Hang onto him. Don't let your imagination screw this one up for you." Kate gave her a look that she couldn't read and said, "I'll call you tomorrow." Aubrey nodded, hugged them both again, and watched them walk through into the security line, fighting back tears. Had she made the right decision? Should she have gone back to New Jersey with them? Maybe visited Harrington's happy couple and wished them well?

For some reason, the idea of Marc and Angie did not give rise to the old sadness. She was over Marco Russo, she remembered in sudden relief. She was free. She looked at Connor, coming across the terminal waiting room toward her. Free to love again.

They went to a pub for fish and chips. Connor was quieter than usual and she felt her senses tingling. Celebrate, he'd told her. She had assumed it was just an offhand remark, but now she began to worry. Did he have something else in mind? Was he going to do something stupid? Connor had been sending her signals for some time now, she had just chosen not to acknowledge them. She had assumed that this was just another adventure for him—the American lass who seemed a bit sad and needed his charming self to lift her up—but what if it was more? What if he wanted more from her? She had never seen him look so nervous.

How did she really feel about Connor MacConnach? She enjoyed his company, definitely enjoyed his kisses, so why was she so conflicted? What the hell more could she want?

"Keep the one who makes you sing," Gladys had said.

It all came home in an instant.

Keep the one who makes you sing.

"What're you thinking so strongly, lass? I can feel the brain waves all the way over here," Connor said. His eyes were warm and golden. And something else. Was there sadness in the depths of those eyes? Did he sense what she was thinking?

"Nothing," Aubrey answered. She had to tell him, make him understand. But she was no good at letting men down. And maybe the "celebration" wasn't what she thought and she wouldn't have to. She really was such a coward.

They walked to the little BMW and he helped her in, his warm hand lingering on her back. He handed her a flask. "A wee dram o' whisky," he said. "You'll like it."

It was Tulach Àrd; she recognized the soft, mellow tones of the whisky as it ran over her tongue. It had a deep, soft honeyed sweetness, with hints of caramel, thick cream, and a touch of citrus. *Listen to me*, she thought, *the single malt expert!* She offered the flask to Connor, but he refused to take even a sip, citing Scottish law that was stricter on drinking and driving than anywhere else in the UK.

"I think it might ruin the fun if I were to be pulled over, aye?" She shrugged and took another sip of Lachlan Mackenzie's family treasure, and then another. As the car sped over the Highland roads she began to feel weightless. It felt good. She asked, voice thick and muzzy, "Where're we going, Connor? You should tell me, yesh?" She felt as if she were floating, supported by clouds. This was some great whisky!

"Oh, aye, darling. You'll find out soon enough." His voice sounded far away. Her thoughts drifted, fractured, came back in bits and pieces, skittered away again. She couldn't hold on to them. She hadn't had enough to get drunk, had she? M'be it was 'cause of th' cabin doxit...her thoughts spun, broke apart, and then floated away altogether as her head fell sideways and she slumped unconscious in the BMW's luxurious leather. Connor drove on, hands tight on the wheel.

Aubrey came awake slowly. Her head was fuzzy again. Had she had a relapse? She was tired of her thoughts eluding her, sick of not knowing where she was. She lay still, trying to stitch together the bits and pieces. Something tickled her cheek. Grass?

She heard voices, hushed and sibilant.

"No! You can't do this! We don't have to get rid of her—I can keep her in line! She's in love with me!"

"You fool! You really have fallen for her, haven't you? Can't I trust you to do anything?" The voice was low, furious. "You heard her tell her friends she saw something. She was right there! We can't take the chance!"

Aubrey opened her eyes.

"Ahh, princess, back in the land o' the living. How nice!" the voice purred.

Aubrey pushed herself through the cloud in her mind, made herself focus. She was lying against a stone wall, her hands bound behind her. Struggling to sit up, she looked around. Somehow familiar, but where? More stone walls rose on all sides, and grass filled the vast space inside. In the corner, the empty carcass of an ancient tower rose against the night sky. Gothic windows with red sandstone mullions stood in proud splendor. She was inside the ruins of Rait Castle.

The shock chased the remaining fog from her mind and she turned her head in the direction from which she had heard the voices. Two people stood ten feet away. Connor watched her, sadness shadowing his features. Next to him stood Isla Gordon, hands on her hips, eyes narrowed.

"My friend Connor thinks he can keep you under control," Isla said. "But we women know that men only *think* they're in control." Her voice was low, even, and cold as ice. Aubrey shrank from the malice in that voice. Gone was the perfect Highland princess. In her place stood a figure clothed in black, her hair pulled away from her face in a simple ponytail. She wore no makeup, and it was this, more than anything else, that sent a chill slithering down Aubrey's spine. Incongruously, Isla carried a designer purse, draped cross-body style over her shoulder.

"W-what do you want from me?" she stammered.

"Oh, I don't want anything from you," said Isla, her voice offhand, disinterested. "But my dear Connor seems to think that you saw something at the distillery. Did you see something at the distillery, darling?" Isla smiled. It was the smile of a snake eyeing its prey.

And suddenly a memory flashed into her consciousness. Something she had seen out of the corner of her eye—had noted even while her conscious mind didn't register the anomaly. Isla, standing behind a door in shadow. Isla, dressed as she was now, blending in with the shadows.

"Oh dear, ye *did* see me. What a shame," Isla murmured. She turned to Connor. "So you see, darling, I can't let you keep your little plaything after all."

"No!" Connor's voice was desperate. "I won't let you hurt her! We were just going to make her promise not to tell! You said she wouldn't be hurt. You promised!" He sounded like a petulant child.

"You are so stupid," Isla said, her voice indulgent. "I knew when I recruited you it was a mistake. You simply can't see the bigger picture. Did you think you could lock her up in a tower so she wouldn't talk? This isn't the Middle Ages, darling." She sighed, reached into her designer bag, and pulled out a sgian dubh, turning toward Aubrey.

Smiling, she reached up and stroked Connor's cheek, and then in one fluid movement, graceful as a dancer, she plunged the blade into his chest and drove it upward. He coughed, eyes widening in shock and disbelief, and opened his mouth, but no sound came out. As Aubrey watched in horror he stumbled forward two steps like a disjointed marionette and dropped to his knees, clutching at his chest where a bloom of red was spreading, stark against the white shirt. He reached a hand out to Isla in confusion, and then time slowed as Connor's body folded and toppled to the grass. He shuddered once and went still, slack face frozen in astonishment. Once so full of life, the lovely amber eyes stared into Aubrey's own, fixed and empty. She turned and threw up into the grass.

Isla waited patiently until she was finished. "So, darling, it's just us girls now." She bent to wipe the blade on Connor's kilt and toyed with the beautiful filigreed hilt of the sgian dubh absently.

"He's dead! You killed him!" cried Aubrey, staring at that still face, feeling hysteria rising to choke her. She tore her gaze away from those staring eyes and the memory of the warmth and humor that had filled them such a short time ago. "Why did you kill him?

Because of me?" She fought for control. "What do I have to do with this?"

Isla laughed. "That's the funny part. You never had anything to do with it. Not until you saw me at the distillery, coming out of the ventilation control room. If you had talked, people would have put two and two together. I couldn't have that, now could I?"

"*You* sabotaged the ventilation system? But why? You could have killed all those people!"

"Well, now, that *was* the idea. We were going to send a message, put Lachlan Mackenzie out of the Scottish independence business once and for all. Not something you'd know about, not being from here, and I don't have time to teach you. But anyway, a few dead tourists was a small price to pay." She frowned in irritation. "Only it took too long for the gas to build up, and that tour guide figured out what was happening. Too bad. We'll do better next time." Her voice was matter-of-fact, bored. Aubrey stared at her in revulsion. She had to keep her talking, even though she knew no one would ever know to look for her here. The last person who had seen her was Nessie, and Nessie would just assume she was out with Connor.

Connor. Oh, God. She forced down a new wave of nausea.

"Was—was he involved?"

"Of course he was involved, fool! Connor and I go way back. Why d'ye think Finn hated him so much?" Isla looked from under her lashes at Aubrey as if they were two teenage girls sharing secrets at a slumber party. "Finn ended it with me because I cheated on him with lover boy here." She glanced down at

Connor and shrugged. "It was fun while it lasted, but I got tired of him and he didn't like that one bit." She nudged the body with a dainty foot. "Did you, love?" she cooed. Her eyes narrowed.

"I tried to get Finn back, but it was over for him. Honest, straight-arrow Fionnlagh. Then he met you, and I could tell he fell hard, but you weren't interested."

I *was* interested, you bitch, Aubrey thought. I was so interested. And now it's too late. Now I'll never get the chance to tell him. She could feel tears welling and forced them back. She would not let this monster see her cry.

"That was why Connor went after you, you know. He couldn't stand to let Finn win. It ate at him. That's why he picked Finn's tour group for the attack, but then he found out you were on the tour and he lost it. Her eyes glinted with malice. "First Finn, then Connor. I made that bit up about him liking you, but I guess the joke was on me." She shrugged. "I only invited you for drinks to see what all the fuss was about." Isla looked down her perfect nose at Aubrey. "Personally, I don't get it, but whatever." She shrugged again and stretched her lovely arms over her head, the knife in her hand catching the faint moonlight that shone through the clouds above the roofless castle.

"Well, I've enjoyed this little girl talk, but I really need to get back to Edinburgh. Have to check in with the boss. He wasn't pleased that no one was killed at the distillery, but it'll still mean ruin for Lachlan, so all's well that ends well. He'll be fighting lawsuits for years. It should keep him quite busy."

She came over to Aubrey and yanked her to her feet, surprisingly strong for such a tiny woman.

"After you're dead, I'm going to put you right here next to dear, sweet Connor," she said, her tone conversational. "Funny, bringing you to this rat's nest was his idea. It gives me the creeps, but now it's working in my favor. I doubt anyone will find you before the scavengers do, but just in case, I'll make it look like a lovers' quarrel. So sad, he attacked you and you managed to turn the knife on him before you died." She gave a dramatic sigh. "I know, it's kind of cliché, but we have to work with what we have, right?" She smiled her lovely smile, perfect teeth gleaming.

But Aubrey was no longer looking at her. Behind Isla, in the corner under the ruined tower, something was happening to the still air. The mist was coalescing, rising and coming together. It began to swirl and undulate, and gradually the amorphous vapors assumed a shape.

Isla seemed to realize that she had lost her audience.

"What?" Annoyed, she turned to find herself face to face with the specter of a woman. Floating just above the ground, the apparition stared at Isla out of eyes black as night. The face was eerily beautiful, but as it leaned closer Aubrey could see anger radiating from its visage. The ghost reached for Isla with long white arms that ended at the wrists.

Isla began to scream, backing into the stone wall of the castle, all semblance of beauty or control gone. The sgian dubh fell from her fingers to be lost in the grass as she gibbered in terror.

317

The ghost turned its head and looked at Aubrey, and its mouth opened.

"Go!" whispered Ailith Comyn...and Aubrey turned and ran, stumbling out through the arched doorway and straight into the arms of Finn Cameron.

CHAPTER 28

JUST DESSERTS

arius Sanderson sat rigid in his leather chair, staring out at the interminable rain. The two-day old newspaper lay face up on the desk, a picture of Isla Gordon splashed across the front page. Droplets splashed against the windows, running down like tears, but he saw none of it. Thoughts raced through his brain in ever-tightening circles, like electrical impulses whose switchboard has been struck by lightning. How had he let this happen? How could he have been so wrong? He'd been so sure that this day would never come. The work she'd done previously for him had been perfect. She didn't make mistakes, didn't allow room for them. He had been looking for someone to replace Ollie Thomson for some time, and Isla Gordon had been recommended as a brilliant operator—cool under pressure, ruthless, a true mercenary. She was all that.

She came from one of the most prestigious families in Scotland, her background impeccable. It allowed her to move in the highest circles, let her come and go unsuspected as anything but what she showed the world. She was one of the lucky ones—young, beautiful, wealthy. A spoiled rich girl. Who would ever have suspected that the lovely young socialite was anything other than she seemed? That behind the perfect face lived a sociopath, a mind so lacking in empathy that no act of violence was beyond the pale, as long as it staved off the monotony of her privileged life?

Darius had met Isla Gordon ten months ago and had been mesmerized by her beauty and intelligence. Sanderson seldom allowed physical attraction to play a part in his decisions, but she was different. He had set her a task. She had accomplished the simple mission with speed and efficiency, and he had given her another. She had handled that one with equal skill, so he had increased the risk and the reward. She had exceeded his expectations. She was like a shadow—ephemeral, invisible, lethal. She always worked alone. He liked that.

And there. That was the mistake. It was not hers, though, it was his. Planting Isla inside *Caledonia First* would never have worked. The Gordons and Sutherlands had supported the English crown through the centuries; it was how they had compiled their wealth and power. No one would have believed that one of their ilk would fight for Scottish

Independence, so she had recruited Connor MacConnach for that role.

Brash, likeable—the stereotypical Highland warrior, MacConnach was embedded in the culture of the independence movement. His family was a sept of clan Mackenzie. He even worked for the chief, trusted like family because he *was* family. The worm in the woodwork. And he was so besotted by Isla that he was easily subverted. He wasn't brilliant, like Isla, but he wasn't stupid either. For the most part he *was* what he seemed: sincere, charming...a man's man. Unfortunately he was also a woman's man. He had allowed Isla to recruit him not for personal gain, or revenge, but because he had imagined he was in love with her.

MacConnach did the heavy work. He moved within *Caledonia First* as Isla Gordon could not. Carrying the banner for his cousin Lachlan Mackenzie, he talked incessantly of the glory of an Independent Scotland even while he recruited the worst filth of humanity to carry out enterprises that would destroy that dream. Saboteurs, murderers, he sent them to Isla. He was not a killer, he told her; he would not be a part of murder. Never seeing the truth through the fog of lust.

Even when Isla tired of him and took others to her bed his loyalty did not waver. Although he hated her alliances with other men, wanted to kill them with his bare hands, he imagined that she would always come back to him. There was a connection between those two beyond what they shared as lovers. Isla was incapable of forming lasting affinities because she was blind to the feelings and emotions of others, but she and Connor had a bond rooted in their shared experience in the shadow world. For MacConnach, her sojourns to his bed were proof of her need for him. For her he was useful, a distraction from the boredom that dogged her existence.

Sanderson knew all this because he was one of those who had allowed Isla Gordon into his heart and his head. He hated himself for his weakness and was surprised by it. He had always suspected that he was somewhat asexual, had never let a woman cloud his judgement or impede his goal. Until this time. He had been surprised at the depth of feeling she stirred in him, wary of it. She was just another beautiful woman, and Darius Sanderson had beautiful women throwing themselves at him every day. But she was different, and he came to realize that what drew him to her like a moth to flame was not her beauty, but her brain. He recognized a kindred spirit in her ability to plan without regard for human feeling, in her lack of empathy. She enjoyed playing with people, hurting them. He understood her—because he was very much like her.

And then something had changed. She had begun to lose her grip on MacConnach. The big Scot had met someone who was different from all the others who had filled his periods of waiting for Isla to come around. His unwavering loyalty to Isla was fraying, and he had begun to emerge from the fog in which he had existed. She was having difficulty in controlling him, and it threatened their alliance. It threatened Sanderson.

The sabotage of the *Tulach Àrd* distillery was to have been their crowning achievement. It should have created such havoc for Lachlan Mackenzie that his perceived negligence would destroy his livelihood and perhaps even put him in prison. The savior of Scottish independence would go up in flames, and people would turn from *Caledonia First* in disgust.

Not understanding how quickly carbon dioxide built up in the fermentation tanks had been Isla's first mistake. Sanderson could have lived with that. But allowing someone to *see* her, in a place she should never have been...that was unforgiveable. Isla had not even known that she had been compromised until Connor MacConnach had come to her railing that his new American girlfriend had nearly died, and that she had told her friends that she'd seen something out of place before her collapse. It meant that Isla had a mess to clean up. MacConnach had been so incensed at Isla for putting his sweetheart in danger that he had failed to see the obvious. He had signed her death warrant...and his.

Isla had promised him that no harm would come to the girl, that all he had to do was drug her and bring her to a place where her silence could be ascertained. The fool! He was so besotted he had forgotten that Isla possessed only one method for ensuring silence. And he had paid for his weakness with his life.

But something had gone horribly wrong. Somehow, that damn chief inspector who had been dogging his steps had known to follow Isla as well. How had he even known about her? He could have sworn that they had never been seen together. None of their meetings had taken place in his office, or even in the same place more than once. But for some reason the man had followed her that night, had shown up at just the right time to rescue the girl. And Isla, discovered standing over the dead body of her lover, had been arrested and charged with murder.

It had been in all the newspapers. Isla Gordon was Highland royalty, and shock waves still buffeted the country. This was national news, and there would be more. She would talk, of course. Sanderson had no illusion that there was anything resembling loyalty in Isla. She would react the way he would in her situation—barter her knowledge to the police in exchange for mercy and sell him out faster than they could write it down. They would come for him...he was surprised that they had not come already. It was over.

Sanderson's fear threatened to overwhelm him. He felt a dull pain in the center of his chest and stood to walk the length of his office to alleviate the anxiety. He was just waiting now, waiting for them to come for him, to destroy his dream, to put him away in a dark cell forever. He didn't think he could bear it.

The pain in his chest increased, a relentless pressure as if something were being pushed into it by a giant's hand. It grew inexorable. A numbness began in his right shoulder and radiated down his arm, and he realized that he could no longer lift the arm. The pain moved to his left side, and it was then that he understood with horror what was happening. This wasn't anxiety. He was having a heart attack!

The numbness in his arms subsided. He needed to get to the phone and call for help. But before he could take a step, a blinding pain in his back forced him to his knees, tears rolling down his face. His muscles seized, the pain so intense it took his breath away. He fell onto his back, unable to move.

Darius Sanderson lay on the floor of his luxurious office, staring at the ceiling. The irony of what was happening to him seeped into his waning consciousness. *This is what Ollie felt. This is what I did to my friend.* The ceiling began to recede as his vision clouded, and with it went the pain. The roof lifted away, and he was staring into the wet grey skies of a Scottish morning. A last thought whispered across his mind. *I'm sorry, Ollie.*

CHAPTER 29

IT WAS YOU

"It's over." Chief Inspector Alan Brown put down the latest newspaper with satisfaction. "With Sanderson's death, the entire ball of yarn has come unraveled. Isla Gordon's been singing like a nightingale, implicating all the players in their nasty little game."

Brown looked at Aubrey, sitting next to Finn at the scarred old reading table in the *Mackintosh Bookshop*. "I'm sorry it took us so long to get to you that night, lass. We were following Isla, not MacConnach, and we got a bit turned about in Nairn and lost her for a bit. Your lad here was fair jumping out of his skin before we found our way up to the castle and heard her telling you what she planned to do with you." He chuckled. "He had some pretty harsh words for me, let me tell you. A citizen should not talk to the police that way, not at all, but I decided to excuse him because he'd been rather helpful." He shook his head, his expression dolorous, and then winked. Finn rolled his eyes and gave Brown an exasperated glare.

"Weel, there's nae excuse fur lettin' mah lassie get kidnapped an' almost kilt noo, is there?" snapped Angus, as he plunked a mug of tea in front of Brown. "If ye kent this Isla person was such' a rotter, ye shood've picked 'er up afore." Brown took the tea carefully, checking to make sure the mug hadn't cracked from the force of its delivery.

Aubrey patted Angus' arm. "Angus, the police can't just pick people up when they *think* they might have done something. That's why they call them detectives. They detect. Sometimes it takes time to build a case and find proof."

"Ach!" Angus clamped his jaw shut on a Gaelic snort.

"Anyway, it turned out all right...except for poor Connor."

Now it was Finn's turn to produce that guttural snort unique to Scotsmen. She ignored him. "I don't think he would have let Isla hurt me if he could have stopped it. He wasn't really a bad person, and he didn't deserve what happened to him."

Finn shrugged. "Aye, I'll give you that much. No man deserves to be killed in cold blood, especially by a wee lass. But I have to differ with you on the bad person part. He drugged you, and he almost got you murdered, Aubrey!"

She let it go, sensing that there was no winning this one. "So," she turned her attention to CI Brown, "it was Isla who was behind all the sabotage? She was working for this Sanderson character?"

"Aye," said the detective. "Sanderson hired her to be his agent in the Highlands, and she recruited MacConnach. They met at Rait Castle because it was out of the way and a perfect cover, due to his position in the preservation group. Isla Gordon was the brains behind the sabotage and the murders. MacConnach wasn't the only one to die. She's responsible for the deaths of five crew members on an oil tanker that was blown up last winter, and three more in an oil fire in March. The latest casualty was a firefighter killed in an explosion two months ago. She hired the saboteurs for that and at least two more incidents. And that's not counting the tourists at the distillery—including you, Miss Cumming—who would have died if their plan had worked.

"She killed Oliver Thomson," he added. "We found syringes and ampules of Succinylcholine chloride in her home." He sighed. "Isla Gordon was a predator and a killer, but I think the worst evil belonged to Darius Sanderson. Thomson was his assistant and best friend, perhaps his only friend, and Sanderson decided to do away with him simply because he wasn't corrupt enough and therefore had lost his usefulness. He hired Isla and fabricated an important document that could only be delivered by his trusted friend."

Brown shook his head in disgust. "Of course, Thomson was eager to do anything for his friend and mentor. Isla was waiting, and when poor Thomson went through the door to the parking lot, she passed him going the other way and injected him with the

Succinylcholine. It's a drug that paralyzes the respiratory system in minutes and mimics a heart attack. A nasty way to die, and nearly undetectable in an autopsy. She should never have kept the stuff—she might have gotten away with that one. She's fortunate that Scotland has abolished the death penalty, but she'll be a very long time in prison. And Miss Gordon will find that designer clothing and fine jewelry aren't a part of the penal system," he said with satisfaction.

The chief inspector finished his tea and stood up. "I have to be going," he said, and then turned to Finn, "but I can't thank you enough, sir, for being my right arm here in Inverness. I know it wasn't easy, but you've done your country a service that can't be repaid." And with those cryptic words CI Alan Brown left the bookshop, his trench coat flapping against his legs.

In the detective's wake, Aubrey turned to Finn. "What did he mean, his right arm in Inverness?"

"Oh, um...well..." Finn looked embarrassed. "Brown looked me up because of my history with Isla. He'd been watching her for a long time, and he asked me to keep in contact with her and track her movements as best I could without making her suspicious." He slanted her a nervous look. "It wasn't hard to do, because she wanted to be with me, but..."

"But it made me think you were still in love with her," Aubrey's voice was soft. "And you couldn't tell me." She reached out and put her hand over his, still surprised by the reaction of her body when they touched. Then she yanked the hand back and glared at him.

"Wait! Isla said you broke up with her because she cheated on you with Connor. But you told *me* that her family wouldn't let you be together. You gave me the sad puppy eyes and made me think you had a broken heart! What was that all about?"

"Well, now, lass," said Finn, a sheepish look on his face, "a man doesn't usually like to tell the lass he fancies that he got cheated on by the last one, ye ken?" He grinned. "And besides, I never gave you sad puppy eyes, and I think you imagined the broken heart part too. You *had* been drinking a rare lot of whisky at the time, if I remember right."

Her eyes went wide. Could that be true? Had all of this heartache and misunderstanding been caused by her over-active imagination and a few drams of single malt?

"So that's why you were picking her up at the airport? Because you were a secret agent for Brown?" Aubrey laughed at the memory. "You looked so miserable, but I never thought—"

"Well, you were being romanced pretty well by MacConn—" He stopped, seeing her stricken face. "I'm sorry, I know he meant something to you."

Aubrey looked at him, sensing the importance of this moment, considering her words. How could she make him understand? She let out her breath. "Finn, I did like Connor. He was nice and funny and sweet, and he was there when I thought you were lost to me...but he wasn't *real*, was he? He was the image of the Scottish hero, but none of it was real. He wasn't what I was looking for, what I wanted." She held Finn's gaze, willing him to understand.

"He wasn't you."

He stared at her, his eyes glistening, and then leaned forward and touched her lips with the softest of kisses. She shivered, leaned back and looked again into his blue eyes, her own going wide.

"It was you!" she whispered. "At the distillery. I was dreaming, and someone was kissing me, and I...it was you!" She reached out to him, and then for a few minutes both of them forgot they had an audience. Angus leaned back in his chair, crossed his arms over his chest, and smiled his beautiful smile.

⁂

Aubrey awoke bathed in perspiration. She could still smell the blood, more blood than she could ever have imagined. She could see the bodies, their dead eyes staring at her out of faces twisted in anguish, blaming *her* for their fate. Could taste the bitter tang of regret, of failure. Feel the unbearable agony of loss wrenching her very soul from her body. The words imprinted on her numbed mind. She would never see him again. *Who?*

Her bleary eyes stared out at her bedroom in Inverness. She wondered how long she could survive like this, with so little sleep, chased through the night by the dreams. This had never happened to her before. The occasional nightmare after a night of too much partying in college, nightmares about forgetting to go to class and showing up for a final exam. Once, just before she'd come to Scotland, she had dreamed that Marc had come back to her, telling her he loved her and begging her forgiveness, and she had awakened crying. But she had never had the same dream twice, and they had never filled her with a terror that lingered into the waking hours, keeping her from sleep. Until now.

As long as she didn't sleep, she was fine. Yes, she thought, remembering Finn's kisses, more than fine. Something was building there; she dared to hope it was something real. Finn didn't have to report to the college for three weeks, so other than the times he was taking a tour for Dougie's they had spent the long summer days since Brown's visit to the bookshop together, learning about each other, liking what they found. And kissing, a lot. She should have been tired enough from all the kissing to sleep like the dead—

It was the dead. They came for her every night. Taunting her, making her watch as they laughed and drank. They raised their tankards and saluted her—and then pulled out wicked blades and began stabbing each other. They made her watch until they were all dead again, lying on top of each other, their limbs splayed in grotesque imitations of a dance macabre. And then they started again.

Isla was in every dream. She stood in the center of Rait Castle's ruined hall, bloody knife in her hand, laughing. "You did this," she would say, laughing. "This is all your fault. Isn't it fun?" And she would come for her, brandishing the knife, and Aubrey would discover that her hands were bound behind her back and she could not move. Then the dream would erupt in a red mist, as Isla's knife flashed upward, over and over and over. There was no pain, but she knew that it was she who was being stabbed. She was dead, knew with a sick certainty that *she* was the Rait Castle ghost, doomed to haunt the ruin forever.

Sometimes in the dream she looked down at her hands... and they were gone. Sometimes she was screaming at Connor, trying to warn him about something, but he stared at her with glassy eyes as his blood leaked into the grass. "I won't let her harm you, lass," he said. "Don't you worry." And then he turned into Finn, and it was Finn whose lifeblood was pouring from his chest, turning the grass red. And all the time Isla's blade flashed up and up, cutting.

After the third time she awoke screaming, Aubrey decided that sleep was overrated. Dragging the comforter from her bed, she stumbled downstairs and huddled in the corner chair in the sitting room, knees tucked under her, sitting upright so she couldn't fall asleep and the dreams might be kept at bay. And it was there that Nessie found her, head pillowed on her arm, crying as if her heart would break.

She looked up, bleary eyes streaming with tears. "I don't know what to do, Nessie! I can't stop the dreams! I can't sleep! Am I haunted? Is the ghost angry because I failed? Because I didn't find a Mackintosh? Am I being punished? There's so much blood!"

Nessie pulled her into a hug. "Let's go t' see Angus."

CHAPTER 30

ALL THE PIPERS

It was three o'clock in the morning, but Angus was in his usual place behind the desk at the bookshop. He looked up as if he had expected them to walk through the door. "Yer lad's comin'. As soon as he gits heer we'll gang."

"Gang? Gang where?" Aubrey's mind was not making connections. Lack of sleep had wrapped her in sheep's wool, robbing her of reason. But still she felt better. Angus was in charge. Angus would make everything all right.

"Th' castle. Ther's someone ye need tae meet."

"No! No, Angus, I can't go back there!" She backed up and put her hands out as if to ward off the idea. "I can't!" It was a wail.

Angus eyed her. "Och, aye ye can. Ye must."

Aubrey looked at him. "But what's the point? I failed. I didn't fall in love with a Mackintosh, and I didn't break the curse. Aren't you angry?"

"Ye think ye ken everythin', dinna ye? Juist trust me, will ye?" He shook his head in exasperation.

Finn arrived, his hair tousled from sleep. He had thrown on jeans and an ancient grey sweatshirt, and his blue eyes were cloudy. He took Aubrey's hand, and the familiar vibration coursed through her. "It's going to be all right," he said, and pulled her in for a hug. They all piled into Finn's old battered Audi and headed out in the darkness toward Nairn. Aubrey sat close to Finn as he drove, counting on the warmth of his body to keep her from falling apart.

"Why are you here?" she whispered. "It's the middle of the night!"

She could feel his shrug. "Angus called. He said you needed me. So I came." Simple, yet profound.

Rait Castle stood against the early dawn, grey tendrils of mist curling around its windows and sliding in and out of the gaping arched entrance like wraiths. The silence was a blanket thrown over the world. No one spoke. As the group drew closer to the great ruined doorway, Aubrey felt her fear begin to fade, her courage return. In amazement, she realized that this place knew her. It meant her no harm.

The four walked together over the threshold of Rait Castle. Aubrey felt Finn's grip on her hand tighten and looked to see his face drained of color, his eyes huge and dark with pain. He gasped, bent over and clutched his stomach.

"Finn!"

He straightened slowly, the color returning to his face. "Don't know what that was," he muttered. "I smelled something awful for a second there...like dead meat or something. Weird. And there was a horrible pain. It's gone now."

Aubrey touched his arm. "Did you hear anything?"

He considered, then whispered, "Something like a beehive. How did you know?"

Her answer was lost in Angus' soft, "Sssshh. Bide ye now. She's here."

The mist in the corner of the keep was coalescing, the threads flowing from other parts of the great space to join together, forming a substantive shape. As they watched in awe, the shadows came together and became a shape, which melded into a body...a woman. They could see long hair, the outline of clothing not of this time and place. She had no color but her face was beautiful, black eyes huge in her white face.

She began to glide toward them. Six feet away she stopped, looked at Aubrey, and smiled. It was a smile that made the heart ache, sad and beautiful and filled with longing. And then she drifted forward again... to stand in front of Finn. He did not move, somehow stayed perfectly still, waiting. Her arms came up, those graceful white arms that ended so shockingly at the wrists, and in the next instant Finn was reaching for her, taking her forearms in his strong hands. There was nothing of substance there, but he was *holding* her.

Ailith Comyn looked into Finn Cameron's eyes. She opened her mouth and whispered, in a voice as breathless as the dawn breeze and yet containing all the love of ages of waiting, "Coinneach." And then she laid her head on his chest, closed her eyes, and faded away, the mist dissipating until there was nothing left. In her wake she left a sensation of completion, hope, and absolute joy.

"She's goan. She will nae be comin' back," Angus said, satisfaction in his rough voice. "She's done whit she had t' do, and she's goan t'be wi' him."

Finn blinked and turned to them. "I felt as if I knew her," he said, in a tone of wonder. "Who is Coinneach?"

Angus looked at him, and then at Aubrey. "Mebbe its time t' look at th' wee book agin, lass."

They left Rait Castle as the sun rose over the eastern Highlands, dappling the grass and the trees with soft color and turning the dew into diamonds. Exhausted as she was, Aubrey noticed something odd about Angus as they walked to the car. For a minute she couldn't wrap her mind around it, but then it came to her. Her old Scot was holding hands with Nessie.

Aubrey leaned against Finn's warm shoulder and slept all the way home. She did not dream.

In the bookshop, Angus retrieved an ancient key and opened a door behind the desk. These were the oldest books in the shop, the collector's editions, the originals. No one went through that door except Angus. He emerged carrying the book Aubrey remembered from the shop in Harrington and laid it on the desktop with reverence. The same book, and yet different, somehow. She wasn't afraid of it anymore. At a signal from Angus she stepped forward and touched the cover.

The pages rifled as they had before, but now the sound was the moan of a lone piper and the smell of heather in all its summer glory. She searched her senses for the taste and found the smoothest whisky, warm and tingling on the tongue. The pages slowed, and stopped.

"Reid it," said Angus, and she began to read the ancient words aloud.

In the year 1442, the Comyn clan did lay claim to the castle that is called Raite, and so also did the clan Mackintosh. Long had the two argued over the castle, and about much other, but the Comyns having possession the Mackintosh at length conceded their ryght. Upon hearing this, the Comyn did invyte the clan Mackintosh to a great feast, the purpose to celebrate the burying of animositye. But there was treacherye in the heart of the Comyn, and the men of the clan had contrived in a plot most foul, that at a signal each would rise up and slay his defenceless guest. The plot had been conceived by the Comyn himself, he who had a heart black as the devil and filled with greed and jealousy. The chief had a daughter, Ailith, who was deep in love with Coinneach, son of the Mackintosh. She did overhear her father speak of the plot, and contrived to warn her love by means of a message in the whispering stone whych didst stand outside the castle. Thus warned, the guests did come ready to defend themselves, and when the Comyns rose up to slay them, they turned their own blades upon the murderers, and *slew them. She who had an honest heart didst turn away from the slaughter, but her father saw, and knew. She ran in fear, but he did follow her to the top of the castle tower, and did there cut off her hands and send her into the darkness. From that night to this the walls of Raite Castle have stood emptye.*

Aubrey stopped reading, and the book snapped shut. "But...but it's all different!" she said, her eyes wide. "How can that be?"

Angus looked at her with that inscrutable expression she knew so well. "It'll come t' ye, lass."

"What exactly is a Pipe Band Championship?" They were on their way to Forres for the European Championships, Finn's bagpipes packed into the trunk of the Audi.

He grinned.

"This'll be the final test of whether you're ready to be a true Scot. If you can stand a whole day of bagpipes and drums, you'll pass. There are other tests, of course. Seeing the Loch Ness Monster, that's one, and you passed that one with flying colors. There's whisky drinking..." He looked sidelong at her and made a face. "You know what you like, I'll give you that, but you do seem to get drunk rather easily. We'll have to work on that one." Aubrey punched him in the arm. "And then, of course, there's the full

Scottish breakfast. I've watched you eat, and I think you can keep up with that one just fine!"

Aubrey was laughing too hard to take offense. Besides, there was truth in it, she had to admit.

They pulled into the parking lot at Grant Park and Finn collected Aubrey's tickets for the event. He left her then to check in with his band, and she stood surrounded by happy chaos, wondering how she was going to make it through a whole day of nothing but bagpipes.

"Aubrey Cumming!" boomed a voice, and she looked up to see Alastair MacGregor stalking toward her. "Well met! Mind if I sit with ye?"

"Please! I'm going to need a lot of help understanding what's going on. You're a godsend!" He beamed and took his place. The happy wanderer was a different man today. No frayed cuffs, no dirt, and he smelled as if he'd taken a bath in Yardley's Lavender.

"Do you come to this event often?" She had to yell to be heard over the sound of hundreds of bagpipes tuning up.

"Every year. Wouldna miss it. Ye like it so far?"

"Just got here. But truthfully, that sound is the worst thing I've ever heard in my life! How can you stand it?"

Alastair roared with laughter. "Th' tuning of the pipes is an acquired taste, lass, and not for most ears. It gets better when they actually play t'gether. Why are ye sittin' here alone?"

"Oh, I'm not alone. I'm here with Finn Cameron."

"Fionnlagh! Fine lad. And one o' the best at th' pipes. Just wait. Yer lad'll do ye proud." A feeling of warmth spread through Aubrey at his words. Her lad.

"So," Alastair assumed his professor role. "There are different grades o' pipe bands, from Grade 1, the best, to Grade 4. But there's a lot more t' see than just pipin'. Lot's o' championships—the Highland Dance, the drum major competition, an' some Highland Games. Wha's th' matter, lass?"

"Oh...nothing. Was just thinking of someone who would have enjoyed competing in those Highland Games. He couldn't make it." Poor Connor, she thought. So much joy in living, all gone. Bad choices and worse company had ruined it all for the big Scot, but she would never forget him, so maybe that could be her tribute to his memory.

Finn rejoined them, now dressed in his performance kilt, and later she listened to *Inver Caledonia* play their way to the finals.

At days end, they stood together in the shadow of the whisky tent.

"There's one more event that you can't miss, and I have to play in it. Then we can go. I know it's a lot for the first time, but I hope you had fun?" Finn's face looked so hopeful. This was his world, Aubrey thought. Could it be hers as well?

"I have fun when I'm with you." That was the simple truth, and when he pulled her in for a long kiss, she knew it was enough. But something still nagged at the edges of her mind.

"Mmmm, Finn?"

"Aye?"

"Why do you think the ghost came to you? Why did she call you Coinneach? Didn't the book say that was the name of her Mackintosh lover?"

"Aye, I believe it did."

"Well, how could that be? You're not even a Mackintosh."

Finn stared at her for a long moment, and when he spoke his voice seemed odd.

"Well, to tell the truth, there's something I haven't told you. My father left us before I was born. I never knew him, never wanted to. My mother married again, and Ferguson Cameron adopted me. He's the only father I've ever known." He hesitated. "My real father's name was Malcolm Mackintosh."

Aubrey stared at him, speechless. Finn smiled at her, then pulled her in and gave her a lingering kiss.

"Angus wouldn't let me tell you. He said it was something you'd figure out for yourself. Said he had faith in you.

"I have to go play," he said. "Wish I could be with you for this one, it's the final event in the championship. It's called the March Past. All the pipers fill the parade ground and play at the same time, and the music can be heard miles away. Pretty amazing." He cupped her face in his hands and bent to kiss her again, his blue eyes intense. "But after that, I'm all yours...if you want me." His smile melted her heart and left her weak.

"Oh, I want you."

As the sun sank behind the mist-draped blue and grey mountains, every band began to play in unison, the sound of the ancient pipes filling the Highland air with their eternal magic. Aubrey felt goosebumps break out all over her body, as Angus' words came to her from a lifetime ago in Harrington, New Jersey.

"*When th' Comyn lass finds 'er Mackintosh, aw th' pipers in Scootlund will begin tae play.*"

She hadn't failed. She had done her job, changed the story. The curse had been lifted. She understood now, and she believed in the magic of Scotland with every fiber of her being. She was home.

"Thank you, Ailith," she breathed. "Thank you for waiting."

SCOTLAND, 1445

Three figures stood looking at the castle's imposing facade. The keep stood tall and unyielding, refusing to acknowledge the truth...that it had been abandoned, left to the mercy of the harsh Scottish weather. Still, only three years after the tragic events that had taken place in its hall, there was little evidence of neglect. Tall grass grew in the bailey, the stable door hung off its hinges. That was all. The stone walls stood firm and untouched, as if to say, "They will be back. I will wait."

The woman looked up at the mullioned tower window and shuddered. Immediately the man moved to block her view, to shelter her in his arms, holding her tight as her body shook with the memories.

"I knew it would be too much," he murmured. "We shouldna have come."

"No," said Ailith Mackintosh. "I had to see it, the one more time. It is all right."

"Mama?" a small voice asked her, distress evident in the clear blue eyes. They were Coinneach's eyes, she thought, as she reached to cradle the small girl. The child burrowed into her mother, sensing that something had upset her but unable to comprehend its significance.

"It is all right, my sweet," Ailith's soft voice calmed the girl. They had named her Jaine, "gift from God" in the old tongue, and so she was. A miracle born of a love that refused to die, their hope for the future.

Coinneach stared at the huge arched door of the vacant keep. He had not seen the slaughter that had stained its hall, waiting outside near the tower for Ailith to come to him. She should not have been at the top of the tower, she was to have come through its lower door, to ride away with him from this place of death and be free. But it had all gone terribly wrong, and he had stood helpless under the tower window as his beloved fought for her life against the monster who was her father. She had hung from the lintel, too frightened to let go...until the Comyn had made the decision for her, and she had dropped lifeless into his arms, her face white, blood pouring from the stumps where her hands had been.

He never knew how he had gotten to the stonecutter's cottage, only remembered his desperate attempts to cauterize her wounds with his sword, plunged into the fireplace again and again until the bleeding stopped and the smell of burnt flesh seared his nostrils. But she had lived. Against all odds, she had lived, and six months later another miracle had been given him in the form of their daughter, Jaine.

"You know how this must end," Ailith said, looking deep into his blue eyes, so like those of their child. "You *know what I must do to lift my father's curse, to find the right one...the one who will change the story. No matter how many centuries it takes."*

He knew. In the three years since the massacre they had lived a quiet life away from his clan, but news reached them despite their attempts to avoid it. A Comyn stable boy had survived, not being in the hall, and had carried the news that the Mackintoshes had slaughtered his clan in cold blood. The lie had spread, and clan Mackintosh had no answer. Worse, with his dying breath the Comyn had cursed the clan, damned them from the hell where he had gone. They had been denied the castle that was theirs, doomed to carry the stain on their name forever. Or until another Comyn loved a Mackintosh as these two loved, with a passion to conquer time...

"I know." Coinneach's voice was gentle. "And I will be waiting. But none of that needs happen now. None of that needs happen while we live." He gathered his family into his arms, his face alight with love. "So let us live."

* * *

FORTHCOMING BOOKS IN THE HIGHLAND SPIRITS SERIES.

The Piper's Warning
The Healer's Legacy

CPSIA information can be obtained
at www.ICGtesting.com
Printed in the USA
FSHW010215061019
62740FS